Armaranos
Fend

First Published in Great Britain 2015 by Mirador Publishing

A copy of this work is available through the British Library.

ISBN: 978-1-911044-12-3

Mirador Publishing
Mirador
Wearne Lane
Langport
Somerset
TA10 9HB

Armaranos Fend

Jasen Quick

~ Dedication ~

For Judith

Chapter One
In The Woods

I sometimes wake up in the middle of the night with an image in my head of my three-year old son dying. He is holding my wife's hand as they walk along the pavement. Behind them, a car mounts the kerb and knocks them down, killing my only child instantly. My wife dies in hospital hours later, leaving me alone in this world.

When awoken in this way, I have to get out of bed, switch on all the lights in the house and make myself some tea to clear the thoughts from my head. I wasn't at the scene of the accident, but I see it in my mind all too frequently. I hate my brain for being able to make up images of something so horrific and severely disturbing. My wife and son *did* die. I wasn't there. Stop showing it to me, brain.

I have an agreement with father time: he is gradually healing my wound and I am endeavouring to move on and live life to the full. Neither of us is keeping up their end of the agreement in a satisfactory manner. After seven years, the wound still hurts and my life is less than full. Not even half full. In fact, I would say it is now three quarters empty.

People are hopeless at comforting the bereaved. My best friends avoided me because they didn't want to say something that might upset me, which made me feel worse. Work colleagues overcompensated by talking too much about inane things. They were stuck in the same office as me, so they couldn't hide. Maybe they felt that talking constantly about rubbish would stop the awkward subject from being raised.

My parents had chosen to divorce during the year of the accident. They went their separate ways and neither of those ways brought either of them closer to me. The only person in my life who has always been there for me is my elder sister, Lucy. She makes up for the void left by my parents. No one can make up for the void left by my wife and son.

Lucy is seven years older than me and has been watching my back all her life. She lives across town with her husband and pets. They have no children but Lucy tells me they are trying. I wish she wouldn't tell me that. I don't need to know they are trying. I don't want my brain showing me yet more unwanted images.

People used to call me brilliant. So many problems had obvious solutions and I found I could quickly pick up any skill. Then, after the accident, I had a mental breakdown and lapsed into a depression so great I spent hours staring at the wall. I lost my job and my home and most of my sanity. If I had been able to channel any skill into one useful purpose I might have been brilliant again but, instead, my life became pointless.

I eventually returned to work and Lucy insisted I stay with her and Jeremy until I was fully up to speed. That was six years ago. I stayed with them for two years until I found myself a small detached cottage to rent. A new job took my mind off things for a while and relative normality returned. And then something occurred to me which changed my outlook on life.

People are morons.

I started to notice that there were a large number of stupid people in the world – some would claim ignorance about subjects that were before their time, as though anything that happened before they were born was forever lost. Selfish and self-centred people would complain that they were not getting what they *deserved* out of life. People seemed to want everything handed to them on a plate. In addition, common sense seemed to be less common than ever it was. Lucy used to tell me it was all in my mind but I saw them everywhere; at work, in the supermarkets, on the streets: morons.

If I could rename this world, Moronity would be my first choice. Welcome to Moronity, where all the morons live. Welcome to the moronisphere. I despise them all.

My faith in humanity dwindled and I shut myself away. I lost another job and sank back into a depression so deep even my sister could not help me through.

And that is where I am now.

My home is in Salisbury, on the edge of town, across the valley from Old Sarum. Behind my modest garden, fields contour the land, right up to a line of trees on the horizon, which marks the start of woodland. The woods belong to a stately home, abandoned in the nineteen eighties.

I used to like to walk there at weekends to get away from reality – away from people.

I haven't visited the woods since my doctor suggested I return to therapy. Funny how the words you say to certain members of society provoke specific reactions. You tell the doctor you want to kill yourself and he suddenly becomes your best friend, full of helpful and sincere advice.

I have decided to leave the world and end the torment.

Walking through the woods, with a rope in hand I scan the trees for a climber. The trees are tall and imposing. I might appreciate their elegance if I was in a positive frame of mind. Instead I am looking for one I can climb to secure the noose.

I have never considered myself to be one who dwells on the negative. However, there's only so much a man can take before he realises he wasn't meant to be on this planet.

"Hello," a female voice from behind me says gently. She startles me and I almost jump with surprise. I know these are private woods but I believed the estate to be uninhabited. I turn around to find a young woman dressed as a cheerleader, standing on a fallen tree.

"What's the rope for?" she asks, her voice almost childlike. She speaks slowly but clearly. I wonder if she is high on drugs.

"You made me jump," I say, my heart pounding rapidly.

"I didn't see you jump," the young woman says, dead pan.

"Well, I didn't literally jump," I say.

"What's the rope for?" she asks again. I look down at the noose, hanging from the coil of rope. Should I tell her I was going to kill myself?

"I was going to climb a tree," I lie.

"You don't need a rope to climb these trees," the young woman says. Her face lights up at the opportunity. She turns and jumps to reach a low branch of a nearby tree and pulls herself up. "Come on!" she shouts. I walk up to the tree and look up at her as she sits on the branch.

"I'm not really in the mood…"

"I'll pull you up," she says, leaning down with her hand outstretched. She has the excitement of a child and I wonder whether she is mentally impaired.

"I'm fine," I say waving my hand to emphasise that I don't need help.

"Let's go to the top," she insists with enthusiasm. She stands on the branch and starts to climb up. I look up and realise I can see up her skirt, so I look away, because I consider myself a gentleman.

I know many men who would relish the opportunity to look up a girl's skirt without her knowing. In fact, I once worked with a man who used to take his phone into supermarkets and take pictures up girls' skirts. What I found almost equally disturbing about his action was the relish with which the other men I worked with lapped up the pictures and encouraged him.

"You coming?" she shouts. I look up, trying to focus on her face.

"I can see up your skirt," I say. She lifts her skirt and flaps it around.

"I'm wearing a leotard, silly. The skirt is for show."

"Aren't you a bit old to be dressed as a cheerleader?" I ask. She is clearly in her mid twenties. She ignores my question and continues up the tree, so I put the rope over my shoulder and climb after her. Branch by branch, I pull myself upwards, each step taking me away from my intended purpose. The thought of hanging a noose from the tree slips out of my mind.

We meet near the top, which seems a lot higher than it did on the ground. The view is amazing. I can see the stately home down in the valley. It is almost totally covered in ivy and the garden is overgrown with brambles. How could anyone let a nice house like that go to ruin? I suppose the fact that people nowadays are happy with bland, identical, small houses, with tiny gardens and no privacy has made houses like that unfashionable. I'm not sure I really believe that. People seem to be obsessed with fame and riches. Surely some aspiring z-list celebrity would want to buy an old stately home.

The tree sways, but I feel surprisingly stable. As I look down, the fear of falling reminds me that I came here to die. I wonder whether jumping from here would replace the need for a noose.

"I told you, you wouldn't need a rope," the woman says. She is sitting on a branch opposite me, holding on to the tree with one hand. The cheerleader outfit has an S on the chest.

I realise I am staring at her chest, which makes me feel self-conscious, despite looking at the letter embroidered on her top and not the shape of her breasts underneath, which I now find myself scrutinising. I look at her face and try to keep my eyes on her smile.

"How old are you?" I ask.

"Twenty-five," she answers.

"Thought so," I reply. "Why are you wearing a cheerleader's outfit?" I grip the tree tightly.

"I fancied being a cheerleader today," the woman replies.

5

She stares at me intently and I wonder whether my sister sent her to follow me. Or maybe it was my doctor. Can doctors prescribe girl-in-her-twenties for patients who have a medical need?

"Where do you live?" I ask. I find myself looking at her hand. There's something pleasing about women's hands. They look perfect. Don't get me wrong, I don't have a fetish for hands, although I have heard that some men do - seems unusual. I just like the look of them.

"In there," she replies, pointing at the abandoned stately home. "I like trees."

"Clearly," I reply. I take another look at the house and wonder whether anyone *could* live in it. "You really live in there?" I question.

"Yes," she replies. "What's your name?"

I'm not sure whether the enthusiasm in her voice is an imitation or whether she is genuinely naïve.

"Nate," I answer.

"Nate?" she questions.

"Yes."

"Nate. Nate is a strange name," she says like an adult child.

"It's short for Nathan. My mum liked the name. In fact my full name is Nathan Glover the third. My father is called Nathan and so was my grandfather."

"Hello Nathan Glover the third," the woman says, as though we have just been introduced.

"What's your name?" I ask.

"Heather," she replies.

"Are you, er, taking any medication, Heather?" I ask, hoping not to offend.

"My tablets?" she questions.

"Yes," I confirm. The branch is sticking into my thigh, so I move to get more comfortable.

"How did you know?" she asks.

"You're not like a normal twenty-five year old," I say. I feel guilty for my choice of words.

"My doctor says I have the mind of a ten year old," she discloses.

"Really?" I reply. "He told you that?"

"Do you think I have the mind of a ten year old?"

"I'm not in a position to say. I'm not a doctor." I wish I had not mentioned medication now. I came into the woods to hang myself and, instead, I am sitting at the top of a tree with a woman in her mid-twenties who is dressed as a cheerleader and has the mind of a ten year old. I've never believed in god but if I did I might think he was sending me a message. Maybe she's an angel, sent to stop me killing myself.

"Do you ever wish you could fly?" Heather asks. She stands on the branch, her head almost above the top of the tree. The wind blows her hair and she looks beautiful. She closes her eyes.

"You're an angel," I say quietly. I stand and hold on to the top of the tree, which pulls us closer together. She smells like perfume. The tree starts to sway more as the wind picks up and I realise the danger we are in.

"We should go down," I say. Heather's eyes open and she presses her face against the thin branch.

"Let's fly down," she suggests. I look down and see the ground a hundred or so feet below. I change my mind and decide that she's not an angel. Angels don't try to get you to jump from the top of a tree.

"I'd rather climb down," I say, lowering myself onto the branch. I start to climb down the tree and Heather follows me. At one point, she accidentally kicks my head with her white trainers. I don't think she realises, because she does not apologise.

The ground feels firm as I jump from the lowest branch. I stand up and put my hand up to help Heather down. She jumps from the branch into my arms and I lower her to the floor, getting a mouthful of her hair. For a second I realise we are in an embrace. I look into her eyes and see the childish grin she is giving me, so I let go of her and step back.

"That was fun," Heather says, pulling the rope from my shoulders. She takes the noose and runs away through the trees.

"Where are you going?" I shout.

"Catch me!" Heather shouts back. I run after her and catch up with the trailing rope. I consider stamping on the rope to stop her but decide not to, in case it makes her fall over. Heather runs into a part of the woods where the trees are fir trees, planted close together. It is difficult to run through them without getting a face full of pine needles, so I drop to my knees and crawl.

I reach Heather, who has stopped running and is lying on her back, panting. I lie next to her and take the rope from her.

"I'm knackered," I say, trying to catch my breath. I'm only thirty and yet she left me behind with ease. There is a moment of silence, during which I watch the sun shining through the dense fir trees.

"Why do you want to kill yourself?" Heather asks, breaking the silence. I realise she is more astute than I assumed. I close my eyes for a second and then answer her.

"I'm not enjoying life," I say.

"Why not?" Heather asks.

"I'm in debt, alone and out of work. People are morons." I say, leaving out the real reason.

"Why don't you get a job," she suggests.

"It's not that easy." I turn and look at her.

"But killing yourself? Why?" Heather frowns with disagreement. I look back at the sky through the trees.

It does seem pathetic. Suicide is not rational. Most people don't understand why someone would want to kill themself.

That's why people who kill themselves tend not to include others. We hide and do it alone.

"Do you really want to die?" Heather asks. She seems quite mature now. I turn and look at her. She is fingering her long hair, making small curls. She looks at me and smiles.

"My family died and I miss them," I explain.

"I'm sorry to hear that," she says. I can't tell whether she means it.

"Do you have family?" I ask, turning onto my back again to watch the sky through the fir trees. A cloud covers the sun, shadowing us in darkness, which is deeper because of the close trees.

"I don't know," Heather replies.

"You don't know?"

"I have my guardians. They look after me," she explains.

"No parents?"

"I should go home," Heather says, getting up. She clearly has issues regarding parentage. I wonder what medication she is on and what its purpose is.

I follow Heather out of the dense fir trees, back into the taller trees. I must learn more about tree types. I know what an oak looks like, but I have no idea what these tall trees are.

"Do you come here often?" I ask. I realise it sounds like a cheesy chat-up line but hope that she won't see it as such. Heather turns and looks at me.

"Every day. You?"

"No. I only came here today to…," I stop and look down at my coil of rope.

"Can I have that?" Heather asks, pointing at my rope.

"You want my rope?" I question.

"Yes. Can I have it?"

"Well, I need…,"

"You need it?" she finishes. I feel stupid admitting it.

"Yes."

9

"I'll give it back to you tomorrow," she says. I find myself handing the rope to her. Either she is very clever and is trying to stop me killing myself or she just likes my rope and wants to play with it.

"What time?" I ask. She looks confused.

"Sorry?" she says.

"What time tomorrow?"

"This time." Heather holds her arms out and looks up at the trees as though conducting an invisible orchestra. "I'll be waiting for you." She smiles and brushes the palm of her hand across my face, teasing me.

I watch her run away through the trees, heading down the sloping woodland towards the abandoned stately home. I want to follow her but decide not to. Once she is out of sight I leave the woods and walk home across the fields, my head filled with thoughts of the strange young woman in the woods.

I don't believe in fate but it seems uncanny how Heather appeared just as I was about to end my life. Now, as I walk home, suicide is far from my mind. I *will* live to see tomorrow - to see Heather again.

I climb over my back fence into my garden and approach the backdoor. Through the window of the door, I see a shadow pass across the far wall and I realise someone is in my home. I quietly open the door and sneak inside.

Chapter Two
My Sister

Standing in my kitchen, I find my sister and a policeman.

"Having fun?" I ask Lucy as I step into the room. The policeman turns to me.

"Are you Nathan Glover?" he asks. The room smells of fresh coffee. I glance at my percolator and see its green light illuminated. The jug is half empty. Lucy runs at me and hugs me.

"The third, yes," I confirm, looking over Lucy's shoulder. "Is something wrong?"

"I was worried," Lucy admits, pulling back to look at me.

"I'm PC Dorak," the policeman says. Lucy steps away, holding my hand. "Your sister was worried about you." The police constable looks at Lucy. "He seems to be fine," he says, grasping for his mug to sip more of my coffee.

"Thank you for coming over," Lucy says to him. "Where have you been Nate?" she asks me.

"I went for a walk. Why? Did you really need to call the police?" I ask.

"You are on your doctor's vulnerable persons list. Because of your last…" PC Dorak starts.

"Attempted suicide?" I say, finishing his sentence.

"Have you been having any suicidal thoughts lately?" he asks. I head over to the percolator and pour myself some coffee. Then I sit down at the small circular table, on which I usually dine alone.

"Yes," I admit. My sister makes a noise which sounds like

she has sucked in a lot of air quickly. It's the opposite of a sigh of relief - a suck of despair. I try not to look at her because it is hardest to admit my failings to her.

"Enough to act upon them?" the policeman probes further.

"I left this house earlier and went to the woods with a noose," I explain. I gesture for the policeman to sit down. "But I left it there and came home."

"What changed your mind?" he asks, as he places his coffee on the table. I look at my sister and see she has tears in her eyes.

"Sit down," I say to her. She shakes her head. She can't look me in the eye. She brought the police over to convince me not to kill myself. She was too late. Heather beat her to it.

"I'm not going to kill myself now," I say to her. I reach over and take her hand to comfort her. I recall my thoughts of how some suicidal people seek attention. Sitting in front of the policeman, I wonder whether I have been fooling myself into believing I am not seeking attention.

"What changed your mind?" the policeman asks again.

"I have a reason to live another day," I tell him. I sip my coffee and then ask, "Do you know the family living in the mansion?"

"The mansion?" he questions.

"What's it called?" I try to recall. "North Silestia House."

"North Silestia House?" the police constable repeats. "North Silestia is empty."

"You sure?" I ask. He nods his head.

"Yes, I'm sure. We send a patrol car up the driveway once a week to make sure vandals don't wreck the place. Why do you ask?"

"I met a woman in the woods who claimed to live there."

"I'll make some enquiries," he says, before drinking the last of his coffee, "but I am certain North Silestia is empty. Did the woman tell you her name?"

"Heather," I reply. "I don't know her surname. I'm meeting her again tomorrow, so I'll ask."

"Meeting in the woods?" PC Dorak asks.

"Yes."

"Are you aware that North Silestia is private property? You shouldn't be going in those woods."

"I have permission from the woman who lives there." I smile. My sister finally looks at me.

"Not if she was trespassing as well," the constable says with an awkward smile.

"Well, I'll find out tomorrow. If she lied about living in North Silestia I promise to stay out of the woods," I explain.

"Who is she?" Lucy asks. "How did you meet?"

"I was walking through the woods, looking for a tree to," I stop myself. "She was walking in the woods as well."

"Did she say why she was in the woods?" PC Dorak asks.

"No. She said she liked to wander amongst the trees. It made sense that if she lived in North Silestia she might do that."

"I'll ask for a patrol car to go down and take a look," PC Dorak says as he stands. He leaves the kitchen and a moment later I can hear him talking on his radio in the hallway.

"I'm fine," I say to my sister quietly, anticipating her thoughts.

"Promise me you will never kill yourself," she replies. I feel awkward hearing the words coming from her. Suicide is a personal thing that involves no one else. I don't want people to know about it.

"The woman in the woods was interesting," I start. "She intrigued me and I want to see her again. You know how I feel about people. I find them a bore, but Heather was different."

"You actually found another person who doesn't bore you?" Lucy clarifies. "I don't believe that for one minute." She smiles through the tears.

"Heather had an aura about her. It's hard to explain," I state. "She seems to have a mental issue, though. She's…"

"Retarded?" Lucy finishes. Her smile has gone. I am surprised by her choice of words. I think for a moment and realise what prompted her comment. Lucy's presence in my life won't stop me killing myself but a strange young woman in the woods instantly changes my mind. I admit it seems unusual. Lucy must see it as an insult to her.

"I know what you're thinking," I say.

"Good," she replies abruptly. "For a genius you can be quite a bastard. So what's so special about Heather?"

"She was like an adult child, which I think was induced by medication. I want to find out more about her. Find out why she's on medication."

"You mean she has the same mental issues you have and you feel an affinity with her?"

"Well, no, but that will do if it makes it easier for you to accept."

PC Dorak pokes his head around the door.

"I'll let myself out," he says. Lucy turns to him and follows him into the hallway, so I stand up and join them.

"Thank you for coming," she says.

"You're welcome," the policeman replies. "Thank you for the coffee," he adds.

"Will you let me know what you find out about North Silestia?" I ask.

"I'll tell you whether it is inhabited," he replies. "I do recommend that you stay out of those woods though. It is trespassing."

Lucy walks with PC Dorak to the front door and lets him out, closing the door behind him. She turns to me and leans back against the door.

"Well Nate?"

"What?" I head into my living room and Lucy follows. I

approach my wall of books and turn to look at Lucy. When I feel at peace, I usually find myself sitting in front of the open fire with a book.

"Were you really going to kill yourself? Do I mean nothing to you?"

"You mean everything to me, but you know I have issues. You don't understand how hard it is for me."

"No, I don't. It's been seven years since the accident. You need to move on." Lucy says, like a teacher reprimanding a pupil.

"I miss them!" I shout. I feel tears welling in my eyes. Lucy leaps forwards and puts her arms around me.

"Hey, it's okay. I just wish you would tell me when you're feeling suicidal." She leans back and looks me in the eye, still hugging me. I don't want to look at her but I do.

"If you die, that puts me in the situation you're in, having lost someone I love. You wanna do that to me?" she asks. I can see through her question. She is a clever woman but I have this thing about reading body language and interpreting the things people say. She's trying to keep me alive by making me feel guilty about hurting her. I feel bad that her words won't work. If she had said that to me before I went to the woods I would have still gone to the woods. Being suicidal is selfish. The only thing that could stop me killing myself was to find something *I* want.

Something like Heather.

"I'm not going to do it now," I say.

"I should feel pleased that this Heather girl has given you a reason to live," Lucy says. "Who is she? Do you fancy her? That would be a good thing, right?"

"I suppose it would," I agree. I haven't fancied any woman since Francine died. "Heather intrigues me. She's like a child in an adult body but she seems to be more astute than she lets on."

"What happens when you get bored of her?"

"I promise not to kill myself without giving you the chance to talk me out of it," I say. I'm not convinced I really mean that. If I start to feel suicidal again I will probably just run away and hide until I decide whether to do it.

"You promise?"

"Yes." (As I said: not really sure I am being honest.)

Lucy pulls me to her and we hug. Then she steps back and releases me.

"You coming to my party?"

"Oh, the party," I say with a negative tone. I hate parties.

"You *have* to come," Lucy pleads. "It's to celebrate my promotion."

"I'll be there for *you*," I agree. "But only for you."

"I'll introduce you to my friend Michaela. She'll put a smile on your face," Lucy threatens.

"Please don't."

Lucy backs away, towards the door.

"What plans do you have for this evening?" she asks.

"Well, since I had intended to go to the woods and end it all, I don't have any plans. I think I'll just get an early night."

"You could come home with me. Have dinner with me and Jeremy."

"Thank you, but no. I am tired and my head is swimming with thoughts. I'm going to open a bottle of wine and drink it in bed."

"Nate, can I ask you a question?" Lucy asks, leaning against the door frame.

"I'm not going to kill myself," I reply.

"That wasn't my question," Lucy replies. "I was going to ask why you didn't leave a note - you know, a suicide note. Were you really going to kill yourself?"

"I intended to, but I'm not sure I was really convinced. After all, I still have some excellent wine in the kitchen." I smile. "I didn't think a note would help you, so I was just going to disappear. Sorry."

"Don't ever do that, you understand?" Lucy says. She looks annoyed.

"Yes."

"Don't ever just disappear. You have to give me the chance to talk you out of it. No matter how much you think you need to disappear."

"Okay."

Lucy leaves the room, and then my house. I don't see her to the front door. She won't say goodbye to me.

Chapter Three
The Soldier

I feel uneasy walking through the woods again, this time expecting to see Heather. My fear is that she won't turn up, whether because she has no more right wandering these woods than I or because she is a figment of my imagination. At the very least, I intend to take a look at the stately home for signs of inhabitants. If PC Dorak was correct, no one has lived in the house for over twenty-five years, so it should look abandoned.

Quite a few of the trees have lost their leaves, despite this being the warmest autumn on record. It seems hard to believe that in a matter of weeks it will be too cold to wander outside without extra clothing.

I locate the tree I climbed yesterday and look up. An image of Heather climbing its branches enters my mind. A rustling sound from the leaves at my feet takes my attention and, without warning, the leaves explode into the air as a figure wearing combat clothing leaps up at me from their hiding place. In one move, the attacker wraps an arm across my shoulder and pulls me backwards to the ground. Then they climb on top of me and straddle my chest, pinning me down.

"Hello again," Heather says, grinning like a Cheshire cat. Still in shock, I try to take a deep breath, which is hard with her on my chest.

"Heather?" I manage to say. Her hands are pressed against my shoulders. "A soldier? What are you now, Action Man? Action woman?"

"I was hiding." Heather says, clearly pleased that I had not seen her.

"Yes you were," I reply. "Where did you get the uniform?" It looks genuine. She is wearing black combat boots, tied around the ankle, with long woollen socks and webbing around her shins and calf muscles. The camouflaged trousers have pockets in the legs and her jacket bears the name Griffin across a chest pocket. She is wearing a scarf made from webbing, which partially conceals her face. On her head a webbing covered helmet completes the outfit. I scan her clothing for signs of a knife or pistol but find none. Her unpredictability is fun but also a little worrying.

"I have a wardrobe of clothing at home," Heather informs me.

"With a cheerleader outfit and combat clothing? What else is in that wardrobe?" I ask. I actually feel comfortable with her sitting on me, and I hope that she stays.

"Tomorrow I might be a Queen, or a nurse." Her eyes light up and I imagine she is picturing the contents of the wardrobe in her mind. "I could be policewoman!" she screeches with excitement. An image of PC Dorak enters my head and I realise that his and her paths may well cross in the near future.

"Probably best not to dress as a policewoman," I suggest. "It's against the law." Heather looks confused and I wonder whether she understands legalities.

"I'll surprise you," she says, rolling off me and crawling like a commando through the leaves away from me. I decide to play along and crawl after her.

"Where are you going?" I ask.

"I heard the enemy," she whispers. "We need to reach the checkpoint and disable the guards." I really hope she is role-playing. I'm not dressed for combat.

"Do you really live in the big house?" I ask, the elbows of

19

my fleece jacket soaking up moisture from the ground as I crawl.

"Shhh," Heather snaps. She stops crawling and pretends to listen to the enemy.

"Can I come to your home?" I ask quietly.

"The enemy has gone. It's safe now," she says, ignoring my question.

"Can I come to your home?" I repeat.

"Why?" Heather asks, turning to look at me.

"I'm curious," I reply. "I'd like to see your wardrobe of clothes."

"Tomorrow," Heather replies. She stands up and turns to me, taking her helmet off her head. She drops it on the floor. Her hair is a mess.

"Why tomorrow?" I ask as I rise to my feet.

"Because we have a mission to accomplish today," she states, placing a hand in her chest pocket. She pulls out a packet of cigarettes and tips one into her hand.

"Smoke?" she says offering the pack to me. I shake my head. There's something ugly about women smoking. My mother smoked throughout my childhood and I grew to hate the vision of her puffing away. It amazes me that she never developed cancer and died.

Heather places the packet back in her pocket and pretends to light the cigarette. I realise she is not going to smoke the cigarette. She's still role-playing.

"You know what, I *will* have a cigarette," I say. I poke my fingers into her pocket and pull the pack out. As I pretend to light one, Heather breaks the end off her cigarette to make it shorter.

"So, who's the enemy?" I ask, puffing imaginary smoke. Even when unlit, cigarettes taste disgusting.

"An army of people from a parallel universe, under the command of a crazy scientist," Heather says, excitedly.

"Sci-fi. Cool," I say. I break the end off my cigarette to make it look like I smoked some of it. Heather breaks more off the end of hers and puffs imaginary smoke into her lungs.

"We missed them," she says.

"In that case, why don't we go and see your home?" I suggest.

"Not today, tomorrow," Heather replies.

"So you said, but why tomorrow?"

"My guardians won't let you in. They'll throw you out." Heather flicks hair out of her face and accidentally knocks the cigarette out of her mouth. She presses her foot on it as though extinguishing it.

"Can't you talk to them? Tell them I'm your friend?" I ask.

"They won't let you in," she says, looking down at the cigarette.

"But they will tomorrow?" I question.

"Tomorrow they have to go out, to buy food," Heather explains. "You can come then." She picks up her helmet.

"What time?" I ask.

Heather looks up.

"Now time," Heather replies, her hair is over her face. Yesterday her hair was tied back in a pony tail. Today it is not. She brushes her hair back with her fingers and puts the helmet back on.

"Now time?" I ask.

"Now, but tomorrow," Heather bangs her knuckles on the top of the helmet and turns to walk away.

"This time tomorrow," I clarify. "Okay," I throw my cigarette onto the ground and follow Heather. "Would you like to come back to *my* house?" I ask.

"Can't," she replies. "Not allowed to leave."

"You're not allowed to leave? Says who?"

"The doctor. He said I'm not well enough to leave."

"We could sneak out," I suggest. Heather sits down on the

leaves and crosses her legs, so I do the same. I haven't crossed my legs in years and it feels much less comfortable than it did when I was a child, so I uncross my legs and sit with them out straight. I put my hands behind me to support myself.

"I'm not allowed to leave," Heather repeats. She holds on to her ankles and stares at me with no expression at all - just a vacant stare. I try to understand what her life is like but I can't figure it out. Someone is keeping her at an abandoned mansion and is giving her medication because she is supposedly ill and she's not allowed to leave the premises. Sounds like she is being held against her will – in fact it seems as though her will has been removed. I wonder whether that's what the medication is for.

"What's your last name?" I ask. "Is it Griffin?"

"Why would it be Griffin?" Heather questions. She looks confused.

"It's written on your jacket." I point at the embroidered nameplate on her combat jacket. "Griffin."

"My name is not Griffin. Griffin was the invisible man." Heather states.

"Invisible man?"

"The book by H. G. Wells: The Invisible Man. His name was Griffin."

"How do you know that?" I ask. I read The Invisible Man, years ago, but I don't remember the name of the character. He was just *the invisible man*.

"I have books," Heather replies. "Lots of books."

"Do you read them?"

"I like to read in bed," she tells me. "Yesterday I read about Cage and Constance."

"Who are Cage and Constance?" I ask.

"Two people who cannot die. They fall in love," Heather says, her expression turning to a smile.

"They cannot die?" I question.

"No."

"Nice," I say. "Do you read a lot?"

"I love books," she replies. She puts her hands together as though they are a book and pretends to read imaginary text. She holds her hands – the book – up so I can't see her face as she reads.

"Is that one of your books?" I ask.

"These are my hands, silly!" Heather replies, wiggling her fingers in front of my face. She touches my cheeks and then holds on to my face with both hands.

"Your face is cold," she says.

"So are your hands," I reply. I like her touching me so I lean forward a little, so that she doesn't have to reach so far. She kneels forward and brings her face to mine, so we are almost nose-to-nose. As she stares into my eyes my heart beats faster. Her green eyes are striking and she is very beautiful. I think I am developing a crush on her. I just wish she was mentally mature.

"Tell me about you," I request.

"Me?" Heather replies, taking her hands from my face. She sits back on the ground and puts her legs across mine, so that her calf muscles are across my shins, forming a diamond shape with our legs.

"Yes, you. What can you tell me about Heather? Where were you born?" I ask.

"I don't know. My tablets stop me from remembering." Heather picks up a twig and plays with it as she speaks, turning it over and holding it like a cigarette.

"How do you know it's the tablets?" I question.

"My doctor said so." Heather's eyes look away as she says the word doctor. I suspect she has bad memories of the doctor.

"And you believe him?" I ask.

"He's my doctor. Why would he lie?" She throws the twig into the leaves.

"Why does he think you *need* tablets?" I ask. I put my hand on her boot and play with the loop in the lace.

"Because I am ill," Heather explains. She looks at me playing with her lace and then pulls on one of my shoelaces, untying it.

"You don't look ill. What's your illness?" I ask.

"I don't know," Heather replies. She unties my other shoe and smiles.

"So you're taking tablets for an unidentified illness?"

"My doctor knows what it is."

"Why don't you ask him what's wrong with you?"

"He said I have the mind of a ten year old and won't understand." Heather looks at me with that blank expression again.

"I don't think you have the mind of a ten year old," I say.

"Why?" Heather asks.

"I think your tablets are making you seem as though you have the mind of a ten year old and if you stop taking the tablets you'll be normal again. I think the doctor is sedating your mind."

"No, he is trying to help me, silly." Heather laughs.

"Stop taking the tablets and see what happens," I suggest. I pull on her boot lace and untie it. If I'm going to have to tie my shoes back up she can do the same.

"No, I can't do that." Heather becomes uneasy at the thought.

"Why not?

"They make me take them. They tell me bad things if I struggle." Her eyes glaze over and she looks frightened.

"They *force* you to take them?" I ask.

"Not now. Now I take them myself."

"Do they watch?" I question, imagining two nasty people bullying her into taking medication she doesn't need.

"Yes."

"Who are they? Can I meet them?"

"No. They look after me," Heather says.

"No," I disagree. "They don't. They force you to take medication."

"It's for my own good."

"Take me home with you and introduce me to them," I demand. I feel like confronting them.

"No!" Heather snaps. She looks annoyed, so I back off.

"Would you like to come to *my* home?" I ask again. Ignoring my question, Heather ties her boot lace back up and stands up. Then she runs away. I jump to my feet and follow her as she runs through the trees. I only get twenty feet before I trip over my shoe laces and land on my face in the mud.

"Hey!" I shout to Heather. "Wait!" I roll onto my back and pull my leg up to tie my shoe lace. Then I start on the other lace. Before I finish I feel the sole of a combat boot on my forehead.

"Oh, come on!" I shout, pushing the boot off my head. She has angered me, for the first time. Standing on my forehead is just wrong. I jump up and face Heather. Her smile disarms me and I find it impossible to tell her that she crossed a line.

"Kiss me," I demand. I grab hold of Heather's jacket and pull her against me, so that we are face-to-face.

"No," Heather replies. I wonder whether she knows I find her attractive. In fact, I wonder whether she has the ability to feel love or affection at all. I lean my head forward to kiss her and she turns her head away.

"What's wrong?" I ask.

"Don't want to," Heather replies. I realise I am being a bully. I have never been a bully before. I am mirroring what the doctor does to her and she doesn't like it. I am forcing her to do something which makes her feel uncomfortable. I feel awful.

"I'm sorry," I say, letting go of her jacket. I step back. Heather looks at me and smiles.

"Do you like apples?" she asks enthusiastically, her grin widening. I feel a little confused. Has she suddenly overcome the distress of my action or was that all put on?

"Yes," I reply. I feel the need to be agreeable so she likes me. I'm not really fond of apples.

"Come with me," Heather says, taking my hand.

We run through the woods, along the top of the small valley in which North Silestia is situated. Eventually we reach the edge of the trees and, after running through a small gate, we find ourselves in an orchard of apple trees, which is spread out across a small field.

"Apples," Heather says, letting go of my hand.

"Lots of apples," I add.

Heather runs up to a tree and pulls on a branch. She tugs at a red apple and pulls it off the tree. Then she turns to me.

"They taste nice," she says, shoving the apple into her mouth and biting off a large chunk. I walk up to her and look up at the tree. Just as I am about to speak I get a face full of apple as Heather thrusts the half eaten apple into my mouth.

"Try some," she says. I bite off a small piece of apple and chew it. Heather takes it from me and bites into it again.

"I hope these haven't been treated with pesticides," I say. The apple actually does taste nice.

"Heather," a voice from behind me calls out. I turn to see a man standing at the gate to the orchard. He is holding a shotgun. I turn back to Heather and see in her face that she is worried. She drops the apple to the floor and nervously kicks her foot into the ground.

She looks at me and then the man.

"Time to come home," the man says.

"Is that your doctor?" I ask. I turn and look at the man, who is still by the gate.

"I have to go," Heather says, walking towards him. I start to follow.

"I wouldn't if I were you," the man says, raising the shotgun. "You can stay there until we are out of sight."

Heather reaches the man and turns to look at me. She lifts her hand just enough to wave at me and then turns her back and leaves the orchard. The man takes a couple of steps towards me but does not approach me.

"This is private property," he says. "If you come here again I will call the police."

I decide to say nothing. He needs to believe I am just a passer-by who Heather has played with. I nod my head and wait for the man to leave the orchard. Then I walk home.

Chapter Four
Wanting More

I don't sleep that night. I feel a strong desire to investigate Heather's life and discover why she is being held in North Silestia House by a mysterious doctor. Seeing the man with the shotgun made me angry and I want to confront him.

At two-thirty in the morning I get up and make myself some coffee, using the last few beans in the packet. I have never understood why people avoid coffee at night. It has never kept me awake. In fact I can drink a large mug of coffee and then fall straight to sleep. It is usually the last drink of my evening.

As I sit at the breakfast bar in my kitchen I think about Heather's reaction when I told her to kiss me and I feel ashamed. What was I thinking?

"Sometimes, Nate, you are such an idiot," I say to myself. The moon is bright and shines through the closed blinds as it emerges from behind a cloud. I put my coffee down, walk over to the window and open the blinds, letting the moonlight shine through. The silhouette of the woods is visible and I wonder what Heather is doing right now.

"I'm going to have a look," I say aloud.

I finish my coffee and get dressed in black cargo trousers, black t-shirt and a black jacket. I don't own a balaclava, so I find another black t-shirt and cover my head, securing it with elastic from the waistband of some old tracksuit trousers I only ever wear at home. I locate a screwdriver and then venture out.

I cross the fields in the moonlight, reaching the woods within half an hour. Then I climb over the old wire fence and enter the woods, making my way to a loosely-defined track, which leads to North Silestia House. The trees descend into the valley, right up to the stately home's back garden, which has a Victorian brick wall around it. The gateway is locked, so I climb over the wall and sneak up to the house. I hope they don't have CCTV.

The house looks deserted. I survey the windows and try to determine which is Heather's bedroom. A large conservatory on the east side of the building has a wooden door, with glass panels, so I take out the screwdriver and try to prize it open. It won't budge. The door has bolts at the top and bottom, so I head around the house in search of another doorway. I find a back door and try the handle. Unsurprisingly, it is locked, so I try the screwdriver on its latch.

After several attempts to force the door I give up.

"Now what do I do?" I ask myself. I have never broken into a house before. I wander around the building, looking for a way in. I notice an upstairs window is open and the wall next to it has a trellis with bushes growing up it, so I climb up the trellis, hoping that it stays attached to the wall.

I peer in through the open window and see that the room is empty. Then I climb through the window and make my way across the large empty bedroom.

The room has a bed and an arm chair, both of which have white sheets covering them. I assume this room is not used. The door is closed, so I carefully open it and peer out across the landing. A large staircase descends in a spiral around a central pillar. I run across the top of the stairs and try the next bedroom door. I open it slowly and peer inside. In a double bed in the centre of the room a single person is asleep. I can't tell whether it is a man or woman. I don't think it is Heather.

I close the door and head for the next bedroom. Inside I see Heather asleep. I wonder whether I should wake her and say hello, but the thought of her making a noise stops me. She might scream at the intrusion, or get excited. In the corner of the room I see the large wardrobe she has talked about. Lying across a dressing table next to it are the combat jacket and trousers Heather was wearing. I close the door and head down the stairs, which seem to be made from stone, or marble. I am relieved - wooden stairs almost always make a noise.

I find the kitchen and browse the cupboards, looking for medicine. If I can get a sample of the medicine Heather is being forced to take I can get it analysed.

After searching all the cupboards I find nothing. I leave the kitchen and head into the dining room, which has a large table in the centre. On a cabinet next to the table are decanters of alcohol, with an assortment of glasses. I walk through the dining room to a door at the opposite end and head into the living room. I walk briskly through the living room and head into a study, which has a large desk against a wall. As I scour the room for medication I hear a noise from upstairs. I stop dead and wait to see whether the noise is from a person. After a few seconds I hear footsteps on the landing. I peer through the doorway and see a second set of stairs just along from the study. They are small and simple: servants' stairs, from a time when North Silestia was owned by the upper class.

The footsteps reach the top of the stairs and start to descend. I quickly run back through to the living room, then dining room and into the kitchen, where I stop and open a window over the sink. I clamber onto the sink and dive out of the window, landing on a bush. I reach up and push the window closed and wait for a moment. Then I run across the driveway towards the walled garden, and make my way home, via the woods.

Once back home, I make more coffee and sit in my living room, energised with adrenalin. The experience of sneaking around North Silestia was exhilarating. Maybe that's what my life is missing – some adrenalin-producing excitement.

Chapter Five
Who's Watching?

Sunshine replaces moonlight, waking me as it shines through the gap in the curtains I had created to allow the moon into my bedroom.

I draw the curtains back and peer out at yet another day I had not expected to see, which reminds me that I never got my noose back from Heather.

Across the street, next to a derelict cottage, a flower delivery van sits with its engine running.

"Someone getting flowers?" I ask myself as I watch the delivery man wander along the footpath towards his van. He gets inside and picks up a clipboard, on which he starts to write. There are only a dozen houses in my street, with seven of them on the same side as mine. The opposite side of the road is mostly taken up by the shell of an old warehouse and the derelict cottage. Rumour has it that the warehouse might one day be turned into a block of flats. However, nothing has happened in the decade since that idea was first proposed and nowadays it sits empty. It is perhaps a sign of the times that a small industrial development and the mansion that is North Silestia House both lie empty.

I open the window to allow fresh air into the room and then head downstairs to the kitchen to make some coffee. When I open the cupboard I find the coffee jar almost empty. Not enough to make a pot.

"Great," I say to myself as I place the glass jar on the worktop, "another trek to the supermarket."

Supermarkets are awful places. People walk around them as though their needs are more important than anyone else. To be standing in front of a shelf of marked down items and have some ignorant self-obsessed moron lean in front of you to take the item you are looking at is incredibly annoying. I even had someone stand in front of me once. I pushed their back so they fell onto the shelf and then told them how obnoxious they were. Then I walked away, leaving them stunned. I suppose they could have pressed charges against me for assault but they didn't. The penny must have dropped and they realised they were exactly what I had described them to be.

Standing in the freezer section of my local supermarket, I examine a ready meal of chicken korma. Food in a box – the packaging really oversells what's inside; a plastic tray split in two with korma on one side and rice on the other. If the food actually filled the box it would weigh a kilogram. I flip the box over and see its weight to be 375g - three hundred and seventy-five grammes of processed food. I put the box back into the freezer and step back. I like the freezer aisle. It's always devoid of people. They tend to congregate in the fresh produce aisle or around the bakery section. No one hangs around the freezer aisle.

A woman wanders into the aisle and I see her look at me briefly before opening a cabinet, which contains desserts. She is dressed in the supermarket's uniform but has a handbag with her, which has a Hello Kitty logo on it, from which her car keys dangle. I like to study people and try to determine what makes them tick, so I analyse the woman further. On the keychain is a Yale key and a mortise lock key: front and back doors. She also has a dangling key fob, with a picture of a building on it. I step closer and pretend to look at the bags of frozen vegetables in the cabinet below the one she is looking in. The building on her key fob is the Campanile di San Marco in Venice. Her skin complexion is very English, so she's not

Italian. I bet she has fond memories of a trip to Italy. Did she meet someone there? - She bought a tacky key fob, which she keeps on her keys. Her name badge says she is called Heather, which makes me smile. I don't think I had met a woman called Heather before visiting the woods, and yet here I find myself standing next to the second one within a matter of days.

"Hi," she says, unexpectedly. I am caught a little off guard. I wasn't expecting to interact with her.

"Er, Hi," I reply. Am I being picked up in a supermarket? By an employee? I smile at the woman, who is actually quite attractive. I once read that many a relationship has started in a supermarket. I'm not sure how that happens but apparently the intention to buy food is easily abandoned when a suitable mate is seen perusing the aisles.

"You undecided?" she asks, pointing at my almost-empty basket. It holds just a jar of instant coffee and a packet of filter coffee.

"Sorry?" I reply.

"Your basket just has coffee in it," she adds.

"So much choice," I reply with some sarcasm. I'm really not sure what to say to her. I have no interest in talking to her.

"I recommend the black bean sauce," she says, pointing at a cabinet of boxed foodstuffs.

"You've tried them?" I ask.

"I live alone" she replies. "Who else buys ready meals?"

"People who don't know how to cook," I reply.

"I never find the time," she says. It's a rubbish excuse. There are many good meals which only take minutes to prepare. Her eyes widen and she smiles, revealing her teeth: clean, white teeth - all perfectly straight. "Do you cook?" she asks.

"Yes, I do," I reply. I won't lie. I do cook. I was only looking at the ready meal out of curiosity.

"Ooh, you can come 'round my house and cook for me sometime," she says with enthusiasm and a wide grin, which reveals those teeth again. Her hand finds its way to my arm and she pats me gently. She stares at me, waiting for my response, still grinning. I consider making her hang there, waiting. How long can she keep grinning if I don't respond at all? Will she just walk away?

I smile back at her, trying to show my teeth. I read somewhere that fake smiles don't show your teeth. I need to check whether that's true.

"So your name is Heather," I state, changing the subject. "I have a friend called Heather."

"Really? What's her surname?" she asks. I have no idea. Make something up.

"Friesian," I reply. It was the first word which came into my mind. I think it's a type of cow.

"Wow that's almost as unusual as my surname," she laughs.

"Which is?"

"Peavicante."

"Heather Peavicante. That *is* a mouthful."

"Don't ask what it means, I have no idea. My parents died when I was young so I couldn't ask them." She stops talking and stares at me. I see her glance down at my left hand and I wonder whether she is looking for a ring. Maybe I should get a ring. Her cheeks blush a little.

"Some friends and I are going to a club on Friday night. Would you like to join us?" she asks.

"A club? I'm not sure what I'm doing on Friday," I reply.

"Well, I'll be working here until eight. If you are interested just meet me here after work," she suggests.

"Okay, I'll see whether I am free." I lie. I think my sister's party is on Friday.

"What's your name," she asks.

"Nate," I reply. "Nate Glover."

"Maybe see you on Friday, Nate," Heather Peavicante says, clutching my forearm.

I step backwards slowly, smiling at her. I wonder whether she can read my body language as I keep backing away. I turn and leave her in the freezer aisle. Once around the corner of the last freezer cabinet, I quickly head for the checkout and pay for my coffee, dropping the empty basket into a stack by the conveyor. That was close. I am not scared of people but I do find them hard to interact with.

In the car park I see the flower delivery van that had been parked outside my house. The driver is sitting inside and he seems to be looking straight at me. He looks away when I look at him, which makes me suspicious. The van is parked in a parking space, so is probably not delivering to the store; otherwise he would be in the loading area around the back. The side of the van has a picture of some flowers and the words 'Flowers To Your Door'. No phone number. The driver is looking at me again, so I pretend not to notice and head for the alleyway which leads to a shortcut home. I admit to being a little paranoid but who knows, one day it might save my life – should I ever want my life to be saved.

The walk home is uneventful and, despite being on the lookout for the flower van, I reach my home without company.

I head to the kitchen and make some fresh coffee, whilst listening to the news on the radio. Since Heather - that is, Heather-in-the-woods - changed my mind about ending my life I have decided to make more of an effort to catch up on what is going on in the world. I still feel depressed, but not to the point that I want to die.

The news is as bleak as I might have predicted. Businesses are struggling, local crime is up and a care home has been closed because of staff cruelty.

As I drink my coffee, the telephone rings. I pick up the handset which I keep in my kitchen and press the green button.

"Hello?"

"Could I speak to Mr Glover, please?" the male voice asks.

"That's me," I reply.

"I am calling from Deedflow North. I would like to tell you about our life insurance policies."

"I don't need life insurance," I say. I haven't had a cold-call salesman call me for years. A life insurance call a few days after I had gone to the woods to hang myself?

"What would happen to your family if something happened to you and you were no longer there to provide for them?" the man asks.

"What makes you think I have a family?" I reply.

"Don't you?" he asks.

"No, I don't."

The line goes dead and I feel quite annoyed. How dare he call me to sell me life insurance to protect a family who were taken from me years ago – and then hang up on me without apologising for the intrusion. I make a mental note to look up Deedflow North and write a letter of complaint.

I finish my coffee and decide to go for a walk to clear my head. I feel the need to collect my thoughts.

Walking is a therapeutic activity for me. I do own a car, but I rarely drive it. I always wanted a Delorean, so I saved my money and bought myself one. I keep it in the garage at the side of my home. It is taxed, insured and serviced regularly - and has only been driven on a public road four times in seven years. Two of those were by my sister Lucy, when her car was off the road.

I don't want to head towards North Silestia House, so I leave my home and walk through the derelict industrial units to the other side, where small-scale industry becomes large scale farming. I follow an old footpath along the edge of the field, heading towards Old Sarum. The sun is shining and there is a cool breeze. Ahead, I see a bird of prey hovering over the field, so I stop and watch it for a moment. It hovers perfectly in the air, its wings keeping it aloft as it scours the land for prey. The bird makes a screeching sound and then swoops across the hedge to the next field where it drops to the ground. I wonder whether it caught anything.

"Well Nate, what to do now?" I ask myself. "On Monday I hated my life, missed my wife and son and I could see no reason to stay alive. On Tuesday I decided to end it – but I didn't. Heather stopped me." I think about her grinning face and I find myself smiling as I walk along.

"She bewitched me," I say, still smiling. I don't believe in witchcraft, but I find the thought of Heather having the power to bewitch amusing. I am looking forward to seeing her again this evening and I wonder how she will be dressed this time.

The blue sky is speckled with small fluffy clouds, like a fleet of alien cotton wool spaceships. On the horizon, dark clouds are looming. I stop and watch the small fluffy spaceships, to determine which way the wind is blowing and realise the dark clouds are heading this way, possibly bringing rain.

I live in a beautiful part of the country, with stunning views across Salisbury and the woodland. However, since losing the will to live I find nothing beautiful at all. My thoughts turn to people living in the cities who never get to see such amazing views and I feel guilty for not being able to appreciate it.

I sit down on rock to rest, putting my hands on the stone. It feels cold under the palm of my hand and I am reminded that my negative state of mind inhibits my ability to find satisfaction in interacting with objects in the real world. I rub my fingers along the surface of the stone and feel its pitted texture. My thoughts turn to Heather and my heart flutters. She excites me and arouses emotions I have not felt in seven years. I worry that such excitement will turn to sadness when the course of our friendship reaches an inevitable conclusion; ending as quickly as it began, possibly by her captors moving her away from North Silestia.

The dark clouds start to scare away the fluffy spaceships and I feel the first drip of water on my face. I decide to return home, to prepare for another trek to the woodland.

I enter my home and close the front door behind me just in time to avoid the rain, which pelts down as though deliberately sent to usher me inside. As I pass my antique telephone table I see the red light flashing on my answer phone, indicating a new message. I press the button to play the message.

"Don't forget the party on Friday," my sister starts. "Ring me when you get this message. I need to know you're ok."

Despite my assurances, Lucy still worries that I am suicidal. I make a mental note to ring her after I have eaten; before I head to North Silestia.

The sound of a vehicle outside takes my attention, so I open the front door just enough to peer out. The flower van is parked across the road. I immediately close the door and step back.

"More flowers?" I say to myself. The flower delivery man is really not very good at being covert. Does he think I am so stupid I might believe flowers are being delivered to my neighbour's house twice in a day? - Unless he made a mistake and has returned to correct it. Maybe he gave the wrong flowers to someone. It is hard to sift out the paranoia from the reasonable assumptions.

I open the door again and stroll across the road towards the van, intent on asking the driver some questions. It is now raining and I am getting wet. Before I reach the van, the driver sees me approaching, starts the engine and drives away, adding weight to my suspicion that he is watching me. On the other hand his eagerness to leave might simply be a desire to make his next delivery without being hindered by an accusing resident.

I return to my home and lock myself in.

Chapter Six
Expecting the Unexpected

After a small meal and a lengthy telephone conversation with my sister, I head to the woods at North Silestia. I still haven't decided whether I should tell Heather I sneaked into her home. With her unusual state of mind I don't know how she will take it.

I find the tree where we first met and wait for Heather.

The dark clouds I had seen earlier have covered the sky and darkened the woodland. The rain has stopped, for now. Through the trees, towards the fields, the sun is low in the sky. Its rays find a gap in the clouds and send a beam of golden light through the trees, turning the woodland yellow. Against the black clouds overhead the contrasting colour should be breath-taking. I am certain there are people near here looking up and mouthing 'wow' this very second. I wish I could feel that.

Rain starts to fall again, pattering onto the leaves of the trees. The experience is so unusual I don't even think to take shelter. I find myself smiling.

"Well Nate, this is what life is all about." I recall the depressed state in which I wanted to kill myself and feel embarrassed. Golden trees and dark clouds have partially succeeded where my sister failed. They make me feel alive. Or is it something else?

Ahead of me, through the trees, a shadowy figure walks casually towards me. She has an umbrella over her head and is singing to herself. As she emerges from the shadow of the large trees the golden sunshine illuminates her like a theatrical spotlight. I become aware of the rain on my face as water trickles over my eyelashes, so I wipe my face with my hand and brush my wet hair back off my forehead.

I wonder what costume she is wearing today. I hope it is not a police outfit. She has an umbrella, so maybe she is Mary Poppins.

"Hello!" I shout to Heather as she walks up to me. She is wearing a raincoat, under which I can just make out a blue blouse of some kind. It doesn't seem to be a costume.

"Hello again," Heather says as she reaches me. She hands me the umbrella and opens her raincoat to reveal a large pregnancy bump. For a moment I am lost for words. Heather rubs the fake belly as though it is real.

"You're, er," I start.

"Pregnant," Heather says. She smiles and takes the umbrella back. "Let's go to the den and get out of the rain," she suggests. Without waiting for my response she runs through the trees. I follow her.

"Where's the den?" I shout. I duck under a low branch and splash in a muddy puddle.

"It's not far," she replies, one hand holding the umbrella and the other tucked under her fake bump to stop it falling out. As we run, the sun disappears behind the clouds, extinguishing the golden light display and sending a shadow through the forest.

Heather leads me down a track, which seems to be heading towards the mansion – is she taking me home? Before reaching the house, she ducks into a small garden and, jumping over the flowerbeds, heads for a gazebo, which has glass windows all round. Heather runs inside and drops onto the sofa, which is against the back wall. She lets the umbrella fall to the floor, still open. I follow her in and close the door, just as a flash of lightning lights up the sky. It is followed by a tremendous clap of thunder.

"That was close," I say, referring to the thunder.

"I don't like thunder," Heather admits. I turn and look at her; sitting on the sofa, with her hand on the bump. It is quite large and makes her look as though she is due to give birth any day. Her outfit is nowhere near as appealing as the soldier or the cheerleader. Having said that, I believe there are men who are attracted to pregnant bellies. I'm just not one of them.

"Sit with me," she requests. Another flash of lightning makes her jump, so I quickly sit down next to her before the thunder scares her. She pulls my shoulder close to her and rests her face on me. The clap of thunder is so loud the glass in the gazebo rattles. I feel her hand tighten on my arm.

"What's that made from?" I ask, looking at the bump. I prod it with my finger.

"Rubber, I think," Heather replies.

"Why on Earth do you have a maternity dress with a fake bump in your wardrobe?"

"It was just there," Heather replies.

"I really wasn't expecting that," I admit. "Policewoman – yes; clown - maybe, but not a pregnant woman."

"It feels cosy," Heather says, rubbing the fake belly. "Do you want to feel it kick?"

I pause for a moment as I consider whether the bump is animatronic.

"Er, okay," I agree. I put my hand on the bump and feel. Nothing happens.

"Did you feel that?" Heather says excitedly.

"No," I say, ignorant of her role-play.

"There it is again," she says. I feel stupid when I realise she is pretending, like when she pretended to smoke cigarettes whilst in the combat uniform. Heather seems different today; not so childlike. She is more pensive; more adult, despite pretending to be pregnant.

"I felt that one," I say, deciding to play along. We sit in

silence for a moment, awaiting the next flash of lightning. When it comes, Heather turns her head towards me and tucks her face under my chin. I pull her face up to mine and kiss her on the lips. She kisses me and the thunder rocks the gazebo. I stare into her bright green eyes for a moment and then realise I owe her an explanation.

"I was just trying to take your mind off the thunder," I say.

"I liked it," Heather replies. Her grin beams at me and I find my heart beating faster. Her smile is infectious and I cannot help but grin back at her. I realise I still have my hand on her fake belly, so I slowly take it away and sit back. Heather puts her hand on my knee and squeezes it, so I place my hand on top of hers.

"You seem different today," I tell her.

"They left me alone," Heather replies.

"Who? Your doctors?"

"Yes. I don't want to be alone."

"Where did they go?" I ask. Heather takes her hand off my knee and looks away from me, at the garden beyond the glass panes.

"Shopping." She looks back at me. "I heard them say they were going to meet someone."

"Who?" I ask.

"I don't know. He might be the man who made me wear this dress on the first day."

"The first day?"

"The day I came here." Heather fingers the material of my trousers around my kneecap and squeezes my knee.

"Do you know when that was?" I ask, rubbing her fingers with mine.

"Forty-two days ago."

"Have they ever left you before?" I ask.

"Not for this long," she replies.

"Would you like to come home with me whilst they are

away?" I ask. Heather smiles and jumps up off the sofa.

"I'd love that," she says, picking up the umbrella and shaking the water off it. "Can I stay the night?"

"If you want," I agree. "I don't want to get you in trouble though. What if they come back and you're not here?"

"You can bring me back in the morning," Heather says. She taps the floor with the tip of the umbrella. Yesterday she said she can't leave. Today she is eager. I wonder whether she has stopped taking the medication.

"Do you want to get changed first and bring some more clothes?" I ask as I stand up.

"No, I'm fine," she says.

"You're sure?" I question.

"Yes," Heather says, smiling. I take the umbrella from her and close it. I throw it onto the sofa as another flash of lightning crackles through the clouds above the stately home which is only a few hundred feet from us. I didn't realise we had got this close to the house. This time the lightning is forked and is followed almost immediately by the thunder. Heather throws her arms around me in fear, so I hold her to comfort her. The rubber bump is pressed against me and I briefly find myself concerned about the pressure our embrace is putting on it. Then I remind myself that there is no baby inside her.

"This storm could go on for ages," I say. "Perhaps we should go into your home. You could show me the wardrobe from which you keep getting these outfits."

"No," Heather objects. "If they come back they will hurt you."

"Okay, we'll go to my house." I pull myself away from her and look out the window at the dark clouds overhead. "Are you sure you don't want to change out of that outfit?" I ask.

"Don't you like it?" Heather replies. I turn and look at her. She is playing the expectant mum again, rubbing her hand on the bump.

"I was just thinking about your comfort," I lie. I feel uneasy having the romantic feelings I feel for her whilst she appears to be pregnant.

Rain thrashes down on the gazebo roof and another ray of golden sunshine cuts through the trees to light up the large grey house.

"I think the storm is clearing," I say. "Apparently, if you are in the rain, you're not under the thunder cloud. The storm must be passing over."

Heather says nothing, so I take her hand and squeeze it.

"You're perfectly safe," I reassure her. I prod the bump with my finger and smile. "Boy or girl?" I ask.

"I don't mind," Heather replies.

"It's a girl," I suggest. It's my turn to role-play. "We can call her Penelope."

Penelope? How about Constance?"

"Constance. Connie. Okay, Constance it is."

The rain stops, so we venture out of the gazebo. The gap in the clouds has grown and the sunshine flooding though is no longer golden. Everything looks normal - wet, but normal. As we leave the garden I scan the house for signs of life but see nothing.

Heather and I walk through the forest holding hands. I think about her medication.

"When did you last take your tablets?" I ask.

"Yesterday," Heather replies.

"Were you meant to take some today?"

"Yes," she says, squeezing my hand. "Do you think I'll get ill?"

"Not at all," I reply. "In fact, I would say you are getting better."

"Better?"

"You seem more adult now," I explain. "You don't have the mind of a child."

"I feel strange," Heather admits.

"Strange? In what way?"

"Thoughts, images, keep appearing in my head. They confuse me."

"I expect that's because you have stopped taking the medication. I really think that's a good thing."

"You do?"

"Yes, definitely."

We leave the woodland and head across the fields, towards my home. I turn and look back at the trees behind us and smile. I am taking Heather home! As we walk through the grass I realise I am falling in love with her.

We reach my back garden and I help Heather climb over the stone wall. Then I unlock the back door and invite her into my home.

"Would you like to change out of your wet clothes?" I ask, wondering what I have that she could wear.

"Can I shower?" Heather asks.

"Of course."

I show Heather to the bathroom and take a couple of towels out of the airing cupboard.

"Would you like to borrow some of my clothes?" I ask, wondering how I am going to wash and dry a maternity dress with a rubber bump in it.

"No, I'm fine," Heather insists.

"You sure?"

"Yes." She pushes me out of the bathroom and closes the door. Whilst she showers, I make tea and relax in my living room. After almost an hour I hear the hairdryer being used upstairs, so I venture up to my bedroom and find Heather wrapped in my dressing gown, blow drying the maternity dress.

"Did you wash the dress in the shower?" I ask.

"No, I'm just drying the rain out," Heather replies.

"I have a tumble dryer to do that."

"It's okay, I'm done," Heather says, turning the hairdryer off. She drops it on the bed and stands up, shaking the dress to straighten it.

"Would you like some tea?" I ask.

"Do you have fruit juice?"

"Orange juice ok?"

"Yes please," she says with a grin. I leave her in the bedroom and head back down the stairs. As I pass the front door I notice a shadow across the glass window next to the door. The shadow moves and I realise someone is outside. The doorbell rings, making me jump.

"Who's there?" I shout through the door.

"Lucy! Who were you expecting?"

I unlock the door and open it to let my sister in.

"What's wrong with you, little brother? You never shout through the door," Lucy says as she enters my home. She kisses me on the cheek and takes off her coat.

"I'm fine," I reply, taking her coat from her.

"I thought I'd check up on you. Make sure you're still thinking positive."

"I am," I say. I hang Lucy's coat on a spare hook on the coat stand at the bottom of the stairs.

"So what's on your mind?" she asks. She kicks off her shoes and stares at me.

"I'm not sure where to start."

"Did you see Heather again?"

"Yes."

"And?"

"I brought her home," I admit.

"You what?"

"She's upstairs." I point over my shoulder at the stairs.

"I thought you said she was under the supervision of a doctor."

"She was. They left her alone so I brought her here."

"You sure that's wise?" Lucy asks. I wonder whether I am about to get a lecture.

"I'll make some more tea," I say to avoid a scolding. As I leave Lucy and head for the kitchen I hear footsteps on the stairs above. Heather comes slowly down the stairs. I stop and wait to introduce her to my sister.

Lucy is shocked to see the apparently heavily pregnant Heather descend the stairs. She turns and scowls at me, then looks back at Heather.

"Hello," Heather says with a smile. "Who are you?"

"I'm Lucy, Nate's sister."

"Lucy, it's not what you think," I say, jumping between her and Heather. I prod Heather's belly.

"It's fake."

"Ooh, I can feel her kicking again," Heather says, rubbing the bump. I regret adding gender to the role-play. I realise that I need to separate the two women so I can explain to Lucy about Heather's tendency to make believe.

"Heather, go and have a seat in the living room," I say, escorting her towards the doorway. "Take the weight off your feet."

Lucy looks disapprovingly at me. I pull her through the kitchen door and shut us in.

"The belly is fake," I say quietly. "Heather is on medication which makes her act like a child. She likes to dress up and play the part. Today she decided to be pregnant and is role-playing. Yesterday she was a soldier."

"Why?" Lucy asks.

"I'm not sure, but she hasn't taken her pills since yesterday and she has already started to become more normal."

"Normal? Rubbing a fake belly and pretending to feel the baby kick is normal?"

"Well, no but she's starting to act her age. When I first met her she was like a child in an adult's body. Since yesterday she has lost that childlike personality. I think someone has been keeping her drugged up for a reason."

"What reason?"

"I don't know, but she said they left her."

"What happens when they get back and find her gone?" Lucy asks.

"I'm taking her back in the morning," I say.

"We should call the police. PC Dorak will know what to do."

"No, I don't want to call the police."

"Why not?"

"I just don't." That's a pathetic excuse. In reality, I don't want to call the police because I am falling in love with Heather and I am worried the police will take her away.

"You sleeping with her?" Lucy asks. Her stare is piercing, like a mother to a naughty child.

"No, I'm not. I'll sleep on the sofa."

"What if she kills you in your sleep?" Lucy considers.

"What?" I hadn't thought she might do that. "I don't think she's dangerous," I take a cup and a glass out of the cupboard.

"How do you know?" Lucy asks. The door opens and Heather enters the kitchen.

"How do you know what?" Heather asks.

"Nate tells me that you have stopped taking your medication," Lucy says to her.

"Yes," Heather replies. She walks up to me and puts her arms around me, hugging me tightly. She rests her chin on my shoulder and I feel awkward. I feel as though I should hug her to comfort her but I can see Lucy is annoyed.

"Really Nate?" Lucy scowls.

"What?" Sometimes I wish she would just speak her mind.

"You're sleeping with a vulnerable, pregnant woman."

Maybe not now, though.

"No, I'm not!" I insist. I push Heather away gently and press the fake belly.

"It's fake," I repeat. Lucy steps forward and puts her hand on the belly. Heather jumps and steps back.

"Connie is kicking hard now," she says, grinning. I step behind Heather and put my arms around her. She thinks I am hugging her. Instead I press the fake belly in so far that Lucy can see it is fake.

"See?" I say to Lucy. She nods.

"Heather, why do you take medication?" she asks.

"To stop me from getting ill," Heather replies.

"What kind of illness will you get if you stop taking the medication?" Lucy asks.

"I don't know."

"Have you ever hurt another person?" Lucy sits on a bar stool and leans an elbow on the worktop.

"I don't think so," Heather replies. She smiles for no apparent reason.

"Do you understand why you are here?" Lucy probes further.

"Nate brought me here," Heather replies. She looks at me and grins, her eyes wide.

"Why?" Lucy asks.

"He wanted to," Heather says, turning back to Lucy. "Why are *you* here?"

"I'm Nate's sister," I care for him.

"That's nice," Heather says.

Lucy looks at me.

"Trust me sis," I say to her. "I know what I am doing and no one is being taken advantage of."

"You do what you have to," Lucy says, heading towards the door. "Just remember, suicide is bad but being murdered is worse." Lucy looks at Heather and then leaves.

"What does that mean?" Heather asks.

"It means my sister is annoyed with me."

Chapter Seven
Return To Normality

My sofa is surprisingly comfortable to sleep on and I awake feeling refreshed. I am excited to see Heather and hopeful that a few more hours without medication have returned her to an adult mentally.

I creep up the stairs, slowly, listening for sounds of movement and trying not to wake Heather. I tiptoe across the landing and stop at my bedroom, slowly pushing the door ajar to peer into the room. Heather is still asleep and is curled up in my bed. Her clothing is in a neatly folded pile on the chair next to the bed. I enter the room and approach the bed.

"Heather?" I say quietly. I'm not sure why I said it quietly. I *want* to wake her.

"Heather?" I repeat, louder this time. "Wake up."

Heather stirs as she starts to wake. She is like a person recovering from a hangover. She groans and wipes her eyes. Turning onto her front she pulls the pillow over her head.

"Mora doo vantea," she mumbles from under the pillow.

"What?" I ask. She is speaking gibberish. Maybe the medication *was* for her own good. "Are you okay? Would you like a drink?"

The pillow is thrown off her head and Heather turns onto her back. She looks shocked to see me.

"How do you feel?" I ask. Her expression changes and she looks confused. "Do you remember me?" I add.

"Oh no, this is bad," Heather says as she pulls herself up. She has only said a few words but I can tell she is no longer the childlike adult who liked to dress up and run around the woods. I am apprehensive about who I am now communicating with. Does she still like me or am I about to be told to leave? "I can't be here," she adds. Her eyes survey the room; then me, my clothes and her own clothes piled on the chair.

I sit down on the end of the bed and wait for her to collect her thoughts.

"Can you remember meeting me in the woods?" I ask.

"Yes," she replies. "It's all very vague, like I dreamt it, but I remember."

"Are we still friends?"

She pauses as she scrutinises my face before replying, "We shouldn't be friends. I'm sorry but you should never have met me."

"But I *did* meet you. We *are* friends." I pause before adding: "I hope."

"I need time to think," Heather says. "Being with me puts your life in danger. I must leave." She looks under the covers to assess her clothing and them climbs out of the bed. She is wearing my pyjamas. Standing by the bed, Heather looks at me, deep in thought.

"If it is any consolation," I state, "I was on my way to end my life when I met you, so being in danger isn't much of a bother to me."

"I'm sorry, Nate," Heather says, disregarding my comment - it is interesting to hear her talking like an adult. "Something is very, very wrong. For your safety, I must leave." She pauses to think. "You should go and stay somewhere else for a few days - a friend's house maybe."

"What is it? What's the danger?" I ask.

"I can't explain. It's complicated." Heather edges towards her pile of clothes.

"Well, I'm not exactly a dipstick." I point out. "I'm intelligent and I have an open mind. Try explaining it to me."

I think the people who kept me in North Silestia were hiding me from someone really nasty. I'm not sure why they were protecting me but I think the medication was to stop me leaving."

"Why didn't they just tie you up?" I ask.

"I don't know. I need to find out why they took me from..." Heather stops mid sentence. "I have questions of my own to answer." She paces around the room, biting her thumb nail.

"If it's so dangerous, why don't you come with me? We could go to my sister's house while you recover from the medication," I suggest.

"I have to go back to North Silestia and talk to the doctors," Heather decides.

"What if they subdue you and medicate you again. You need me to come with you, as backup," I argue. I am aware that my temporary respite from depression is just that: temporary. Heather intrigued me and gave me something to focus on. If I lose her now I will certainly return to the state I was in when I first met her in the woods.

"Nate," Heather says with a concerned expression. She stops to think, scrutinising me as she considers her options.

"I'm not afraid to die," I say. "My life has been pretty crap lately and I have been wallowing in self pity. You have given me a reason to live. I want to help you." That sounded much better in my head.

Heather steps closer to me and touches my arm gently.

"Can you trust me unconditionally?" she asks.

"What do you mean?"

"If I told you it was safe to jump through a window, would you do it?" Heather stares into my eyes. She is serious. Whatever memories she now recalls, she really is worried about my safety.

"Despite logic and experience telling me that I will cut myself?" I clarify.

"Yes."

"Is that something you're likely to tell me to do?"

"No, but I may well expect you to act against your better judgement," Heather says. She takes her hand off my arm and turns to look out of the window.

"Well, as long as I can be confident that you know what's going on, I suppose I could trust you in that respect," I say.

"You have to trust me completely," she says, turning to me. "Once we leave this house and go to North Silestia the world as you know will change."

"Really? The world?" I question. She's either being very melodramatic or I really have poked the biggest wasps' nest known to man.

"The world," Heather confirms.

"When I entered the woods with a noose I was looking to leave the world I knew, so having it replaced appeals somewhat." I admit. I wonder whether now is a good time to ask for my noose back.

"I need clothes." Heather picks up her maternity dress.

"You were wearing that last night," I remind her.

Heather pulls the rubber bump out of the dress and drops it on the floor. She holds the dress against her front and looks down at it.

"Can I borrow some trousers?" she asks.

"There are some cargo trousers in that drawer," I say, pointing at my chest of drawers. "You'll need a belt, though. My waist is considerably bigger than yours."

"That would be good, thank you." Heather replies. She rips the dress in half.

"Would you like some tea?" I ask.

"Yes please." She starts undoing the pyjama top, so I leave her and head for the door.

"Nate?" Heather says just as I am about to leave. I turn and look at her.

"Yes?"

"Thank you."

"No problem." I leave the bedroom and head downstairs to the kitchen.

I make some tea and fry some bacon. Whilst I pour the tea, Heather comes down the stairs and enters the kitchen. She is wearing a pair of my black cargo trousers, with the top half of the maternity dress.

"That smells nice," she says, looking at the frying pan.

"You like bacon?"

"Love it."

"Good. One bacon sandwich coming up." I pass a mug of tea to Heather and lean back against the worktop on the opposite side of the kitchen. Heather sips the tea carefully before sitting on a bar stool at the worktop.

I'm not sure what to say but I feel awkward not chatting. I want to ask her about her memories but I suspect she will avoid answering. I look at her, still considering what to say and she looks back at me, without emotion, staring as though I am nothing. I feel uneasy, so I smile. Heather just stares at me.

"If I asked you just to tell me everything, would you at least consider doing so?" I ask.

"No," Heather replies bluntly. "Don't misunderstand me, Nate, I am not keeping secrets because I don't want you to know. Now I have my memories back I need to decide how to proceed. I can't tell you anything until I am certain it will not jeopardise our lives."

"Is it that serious? Why did they need to drug you and keep you in North Silestia? Were you an assassin?" I ask. If something sinister was going on I might as well believe Heather to be dangerous and exciting.

"No. My background is in science."

"You're a scientist?"

"Yes," Heather says, rubbing her fingers down the handle of her mug.

"What field?" I ask. Heather hesitates and looks out of the window behind me, briefly, before answering.

"Neuroptics," she says.

"Neuroptics?" I question. "Like eyes?"

"Not eyes. Light at a quantum level," Heather divulges. I want to keep her talking.

"I studied physics at university," I tell her. Heather nods her head and then drinks some tea. She turns away and looks at the painting of a steam train I have on my kitchen wall. I liked the painting because it is not a tidy, elegant looking machine. It's a dirty, dark, industrial machine.

"Can you tell me any more?" I ask. Heather shakes her head and looks away from me. She flicks a blue feather which is sticking out of a small cup on a corner shelf. Then she turns and looks at me.

"I don't want to talk about that anymore," she says.

"Okay. Then, may I compliment you on your beauty?" I say with a smile. Humour usually gets people back on my side.

When I first met my wife I was really nervous in her presence. I wanted to say the right thing and ensure that I came across as cool and sophisticated. Nerves made that impossible. However, with Heather I feel relaxed about telling her she is beautiful. I think it is because she has admitted she has secrets and cannot tell me what they are. Somehow, that makes her the uncool one, which makes me feel more relaxed about my own self image. At least that's what I choose to believe.

"Thank you," Heather replies. She takes the feather out of the cup, smells it and then replaces it in the cup.

I turn to the frying pan and flip the bacon over. Then I butter some bread. Behind me, Heather wanders around my kitchen, examining my belongings. I feel her beside me, watching me cook the bacon, silently observing: no comments about my home, the decor, the tea. Nothing. I bet she is great at psychological games.

I make two bacon sandwiches and cut them into triangles. I pass one to my mysterious guest. She puts her plate on the table.

"Mercy," Heather says breaking the silence. She takes a bite of her sandwich.

"Do you speak French?" I ask.

"Yes," she says with a muffled voice, as she chews the bacon.

"Is that pertinent to our situation?"

"Non. I learnt French a long time ago." She takes another bite of the sandwich.

"Anything I should know before we head for North Silestia?" I ask.

"You might not live to come home," she replies. I turn and look into her eyes. Is she mocking me? She looks serious.

"Whilst you were medicated," I reply, "I visited you in the woods several times and no attempt was made on my life. I even met your doctor and he told me not to come around again - but nothing life threatening. So, why do you think North Silestia is a danger now?" It is my turn to bite a sandwich. The bacon tastes good.

"Because they know I haven't been taking the medication and by now will have returned to my normal self. They have to deal with that."

"What are you going to do?" I ask. I jump up and sit on my worktop.

"I'm going to ask them questions and then get out of there as quickly as I can," Heather replies.

"What about me?"

"You should stay here. In fact, we should never see each other again."

"Yeah, but the problem I have with that is that I have a massive crush on you and I can't stand for us to be apart."

"You don't even know me," Heather dismisses. She drinks some tea and holds on to the mug.

"The little I do know is enough to make me like you. When you were medicated you were a fun-loving, childlike adult who returned my will to live. Now you're normal again, I may well be falling in love with you."

Heather puts the mug down and steps into my personal space. She cups her hand around my chin gently.

"Nathan Glover the third, you don't know who I really am. You are falling in love with the idealised image of who you think I am, because the childlike version of me made you feel happy."

"Kiss me," I say, knowing what the answer will be. As I said, I feel relaxed about saying things like that to her.

"No," Heather replies. She taps my nose with her finger and steps back.

"I want to come with you," I insist. "I can look after myself." Heather takes hold of my hand.

"Nate, do you ever envisage scenarios in your head showing all the possible outcomes of an event?" she asks.

"All the time. Why?"

"I do too, and I cannot envisage a scenario in which you come out alive or happy, other than me leaving you here and never seeing you again. If you were me, what would you do?"

"I would say what the hell. If it's going to end badly for him I might as well tell him everything." I smile. "Besides, if you leave me I'll be back in the woods with a noose before the day is out." As soon as I have said that, I hate myself for doing so. It sounds like emotional blackmail.

"Nice try." Heather smiles and I am reminded of the cheerleader I met on Tuesday.

"I really do like you," I say, playing down my feelings.

"I like you too, which is why I want to protect you."

"I would rather die by your side than sit at home with just my thoughts for company."

Heather stares at me for a moment, so I give her time to think.

"Very well. Come with me to North Silestia, but please, do exactly as I say once we get there."

"I promise I will," I agree.

We finish our bacon sandwiches and I wash up the plates, cups and frying pan, whilst Heather dries them with a tea towel.

"Do you own a car?" Heather asks.

"Yes, why? Do you want to drive to North Silestia?"

"Yes. We can get away quickly in a car."

"Okay. It could do with a run."

The Delorean is my pride and joy. I bought it just before I met my wife, Francine. I can remember when I first sat in the car. I couldn't stop grinning. After Francine died I stopped driving it, but I kept it road legal.

I introduce Heather to my Delorean and drive us to North Silestia - it is further by road. Heather's eyes are like a hawk. She constantly twitches and turns her head, looking at everything we pass.

We reach the entrance to North Silestia, which consists of two large iron gates attached to stone pillars, with the words North Silestia House carved into a piece of marble on each side.

"Leave the car here," Heather says, taking her seatbelt off.

I park by the gates and turn the engine off.

"How long is the driveway?" I ask. When I visited the other night I came down through the trees.

"It winds through the grounds, but we can cut through the garden, which will take us straight to the house. Heather opens the gull wing door and climbs out of the car.

"Is that the garden with the gazebo?" I ask as I climb out of the Delorean.

"No, that's on the other side," Heather says across the roof of the car. We both close the doors down.

"I'm not sure whether you need to know this, but I've been inside the house," I admit.

"When?" Heather looks concerned. I'm not sure whether I have seen her frown before.

"Night before last. The day you were dressed as a soldier. I sneaked back that night and climbed in through a window." I lean my arms against the roof of the Delorean.

"What did you see?"

"I saw the doctor asleep and you, in your room, asleep. I went downstairs and then heard someone moving around, so I climbed out a window and went home."

"They may know who you are," Heather contemplates. She looks towards the house, deep in thought.

"They didn't see me," I assure her.

"You never heard of telesurveillance? This place has cameras everywhere. Why do you think the doctor came up to the orchard to tell you to clear off?"

"I was careful. No one followed me home."

We head in through the large gates, leaving them slightly ajar.

Heather leads me through the once ornate flower garden, which is now riddled with weeds and debris from the surrounding trees. We reach the house and approach the front door.

"Nervous?" I ask Heather.

"Yes," she replies. She pulls on a doorbell handle, which doesn't seem to make a sound.

"You want to know whether I am nervous?" I ask.

"No," Heather replies. We wait for someone to open the door.

Nothing.

Heather bangs on the door and pulls the doorbell handle again. After a couple of minutes, we realise no one is coming.

"They still out?" I ask.

Heather tries the handle and finds the door unlocked. She slowly opens the large wooden door and slips inside. I follow her in and we wander through the hall to the bottom of the main staircase.

"Hello!" Heather shouts up the stairs. No one answers.

"Doctor Robert!" she shouts again.

"Doctor Robert?" I question. "That's one of my favourite..." Heather cuts me off with a wave of her hand.

"Shh." she says, listening intently.

"Maybe they never came back," I say.

"Something is wrong," Heather realises.

I follow her through to the kitchen, where a meal is laid out on the table. It appears to be roast beef, with new potatoes, vegetables and Yorkshire pudding. In the centre of the table is a bowl of purple fruit, which I am unable to identify. Heather touches the meat on one of the plates and then sniffs it.

"Cold," she says. I lean forward to pick up one of the fruit, but Heather slaps my hand before I can touch them.

"They might be poisoned," she warns me.

"You just touched the meat," I state. Heather ignores my comment and turns to look around the room. A door is ajar.

"That door is usually locked," she says, pushing it open slowly.

"What's in there?" I ask.

"The medication," she replies, stepping into the small room, which is dark. Heather steps to one side to allow me to enter the room.

"You okay?" I ask.

"I'm fine." Heather replies. "The light switch is on the right."

I take a step to my right and feel for the light switch. It clicks under my fingers and the room lights up. To my horror, the wall opposite is covered in sprays of blood. On the floor are the bodies of two people; the doctor and a woman. Their heads half missing where something shot them.

"They were protecting me," Heather says.

"Okay," I say, trying to stay calm. I try to think logically. "Firstly, you didn't kill them did you?"

"No I didn't. Someone must have come here whilst I was at your home."

"Lucky I took you home." I say. Heather turns and looks at me. "I would be dead now, if you hadn't."

"Does that deserve a kiss?" I ask, smiling. Heather ignores my comment and looks at the corpses.

One of the advantages of suffering from clinical depression - to be so low as to want to die - nothing really bothers me. Right now I should be vomiting or running around in circles shouting, oh my god there's dead people in there. But, apart from the surprise of seeing dead bodies, I don't feel anything.

"Should we call the police?" I ask.

"No." Heather replies. "They can't help." She steps closer to the bodies and examines them.

"Why not?" I question. I step forward and have a closer look myself. I have never seen a gunshot wound before.

"This is beyond their remit." Heather says, turning to head for the door. She seems very calm.

"Really? I thought murder was exactly what the police deal with."

Waiting at the door, Heather says: "We need to get out of here."

"We could go to my sister's house. It would be safer there."

"Will she mind?"

"Of course not."

Chapter Eight
Flower Delivery Van

I step through my front door once again, having left with an expectation of not returning for a second time. This time, I am dragging a suitcase of Heather's clothes, retrieved in haste from North Silestia.

"I'll put these up stairs," I say to Heather as she closes the front door behind us.

"We should keep quiet and be vigilant," Heather suggests, closing the small curtain over the side window next to the front door. "Whoever killed the doctor may well find us here. It's too close to North Silestia."

I turn and let go of the suitcase. Heather kicks her shoes off to reveal her bare feet.

"I've never seen someone shot in the head before. If they were killed last night whilst you were here with me, the killers would have had time to track us down. They should have found us by now."

"Even so, we must remain vigilant."

"I agree." My thoughts turn to the flower delivery man, who may or may not have been watching me. Being paranoid doesn't help with making logical decisions about these kinds of things. I wonder whether I should tell Heather about him. On the other hand, Heather has a whole world of secrets she's keeping from me, so maybe... I should tell her. One of her secrets might involve a flower delivery man. She needs to know what I know.

I pick up the suitcase and drag it up the stairs.

"I'll make some tea," Heather says as she heads for the kitchen. I feel pleased. I am fully aware of my ignorance of the severity of what is happening around me. Having Heather in my home is a pleasure, especially now she is back to normal. As I said to her earlier, I would die by her side.

I reach the bedroom and leave the case just inside the door. Then I head downstairs to the kitchen.

Heather is sitting on the floor in the dark, with the blinds closed.

"You okay?" I ask.

"I don't want to sit in front of windows," she replies. The kettle clicks, so I pour the water into the two mugs Heather has prepared.

"You think the killer is a sniper?" I ask.

"I think the killer could shoot a person through a keyhole if needed," Heather replies. "With thermal imaging, nowhere is safe."

I find myself semi-crouching at the thought of a sniper outside, watching us through a thermal imaging camera. I quickly finish making the tea and sit on the floor next to Heather, as close to her as I feel I can get away with. Our knees touch as we sit with them raised. To my surprise - and pleasure - Heather puts her hand on my knee.

"When we go to your sister's house, we must make sure we are not followed." Heather states. "We don't want to drag trouble to her front door."

"There's something I should mention," I say, deciding that now is a good time to mention the flower van.

"What?" Heather replies, she sips some tea and puts the mug on the floor.

"Yesterday, a flower delivery van was parked outside. The man was delivering flowers to someone in this street, so I thought nothing of him. Then I saw the van in the supermarket and again outside my home later on. I went out to talk to him but he drove off. I don't know whether he didn't see me and was about to drive off anyway or whether he didn't want to talk to me."

"Have you seen him since?" Heather asks.

"No."

"Did you see what he looked like?"

Not, very well. The best view I got was from my window when he was walking back to his van. After he drove off I came to meet you in the woods and brought you back here."

"I don't recall seeing a flower delivery van at any time whilst in North Silestia," Heather remembers. "If he was watching you he would know I am here. So why kill the doctor?"

"Maybe he's on our side." I suggest.

"Or he was simply delivering flowers." Heather considers. She takes her hand off my knee and ties her hair into a bun. She has lovely hair. I take the opportunity to drink some tea.

"Do you want anything to eat?" I ask.

"No, I'm not hungry," Heather replies. She stretches her legs out and wiggles her bare feet.

"Are we going to stay on the kitchen floor all day?" I ask. "Lucy doesn't get home until six o'clock and it's only eleven now." I dare myself to put my hand on Heather's knee but am unable to lift my hand. The nerves which had hindered my ability to be slick in front of my wife are now starting to kick in. I lift my hand and put it on my own knee, as close to hers as I can get. Then I lean my knee towards Heather's knee, so that the side of my hand is touching her. Just need to flip my hand across...

Heather leans forward and crawls under the kitchen table towards a French dresser I bought at an antique auction. She reaches up and takes a book off the dresser, then crawls back to me with it.

"I bought that last week," I say as Heather kneels in front of me, her back against one of the chairs. "It's about the mythology of angels."

Heather stares at me for a moment and then says: "You believe in this stuff?"

"Not at all. I just saw the book and thought it might be interesting. How about you?"

"No. I don't believe in anything paranormal." Heather flicks through the book. "Have you read it?" she asks.

"A few chapters."

Heather closes the book and rubs her shoulder.

"Have you hurt your shoulder?" I ask.

"No, just an ache." she replies.

I lean forward and put my hand on her shoulder.

"How about a massage?" I say as my fingers touch her back.

Heather jumps, dropping the book on the floor. It hits her mug and knocks it over, spilling tea across the floor tiles. She turns her back away from me and holds her hand up in a stop, gesture.

"Please, don't touch my back," she says.

"Okay. I'm sorry," I say. I'm glad I stopped myself touching her knee now. If I touch her breast, will she beat me to death?

Heather picks up the book and hands it to me.

"Don't apologise," she says. "It's my issue. You weren't to know."

"Is there something wrong with your back?" I ask. I try to recall what it looks like - no hump as far as I remember.

"No, not at all." Heather turns away from me and lifts the modified maternity dress up to show me her back. It looks normal. Like any woman's back: no scars, no hump, nothing. So why so protective of it? The only thing obvious about her back is that her spine is visible under the skin - but then it often is with slim people.

"See?" Heather says, dropping the dress back into place. As she turns and looks at me my inquisitive body-language-reading-skills kick in.

Why did she feel the need to show me her normal back? If she hadn't, I would have accepted her explanation. She needed me to see that her back was normal, which makes me think it isn't. Maybe she has an injury between her shoulder blades – I didn't see that area. There must be something about it she is hiding, otherwise she wouldn't have overcompensated. Now I am really intrigued.

"I study body language," I say. Heather picks up the mug and places it on the worktop. "You just overcompensated," I add.

"Overcompensated?" Heather replies. She sees a tea towel hanging on a pole under the worktop and takes it. "Can I use this?"

I nod and watch as Heather mops up the tea. I lean back against the table in the centre of the room.

"You didn't need to show me your back," I explain.

"I wanted you to see I am not injured," Heather replies.

"Why would you be injured?" I ask. Heather throws the tea towel over the worktop into the sink and sits back against the worktop, facing me.

"I would like to stop talking about this now," she says. I look down at her feet and, without hesitation, take hold of her toes and massage them. I can do it when I am not trying to be flirty. Heather doesn't jump or shout at all.

"You have nice feet," I say, wondering what Heather is thinking.

"Thank you. You've seen a lot of feet, have you?" she quips. I keep rubbing her feet.

"If we're going to spend the day on the floor, we might as well go to a room where there is carpet," I suggest.

"Good idea," Heather says, pulling her feet away from my

hands and crawling towards the door. I swig down the last of my tea and stand up. I put the mug in the sink and walk towards the door, where Heather is on her hands and knees. She looks up and sees me standing, so she stands up and runs out of the kitchen and into the living room. I follow her through to the living room, where she is lying on the floor next to the sofa, looking up at me with her hands behind her head.

"Sofa?" I question. Heather shakes her head, so I drop onto the sofa and turn on my side to look down at her.

"You okay lying on your *normal* back?" I mock.

"Very funny," Heather replies.

"So what can you tell me about Heather?" I ask. I stretch out along the full length of the sofa.

"Not much," Heather replies.

"There must be something about you I might find interesting. Where were you born? What subjects did you enjoy at school? Did you go to university? What jobs have you done?"

"I really cannot say," Heather answers.

"Has your memory not fully returned?" I question.

"I think it has. I can remember everything up to being kidnapped."

"Okay, so you were kidnapped. Where were you and can your remember how they apprehended you?" I ask.

"I was walking and they zapped me with something."

"Like a taser?"

"Yes. Then I woke up in the back of a car, dressed in the maternity outfit. A man sitting next to me told me the dress was a disguise and that I must not do anything irrational. I had been medicated so I don't think I really knew what to do. I had some dark sunglasses on and when I took them off he got angry and pushed them back onto my face."

"Where did they take you?"

"North Silestia House. It didn't seem to take long to get

there, but I don't know how long I had been unconscious."

"Do you know how long ago that was?"

A couple of months, I think."

"So, now you're back to your normal self, can you think of any reason why someone would kidnap you?"

"Yes. I know exactly why a particular party might do that. What I don't understand is why someone else did it instead."

"How do you know they weren't working for *that* party?"

"Because they were protecting me," Heather replies.

"From whom?" I quiz.

"Now we're entering into a part of the story I need to keep secret," Heather states.

"Okay," I say, my head filled with questions. "Is there anything else you can tell me at all?"

"If I hadn't met you, I would probably now be dead."

"The irony is that I went into the woods to kill myself. So, if I hadn't met you I would be dead as well."

"Why did you really want to kill yourself?" Heather asks.

"My wife and son died seven years ago in an accident. I sank into depression and lost the will to live. My sister has been really supportive but I got to the point where I couldn't stand to wake up in the morning."

"So why didn't you go ahead with it?"

"You took my noose." I smile at the memory.

"You didn't have to give it to me."

"You intrigued me. There was something about you I liked and I decided to put off dying."

"You still depressed?"

"Yes."

"You still want to die?"

"Not whilst I have the mysterious Heather to distract me."

"Is that why you were so eager to come with me to North Silestia this morning?"

"Yes."

"It seems to me that you came to North Silestia because you want a reason to live. I don't think you want to die at all."

"I must admit, I don't now and that's all down to you. You're not like the other women I have known and I never want to be apart from you. Does that sound creepy?"

"Creepy?" Heather pauses before continuing. "I don't know what you would class as creepy. Would it make a difference if I told you that I could never love you? We can never be more than friends."

"Is that something you are likely to say?"

"I just did."

"I should point out that, as a man with a crush on you, I see that as a challenge and I will make it my aim to convince you to love me."

Heather closes her eyes. When she opens them, she looks serious.

"Nate, if you try to seduce me I will walk away and you'll never see me again. Do you understand?"

"I suppose so," I say with a sheepish tone. I am being told off.

"I am grateful for the help you have given me but it is really important that you get any ideas of loving me out of your head."

"Okay." I lie back on the sofa and look up at the ceiling. I feel Heather's hand on my arm.

"We can be friends," she says.

"Friends with a beautiful woman; just what every man wants," I say sarcastically.

We are interrupted by the telephone ringing. I have a retro 1920s candlestick phone, which rings with an actual bell. I jump up and step over Heather to get to the phone, which is on a side table by the door. I have a telephone in every room, despite the fact no one ever calls me - even Lucy only ever calls me on the mobile phone.

"Hello?" I say into the phone.

"Nate, it's me. How you doing?" Lucy says.

"I'm at home with Heather. Why are you calling the landline," I question.

"Your mobile is going straight to answer phone," Lucy explains.

"I haven't charged it. I didn't think I would need it after…" I stop myself. "Luce, could we come and stay with you tonight."

"Of course?" Lucy agrees. "It's my party tonight," Lucy reminds me. "I took the afternoon off to prepare, so you can come over when you want."

"Great. We'll come straight over."

I hang up the phone and turn to find Heather standing next to me. She is watching the back window.

"That's good news," she says.

"What shall we do with your clothes? Did you want to change or shall I put the case back in the car?"

"I'll quickly change. You stay low."

Heather runs out of the living room and I hear her stomp up the stairs.

I leave the living room and head to the front door, to wait for her. I put my shoes on and then, out of curiosity, I pull the curtain back and peek through the window. My Delorean is waiting on the driveway. Beyond it, parked across the road, is the flower delivery van. I quickly close the curtain and run up the stairs.

"Heather!" I shout, as I fly through the door into the bedroom. Heather is buttoning up her blouse and looks radiant with the sunshine flooding through a gap in the closed curtains behind her. She is wearing a long skirt, which reaches her feet and a blue long-sleeved blouse. She picks up a wool jumper and slips it over her head.

"What?" she asks.

It occurs to me that the flower delivery man might have

70

placed a bug in my house to listen to our conversations, so I decide to be cryptic.

"You know what we were talking about earlier? I said I saw it and you said it might be nothing?"

Heather puts her arms through the sleeves of the jumper and nods her head.

"Yes," she replies. Heather points towards the front of the house, so I nod to confirm he is outside. Heather rushes out of the room and heads down the stairs. I follow close behind. At the front door, Heather stops and turns to me.

"How good is your driving?" she asks.

"I'm a bit rusty but I'm good. Why?"

"Give me the keys." Heather opens the front door a couple of inches and peers out. I pick my keys out of the bowl on the shelf by the front door and give them to Heather. She opens the door fully and turns to me, smiling. "I'll get the car warmed up. You go and do what you have to," she says, winking at me.

"Okay," I agree. I'm not really sure what she is referring to. "You a good driver?" I ask.

"Yes." she says.

"What am I doing?" I ask. Heather points at the van discreetly.

We leave the house and split up. I run towards the flower delivery van and Heather jumps into the driver's side of my Delorean. I hear the engine start as I near the van. Approaching from the driver's side I catch a glimpse of the man's ear and hat in the side mirror. Before I reach it, the van pulls away; its tyres screeching on the dry tarmac as the driver floors the accelerator. I turn and find my Delorean beside me, purring, with Heather at the wheel. I lift the door and jump in, which is not an easy manoeuvre. Before I can buckle myself in we are moving, chasing the flower delivery van.

Heather's driving is excellent. Despite the Delorean not being as fast as its sleek design might indicate, she manages to keep up with the van as he drives out of Salisbury and along a country lane.

After a couple of miles, the van turns sharply into a field and crosses the grass, its wheels sliding. Heather struggles to keep the Delorean straight as we cross the grass, so she compensates with erratic steering wheel control.

"You're good," I say. "You been in many car chases?" Heather is concentrating too much to hear me.

At the far side of the field, the van passes through a gateway onto a gravel track and speeds up the hill, leaving a trail of dust in front of us. Heather drops a gear, from fourth to third and the Delorean's engine screams, lurching us forward, climbing the hill with ease.

The track leads to a main road, which the van driver slides onto with what I assume to be a handbrake turn, his rear wheels motionless as the van slides sideways turning in the direction of the road he is now joining. Heather yanks the Delorean's handbrake up, locking the rear wheels, whilst simultaneously spinning the steering wheel to the right briefly and then fully to the left. The effect makes the Delorean slide sideways onto the main road. We are facing oncoming traffic, so Heather adjusts the steering wheel to bring us onto the correct side of the road, narrowly missing a lorry, whose driver sounds his horn at us. Just a few metres ahead the van is letting out a cloud of smoke in its wake. The driver is slowing down.

"He's stopping," I say, watching the van as it pulls over to the side of the road. The driver turns the front of the van to the left, so his door is on the far side from us. Heather stops the Delorean on the grass verge and we jump out, running towards the rear of the van. I hear the driver's door open. As we head around the side, carefully checking the driver isn't waiting for us with a gun, there is a flash of lightning. I look up at the dark clouds overhead briefly and then at Heather, who is now standing by the driver's door.

"He's gone," she says, slamming the van's door.

"Which way did he run?" I ask.

"We won't catch him," she says, showing the first hint of defeatism.

"What? Which way did he go?" I repeat. I am prepared to chase him on foot but Heather is not and I wonder why.

"We should get to your sister's," Heather says, returning to the Delorean. I follow her back and climb inside.

"If you don't mind me saying, I think you gave up too easily," I say to Heather as she starts the engine.

"Remember when I told you to trust me?" she asks.

"Yes."

"This is one of those moments. We could not catch him."

"Okay, but you must understand that I am now going to be trying to work out why, until I come up with something that makes sense."

"Nothing will make sense."

Heather floors the accelerator, throwing the Delorean forward and leaving a spray of mud and grass behind us.

Once fragile and childlike, she is now a strong and determined woman - in control of my destiny.

Chapter Nine
First At The Party

My sister's home is across town in a more expensive part of Salisbury. It has a good view of the cathedral, which probably bumped up the value of the house to some degree.

Heather parks the Delorean on the spacious driveway. The house is in a cul-de-sac, with a dozen other houses in a semi-circle. Each has a large driveway and front lawn.

As we approach the front door I think about the party Lucy is having for friends and work colleagues. I hate parties. The people who love them seem to be the kind of people I have difficulty being around. They can be obnoxious, predatory, bullish and over-confident. Then they start drinking alcohol and become the worst kind of morons. I stopped drinking alcohol a long time ago because its affects were making me really miserable. Unfortunately, being alcohol free didn't stop the misery. The thought of being around partygoers fills me with dread and I wonder whether Heather and I could hide in a back room until it is over. But I can't – it is Lucy's celebration. She worked hard and got promoted at the solicitors' office – one step away from becoming a partner, apparently. I have to be there to show my support for her.

"Nate!" Lucy shouts as she opens the front door to let us in. She throws her arms around me and we hug.

"Luce," I reply. Lucy turns to Heather and smiles.

"Hello again," she says, unaware that Heather is not the same person she met yesterday.

"Hello," Heather says.

"Not pregnant today?" Lucy asks.

"Er, Heather is back to her usual self," I quickly say.

"The medication has worn off," Heather confirms. "It is unfortunate that we met whilst I was still under its effect."

"And you're still with Nate?" Lucy comments. She is suspicious of Heather and I imagine she is lining up the questions.

"I wouldn't let her leave," I say, stepping into Lucy's home. I turn and find Heather waiting to be invited.

"Come in," Lucy says to her. Heather enters the house and joins me.

"What are you a vampire?" I say quietly to her. She smiles at me and I find myself looking at her teeth, just to be sure. Then I remind myself that vampires are fictional. We both turn to Lucy, who has shut the front door and is looking at us.

"I have a lot of preparing to do," Lucy says. "Later on I would like to sit down with you both and chat about what you've been up to. But, would you mind if I get on and leave you to make yourselves at home?"

"That's fine," I agree. "You get on and I'll make some tea. Is Jeremy home?"

"He was in the kitchen." Lucy points towards the kitchen, despite the fact I lived here with her for a while.

I lead Heather through to the kitchen, followed by Lucy. Jeremy is not in the room, so I pull a bar stool out for Heather to sit on.

"Could I use the toilet?" Heather asks, spinning around to talk to Lucy.

"There's a downstairs toilet through there," Lucy says, pointing at a door on the other side of the kitchen. Heather smiles at her and then heads to the door, leaving me with my sister.

"You okay, Nate?" Lucy asks, as I sit at the breakfast bar. There is a bowl of peanuts on the bar, so I help myself to a few.

Since discovering that I have suicidal thoughts, Lucy has been trying to ensure I only receive positive feedback from her. I dare say she has briefed her husband to do the same. I am expecting him to be extra friendly and overly concerned with whether I am enjoying the party or in need of anything.

"I'm fine," I reply, throwing a peanut into the air. I catch it in my mouth and crunch it. I feel a reassuring hand on my shoulder as Lucy walks behind me.

"And Heather?"

"She is amazing. We have so much to tell you." I turn to look at my sister.

"But you're okay, mentally?" she asks.

"I haven't felt so alive since..." I stop myself from mentioning the accident. "I'm good. I have something to focus on now."

"What happens if things don't work out with Heather?"

"I'll jump off that bridge when I come to it." I take a few more peanuts. As I put them in my mouth I see Lucy is not amused by my comment. She looks annoyed.

"Let me know if you need anything," she says, slipping away to the utility room. With the door open I can hear the washing machine making its final spin and then silence as Lucy pulls the door shut, blocking the sound. Good quality door.

"Hey Nate," Lucy's husband, Jeremy, says as he enters the kitchen behind me. I turn to him. "How you doing?"

"Fine," I reply. "And you?"

"Yeah, good." Jeremy grabs a handful of peanuts and throws them into his mouth and then picks up the kettle and starts filling it with water. Why do we throw peanuts into our mouths?

"Lucy's excited about the party," Jeremy says with his back to me. It's one of those uses of a sentence where the meaning is totally irrelevant. Lucy being excited about the party is not what Jeremy wants to tell me. He's telling me that he doesn't want me to ruin the party for her by being negative. However, because he has been made aware of my trip into the woods, he knows he cannot say anything remotely accusational to me. So, instead, he emphasises the positive aspects regarding the party and Lucy's excitement towards it. His statement has to mention Lucy because she's the emotional link for me. He knows I wouldn't want to upset her. Well, that's my assumption.

"I won't," I reply, to the inferred meaning of his statement.

"Sorry?" Jeremy says, turning around with a full kettle in his hand.

"I won't ruin the party for her."

"I wasn't suggesting that you…" Jeremy starts.

"It's okay," I interrupt him. "I want her to enjoy the party as well."

Jeremy nods his head and then switches the kettle on. With his back to me he says, "Lucy said you were always good at reading body language."

"It's something that interests me," I admit. "But I'm no expert."

"How do you know you're right?"

"People are sheep. On the whole, they follow certain patterns and it's easy to recognise some of those patterns. The body gives away what the brain tries to hide. It's all about guilt."

"Does that mean you would be able to manipulate your body language, since you know how it works?"

"Not really. It would take a lot of concentration to totally control the subliminal tells your body gives off."

"Give me an example," Jeremy says.

"Of what? Controlling body language?"

"Read my body language," Jeremy requests.

"Body language is just one aspect of reading a person. You

have to consider motivation, verbal use of words, and the situation. Right now, you might want to know how to read body language so you can hide something. The question is, would that be to hide something from me or Lucy?"

"I have nothing to hide. I'm simply interested to know how you do it."

The kettle boils and clicks off. Jeremy finishes making the tea in silence, with his back to me. I wonder what is going through his mind right now. Behind me the utility room door opens, allowing the sound of the washing machine's rinse spin into the kitchen again.

"There you are," Lucy says to Jeremy. He turns and looks at her, with a mug in his hand.

"Here you are my love," he says, leaning over the worktop to hand the mug of tea to Lucy.

"You're over-compensating," I say quietly to Jeremy. I give him a smile.

Heather comes through the door from the toilet and shows her first sign of nervousness as she enters the kitchen and sees Jeremy, Lucy and myself together. I jump up and welcome her.

"Hey, you okay?" I ask her.

"Now who's over-compensating?" Jeremy says. Even with my back to him I can tell he is grinning. I lead Heather to the breakfast bar.

"Heather, this is Jeremy, Lucy's husband," I say.

"Hello Jeremy," Heather greets him. Both Lucy and I watch Jeremy for his response. Heather is beautiful and at least fifteen years younger than Jeremy, so he is bound to like her. It is during these kinds of social interaction I find people the most interesting. In fact, what interests me most, is why Lucy is staring at her husband intently. Has her trust for him been weakened?

"Hello, Heather," Jeremy replies, deliberately keeping things simple.

"Heather is off the medication," Lucy informs him. They have been talking about us.

"Are we going to be in the way?" Heather asks. "Because we could find somewhere else to stay."

"Not at all," Jeremy replies. "Make yourself at home and enjoy the party."

"Vs," I say to him. I follow it with a wink.

"Sorry?"

"Make *yourselves* at home. There are two of us."

"Well, Nate, you're family, so it goes without saying," Jeremy covers.

"Of course," I pretend to agree.

I don't really like or trust Jeremy. Lucy loves him, so I tolerate him for her sake but I sense there is something he is keeping from her and I wonder how long before I get the phone call from Lucy telling me she has left him - or he has left her.

I turn to Heather.

"Shall we tell them what we saw in North Silestia?" I ask.

"No, I think that can wait," Heather replies. She looks at me intently, so I give her a smile to show I was joking.

"How about the flower van?"

"Flower van?" Lucy questions.

"We chased a flower van," Heather tells her.

"He was spying on me," I explain.

"Why would he be spying on *you* Nate?" Jeremy asks. His tone of voice bordering on mocking.

"Great," I say to Heather, "now they think I'm having paranoid delusions. You going to back me up?"

"You're asking a woman who spends the day dressed as a pregnant woman to back you up?" Lucy asks.

"Okay, so Heather and I are both crazy. Doesn't mean we're wrong."

"I don't think you're crazy," Jeremy says. "Just not at your best right now." I feel Heather step away from me, so I turn to look at her. She is looking out the window at the garden.

Jeremy is wrong - about Heather; though perhaps not about me. Heather is at her best. The way she drove my Delorean in pursuit of the flower van was spectacular. She showed determined control and foresight. I hope she finds a reason to tell me her secret. I wonder what else she is brilliant at.

"I still have a lot to do, so I'm going to get on," Lucy says. "You can go and relax in the garden if you want."

"Would you like some tea, Heather?" Jeremy asks. She turns and looks at him.

"No, thank you."

"Shall we go and relax in the garden?" I ask. Heather nods, so I lead her through the French windows onto the patio. Lucy's garden is large and has many varieties of trees and shrubs, allowing the garden to have nice little nooks to relax in.

"Is there anything you can tell me?" I ask Heather as we make our way to a garden bench. As we sit down, a squirrel scuttles up the tree in front of us.

"I think I need to leave," Heather says.

"What, now? We just got here."

Heather turns and looks me in the eye.

"I mean, leave you and go home."

"Back to North Silestia?"

"That's not my home."

I pause for a moment, trying to think of a way to get her to stay with me.

"Can I come with you?" I ask.

"No," Heather replies, her face screwed up with the discomfort of having to turn me down. She is concerned for me.

"So, is that it? What about the flower van?"

"You're safe here, with your family." Heather puts her hand on my knee. "I'll come back and see you."

"When?"

"After I've sorted all this out."

"You don't understand." I say to her. "I need this. I need to help you sort all this out. I have nothing to live for without you and this mystery. People were murdered. I can't walk away from that."

Heather turns away from me to think. I wait, patiently until she looks back at me again. She pauses before speaking.

"I am sworn to secrecy," she explains. "I can't break that."

"Can I come with you?" I ask. I don't want her to leave me. I may never see her again.

"No. You're making this hard for me." Heather looks away.

"I'm being selfish," I say. "I don't really care about anything other than being with you."

"I told you we can never be more than friends," Heather reminds me. She looks at me again.

"I know, but I can never stop trying to change your mind," I explain.

We are interrupted by Jeremy, who strolls across the garden with a woman I do not recognise."

"Nate, I'd like you to meet Leia. She works with Lucy."

Heather and I stand up and approach Jeremy and Leia.

"Nice to meet you," I say, holding my hand out to shake. Leia gently shakes my hand. Weak handshake; she didn't want to meet me. She works in an industry where there is a lot of handshaking, so she knows how to do it properly.

"You're early for the party aren't you?" I say.

"I promised Lucy I'd help her set up." Leia replies.

Jeremy and Leia return to the house, leaving Heather and me in the garden. I turn to Heather and take her hand.

"Will you stay for the party? I hate parties."

Heather looks at me for a moment and then at the house. "I am worried," she admits.

"We make a good team," I say, hoping to convince her to stay. "I have your back. Stay with me and let me help."

"I wish I could tell you everything," Heather says, taking hold of my fingers. She squeezes them tightly.

"Try me," I suggest.

"I really can't."

"At least stay with me until the party is over," I plead.

"Very well," she agrees. She starts walking towards the house, pulling me with her.

Inside the house, Jeremy and Leia are preparing the food for the party. I hear the doorbell ring and then the sound of the front door opening. Lucy is talking to more party guests who have turned up early. I look at my watch to check the time.

"Can we help with anything?" Heather asks Jeremy.

"No, we're fine. Just relax," Jeremy replies. Leia seems to have no interest in talking to me, despite being the brother of her work colleague. I wonder whether that is because she knows I have issues or because she is sleeping with Jeremy.

I turn to Heather and pull her across the kitchen away from Jeremy and Leia.

"You any good at reading body language?" I ask quietly.

"Why do you ask?"

"What do you think of those two?" I say quietly so Jeremy can't hear.

"You think Jeremy is being unfaithful?" Heather whispers.

"Possibly." We head into the hallway where Lucy is talking to the new arrivals.

"It's not your problem," Heather says. "Stay out of it."

"Nate, this is Frank O'Toole and his partner Dana," Lucy says, walking towards us.

"Hello," I say to the couple. The man smiles and puts his hand out to shake, so I comply. He has a strong handshake.

"Nice to meet you Nathan," he says. He looks familiar.

"Call me Nate," I insist.

Frank turns to Heather and offers his hand. "Hello," he says. Heather shakes his hand and says hello to him.

"So how do you know Lucy?" Heather asks. I am surprised by her familiarity.

"I don't," Frank replies. "Dana works at the law firm." His partner, Dana, smiles, silent.

"Dana is new," Lucy explains. "Started just this week."

"I hope they are treating you well," I say to her as she and Frank head into the kitchen.

"You two okay?" Lucy asks me and Heather.

"Fine," I reply. "Your guests are arriving early. Is that normal?"

"A number of us took the afternoon off." Lucy steps towards the kitchen door. "Help yourselves to drinks." She says, leaving us in the hallway.

"I forgot my tea," I say to Heather.

"You want to get a fresh one?" she asks.

"Actually, I want to know why Frank looks like the delivery van driver." I reply, looking at Frank through the kitchen door. Heather turns and looks at him.

"I thought you didn't see him properly."

I didn't, but I saw his hair and part of his face. Frank looks just like him."

"You think he found his way here?" Heather questions. She watches Frank carefully.

"Could be a coincidence," I admit.

"I never saw the van driver," Heather says, "but I have a feeling Frank is not here for a party."

"Why?"

"Call it intuition."

"Is your intuition usually right?"

"I came home with you the night my captors were murdered. Worked then and I was still half drugged."

"In that case, let's go and make friends with Frank."

Chapter Ten
The Last Party

After more tea and an afternoon chatting with Frank and Dana - who both seem to have plausible answers to our probing questions - Heather and I head into the garden, where most of the partygoers have assembled to chat and drink. Lucy is laughing at a joke one of her colleagues made, whilst Jeremy is sitting on the bench, next to Leia - with an acceptable distance between them.

"You bored yet?" I ask Heather.

"No, are you?"

"With the party, yes. I like having you with me though."

"I was just going to suggest that we split up and mingle," Heather says.

"You want to mingle?" I question.

"No, I'm just kidding." she slaps my shoulder gently and I am reminded of the medicated Heather. It's nice to see she has retained her sense of humour. "I agreed to stay for the party, so what would be the point of leaving you to mingle? I might as well just go."

"You're not going to leave yet though, are you?"

"Not until I am satisfied Frank is genuine." Heather looks around for Frank.

"You still have suspicions about him? He seems to check out."

"To you maybe, but I'm not convinced." Heather is still looking over my shoulder for Frank.

"What am I missing?" I ask.

Before Heather can answer Frank comes into the garden, followed by Dana. Lucy heads over to the couple and they chat.

"His confidence," Heather answers. I watch Frank and Dana.

"Some people are like that," I reply.

"Dana works with Lucy but she is following *him* around."

"But she only started this week. She doesn't know everyone here," I say.

"Let's join that conversation," Heather suggests, edging towards Frank, Dana and Lucy.

"Okay," I agree. We join the trio, who are talking about the weather.

"Hello," I say to all three.

"Hey Nate," Lucy replies. "You two okay?"

"Fine. You run out of things to talk about?" I smile at each in turn.

"Why?" Lucy asks.

"You resorted to discussing the weather," I reply.

"Frank thinks we'll get thunder."

"I saw lightning earlier," I recall, "but there was no storm."

"Really?" Frank replies. Heather stands silently by my side, watching and listening.

"Lightning?" Lucy queries. "You sure?"

"Absolutely."

"Well, let me leave you all to start a more interesting conversation," Lucy says. She pats Frank on the back and he flinches. I've seen that flinch before. I turn to Heather and give her my quizzical frown.

"Frank, do you have a bad back?" I ask him.

"I dislocated it when I was young," he replies.

"How did you do that?" Lucy asks, as I pull Heather away and whisper to her.

"Why didn't you want me touching your back earlier?" I whisper.

"Without telling you too much," Heather replies - her voice almost a whisper, "you are asking exactly the right question for the right reason but I cannot give you an answer."

"So what now?" I ask.

As we talk, the birds stop singing and silence embraces the evening. Then the air crackles with a static electricity sound, the wind drops and silence steals the audible world. None of the party guests seem to notice the change. From the corner of my eye I see what appears to be a ball of light, sparking and crackling with electricity. It hovers in the air at head height and slowly drifts into the garden. Heather sees it too and I feel her hand on my arm as she points at the strange orb. She moves behind me, which makes me feel brave; protecting her from the unknown. I turn to Lucy, who is talking to Frank, and point at the orb, which is now hovering near the large oak tree at the end of the garden. Then I notice something unusual. Frank steps behind Lucy, in the same way Heather has done with me. Is he scared? What does he know?

I turn and look at the orb, which still seems to have gone unnoticed by the rest of the partygoers, and watch as more orbs float into the garden. The orbs move towards us, each one heading for a person. They pass into the heads of the people nearest to them. Each person, in turn, is paralysed as their brains seem to be turned off. Their eyes roll upwards and they fall to the floor. For a brief moment, panic ensues as partygoers run from the orbs. I turn to Lucy and see Frank put his arms around her, gripping her tightly. I feel Heather's arms wrap around me tightly as I watch Frank's back illuminate with a bright beam of pink light, which rises above him like electrical angel's wings. The angel wings encompass Frank and Lucy. My Peripheral vision catches sight of a similar bright light surrounding me. I try to move, but can't. I wonder whether I have been penetrated by an orb and, for a split second, assume I am about to die.

But I don't die. Instead, I find that the light engulfs me. Every cell in my body tingles for a few seconds until I feel Heather's arms release me. After a moment of temporary blindness my vision clears and I find myself standing on grass, looking towards a familiar sight. I am still in Lucy's garden, but the garden has gone. I spin around as Heather steps backwards. In her expression I see anxiety. Lucy and Frank are close by. Lucy is visibly confused; looking around for the partygoers, the garden; her home. None of it is here anymore.

"Stay calm," Heather says softly, raising her hands. She turns to Frank, her expression turning to anger. "Who are you?" she demands.

Frank lifts his hand and raises a finger at Heather. "Stop," he demands, as he walks towards her, leaving Lucy alone. I run over to Lucy and hug her.

"You okay?" I ask.

"What just happened?" she asks. We both turn to Heather and Frank, who are now facing each other, squaring off.

"I was sent to find you," Frank says to Heather.

"Did you kill the doctor?" I shout. Frank turns to me and shakes his head.

"No."

"Kill what doctor?" Lucy asks. She is shaking with fear.

"What the hell just happened?" I demand.

"Your world just ended," Frank says with a matter-of-fact tone. Heather cringes at his use of words.

"The world just ended?" I reply. I know what the words mean but I'm not sure why he said them.

"I'm sorry," Frank says turning to me. "The glowing orbs of light were created to kill everyone on Earth. I thought we had more time."

"Where are we?" Lucy asks, her voice trembling. Frank and Heather look at each other. I can tell from their expressions that they know where we are and neither of them wants to tell us.

"Why don't you tell Nate who you are," Frank says to Heather. "Tell him what you were working on before you were kidnapped."

Heather turns to me, tears in her eyes.

"Heather?" I question.

"You're in our world now," Heather says. She looks at Frank.

"Your world?" I question.

"We brought you to our world," Frank clarifies. "Think of it as being like a parallel universe. We left your reality and we are now in ours."

"We're in a parallel universe?" I repeat.

"No, not really, it's more complicated than that," Heather replies.

"What about Jeremy?" Lucy asks. "We need to go back and get him."

"We can't," Frank explains. "Jeremy is dead. Everyone on Earth will be dead before the hour is up. It's not safe for us to go back now. If we materialise near one of those orbs we'll die."

Lucy starts to cry, so I hold her hand.

"You take me back right now!" she demands.

"No!" Frank replies. "Jeremy is dead."

"Okay," I interject. "You're obviously not used to breaking bad news to people. You're telling us that everyone - everyone on Earth - is either dead or about to die and there's nothing we can do about it?"

"Yes, that is what I am saying and you can thank your girlfriend here for killing everyone." Frank points at Heather.

"Heather?" I say.

"The orbs were designed to systematically move around the planet killing all human life." Heather confirms. "The expected duration of extermination was no more than one hour from the introduction of the orbs, to the end of humanity. We don't know how long those orbs had been active before reaching us but chances are everyone on Earth is now dead."

I understand what Heather is saying but I don't have the kind of emotional reaction to the news that I probably should have. Depression has numbed my empathy. Lucy, on the other hand, is distraught. She falls to her knees, screaming. I'm not sure how to comfort her, so I look to Heather. She seems to be having the same problem as me; she is not crying and doesn't seem to be affected by the genocide of an entire planet. She looks lost, unable to decide how to deal with the sobbing human woman; my sister.

I look down at Lucy and consider whether patting her on the back will help.

"I don't know what to do," I say to Heather and Frank.

"I'm arresting you for genocide," Frank says to Heather. He grabs her arm tightly and starts walking, pulling Heather with him. Heather puts up no resistance.

"She didn't do this," I shout at Frank. "She has been with me all week." Frank ignores me and keeps walking. I turn to Lucy and pull her to her feet.

"We have to go with them," I say. "Be strong, big sis." Lucy reluctantly rises to her feet and holds tightly onto my arm. We quickly catch up with Frank and Heather.

"What happened to your friend, Dana?" I ask Frank.

"She died with the rest of humanity," Frank replies. He doesn't seem bothered.

"Couldn't she transport herself here as well?" I ask.

"No, I only met her yesterday," Frank admits. "I needed someone to get me close to you."

"They can't be dead," Lucy says, still crying. Frank looks at her but says nothing.

"What was that light?" I ask. "When you transported us here."

"You are now on Periphera," Heather explains, turning to

look at me. "That's what we call our version of Earth. All Peripherans have the ability to travel from here to your Earth and back using a process called Armaranos Fend. It's a quantum state of being created by our spinal columns. Looks like wings made from light."

"And that's why you don't like having your backs touched?" I assume.

"It's a sensitive area," Heather admits. Frank pulls on her arm to keep her with him as we walk across the grass.

"So, why does Frank think you killed humanity?" I ask.

"I'm a scientist," Heather explains. "I was hired to work with a team of physicists to create the orbs. The people who employed us kept the reason for the work secret. When I pointed out that this technology would be uncontrollable and would effectively turn off any human brain it came into contact with, I was ignored. Once I realised the man I was working for intended to wipe out humanity I ran, taking my research and an important part of the device with me - enough to stop them from continuing their work."

"That's your side of the story," Frank says.

"So what do you think, Frank?" I ask.

"It doesn't matter what I think. I was hired to find Heather and bring her to the authorities to stand trial. Ten minutes ago the charges would have been conspiracy to create a genocidal device. Now it's actual genocide."

"Do you have evidence against her?" I ask. I want to believe Heather is innocent.

"Yes," Frank stops walking and looks at me. "Plenty."

"Heather?" I say.

"I stopped working for those people when I realised what they were doing," she claims.

"So how did you end up in North Silestia House? Did they find you and put you there?" I ask.

"If they had found her she would be dead," Frank says.

"Like the doctor?"

"The doctor?" Frank questions.

"The doctor who was medicating Heather was murdered," I explain. "Who did that?"

"Possibly my employer," Heather answers. "Had I not come to your house they might have killed me too. The baltron's brain was in North Silestia. They must have found it and completed the orbs."

"Okay, so you worked for a dodgy gang, building a weapon of mass destruction, you left and got kidnapped, drugged and kept in North Silestia House. But not by Mr Crime Lord, because he wanted you dead and his calculations back. So who put you in North Silestia?"

"I have no idea," Heather admits.

"Someone wanted Heather to be kept safe," Frank adds. "I work for the Peripheran intelligence and it wasn't us."

"One of the other scientists you were working with, maybe?"

"No," Frank confirms. Those who are still alive are in custody. Several were killed by the - what did you call him? - crime lord."

An aircraft can be heard in the distance, getting closer. I look up to see what it is and, after scouring the sky, I see a small plane heading towards us. It descends as it approaches and I realise it is not like the aircraft I am used to. It is a cylindrical shape, with four sphere's protruding from the sides, two on each side. Each sphere is glowing with a blue light, like a blue flame, and a heat haze is visible below each sphere.

"Wow, look at that," I say, to no one in particular.

As the aircraft nears us, it descends to the ground and lands in the next field. Two men jump out and run towards us. Frank greets them and hands Heather over to them. They take her to the aircraft and push her inside. As she climbs in she turns and looks at me, her eyes sorrowful. I feel helpless. I want to defend her but have nothing. I don't even understand where I am. Who are the Peripherans?

"So what now?" I ask Frank.

"You both need to come with me. I'll hand you over to the authorities who will debrief you and explain your position here on Periphera."

"I want to go home," Lucy demands.

"You cannot go home," Frank states. "You have to stay here until it is safe."

A second aircraft approaches from the same direction as the first. As it descends to land, the first aircraft lifts into the sky, taking Heather away from me.

"Will I get to see her again?" I ask Frank.

"That's not for me to say but I would doubt it."

The second aircraft lands nearby and the side door opens. A woman climbs out and approaches us. She is very tall; about six foot four, and slim. Not very attractive but also not quite manly. I don't realise just how tall she is until she reaches us. She is wearing trousers which seem to have a large flap hanging down the back, covering her bottom.

"Francona," she says to Frank - so that's his real name.

"Edruth. Do you know how many survivors there are?" Frank asks. The woman looks at me and Lucy before answering.

"It's low. No official figure yet."

"Low?" I question. "A hundred people?"

"Probably lower," she answers.

"Fifty?"

She shakes her head. I look at Lucy and then at the tall woman.

"Two?"

"We know of twenty-four so far."

"Humanity has gone from seven billion, to just twenty-four?" Lucy questions, still crying. "What about Jeremy?"

"Jeremy?" the woman queries.

"Jeremy was Lucy's husband," Frank explains. "He was with us when the orbs struck."

"You need to come with me," the woman says to Lucy and me. She holds her hand out.

"Who are you?" I ask.

"My name is Edruth and I have been asked to take you in to help you adjust. Please get into the aircraft."

"Aircraft?" I repeat. "How come you all speak English?"

"We evolved alongside humanity," Edruth explains. "We have our own language but we all speak yours."

"And other human languages?" I question.

"Yes, we speak other languages - Those who need to." Edruth ushers us towards the aircraft.

"And you call that an aircraft?" I say, pointing at the humming cylinder, with glowing orb-wings.

"Only when I am talking to you." Edruth admits.

I escort Lucy to the aircraft and we climb inside. The interior is like a luxury helicopter, with leather seats and varnished wooden side tables. The sound of the engines disappears when Frank closes the outer door. He and Edruth sit opposite Lucy and me. There are no seat belts.

"I have a lot of questions," I say to Edruth, whose towering frame makes Frank look quite small.

"I have lots of answers," she replies.

The aircraft lifts into the air and I find myself at the beginning of an experience even more surreal than meeting a crazy woman in the woods dressed as a cheerleader.

Chapter Eleven
Those In Charge

Lucy stares out of the window, her head resting against the glass. I put a reassuring hand on her knee. Frank and Edruth sit silently, watching Lucy and me.

"So, can you tell me a bit about your world?" I ask Edruth. "How come I have never heard of you people before?"

"Because we never wanted you to hear about us. We have been living in parallel with humanity for thousands of years and it was decided a long time ago to keep our presence secret from your race."

"Why?"

"Your race is destructive," Frank answers.

"Really?" I say with a sarcastic tone. "Whose race just destroyed the other?"

"Our race evolved at a quicker rate than yours," Edruth interjects. "We have had aircraft for a thousand years."

"And you didn't feel the need to share?"

"No."

"So what's with the teleportation? Do your spines light up?" I ask. I once imagined what it would be like to meet an alien race and I imagined I would be more forgiving of them. However, since this race just destroyed mine I feel somewhat annoyed by their arrogance.

"Our spines are an extension of our brains," Edruth starts.

"Yes, so is mine," I interrupt.

"But our spines act like a brain and interact with the universe at a quantum level, allowing us to create an envelope to pull us out of our space-time and into yours," Frank explains.

"And you can all do that?" I ask.

"Yes," he replies.

"Anything else you can do?"

"There are differences between our races. You will receive education at the appropriate time," Edruth tells me.

"So what happens first?" I ask.

"We're taking you to Asten," Edruth says.

"Asten?" I question. "Is that a place?"

"It's a building. It's not far," she replies. She doesn't show much emotion.

"Do you call England, England?" I ask.

"No," Frank replies. He looks at Edruth and smiles to show her that he is happy to answer my question.

"What you call Great Britain, we call Mistep-Hoak. Europe is one country, called Ariastep and it includes Russia, China and India. America and Canada are one country, which we call Pelerush," Frank explains.

"Odd name for a country." I say. "So, the land is not divided into countries?"

"Only into regions. Unlike your world, we don't see people from the other countries as foreigners. We're all one race."

"Nice," I say with a little sarcasm.

"You don't like that?" Edruth asks.

"Yes, I think it's great but it seems a bit idealistic. In my world there are people who aspire to making us all one nation but it doesn't work. People like to group themselves, despite what the politicians try and force upon us."

"That's where your people and my people are different. We don't need small groups. We are comfortable as one nation."

"Really?" I question. Are they really all happy about it?

"Yes," Edruth replies. She stares at me until I look away. I regret looking away, so I look back at her and see she is still looking at me.

"Do you like humans?" I ask. It seems strange asking a person whether they like humans.

"Not particularly," the tall woman replies. At least she is honest.

"Would it be fair to assume that the rest of your race shares a similar opinion?" I ask.

"Not at all," Frank interjects. "Many of our people have a fondness for your people."

We fly over a city, whose skyline makes Tokyo look old-fashioned. The skyscrapers are all white, with reflective white windows, making them look like models. As we pass over the city - which seems to stretch entirely across an area which, on Earth, was Salisbury Plain - I look downwards through the window, leaning over Lucy to get a better view. From the corner of my eye I see she is also looking at the view. The streets are arranged like the layout of Venice, with winding pathways and alleys mixed with a system of canals.

"Canals in Wiltshire?" I say to Lucy.

"It's not Wiltshire," she replies, her voice morose.

"There is a lot of water on the plain," Edruth explains. "Our version of Salisbury Plain supports Mistep-Hoak's capital city."

"This is the capital of, Mitswak?" I clarify, deliberately mispronouncing the name of the country.

"Mistep-Hoak."

"So what's in London?" Lucy asks. I am pleased to hear her talk. I hope she is coming to terms with what has happened. I am still unperturbed.

"What you call London, we call Skereks," Frank answers. "It's a city, but not as big as the capital, Verorlanden." He points at the view out the window.

"Verorlanden?" I repeat.

"Yes. Twelve million people live here."

The aircraft lands on the top of a building and the doors open. I jump out of my seat and climb onto the rooftop. The sun is shining and there is a cool breeze. Frank, Lucy and Edruth follow me out and stand beside me. The view is amazing. The skyscrapers extend away for over a mile and, as the hillside climbs over what would be Salisbury Plain on Earth, smaller houses and towers extend to the horizon. Everything looks very clean.

I take Lucy's hand and squeeze it tightly.

"We're not on Earth anymore, sis," I say to her.

"Does it not bother you that everyone on Earth is dead?" Lucy replies. I turn and look at her.

"I'm sorry, Luce, but, no, it doesn't. I know it should, but I suppose being of the frame of mind to want to die makes a man less bothered by the things that concern others."

"The kinds of things you bloody well should be bothered about. Our entire race is gone."

"Not entirely," I reply. Even as I say the words I know they will not be gladly received. Lucy pulls her hand out of my clutching fingers and turns away from me. I decide to give her space - partly because I am not very good at consoling people and partly because I can't think of any words to say to her. I turn to Frank.

"What's going to happen to Heather? She's not going to be killed is she?"

"Killed? No. If she is found guilty she'll be banished to a prison island."

"Do you think she was telling the truth about getting out before they finished the orbs?"

"Not my concern," Frank replies. He puts his hand on my shoulder and looks me in the eye, intently staring.

"We have a council of law makers who will look at her case and decide what she is guilty of."

"Can I see them?" I ask.

"You're standing on their rooftop," Frank says, with a smile. "We're not morons. We give everyone a chance to speak their case and since you have spent the last few days with Heather, your words will be well received by the council."

"Do you call them the council, because that sounds a bit sci-fi," I ask.

"We call them Alwarniforshuzrakas," Frank states. As I try to repeat the word in my head I see Frank's face crack a smile. "I'm just joking," he says. "Yes, we call them the council. Since we have evolved alongside humans some words have crossed over from your language into ours. We also use the French word, mange, to say we are eating. There are quite a few words we use in common with humanity."

Of all the words in the language I wonder why he chose to tell me which word they use to mean eating. I glance at my watch and see the time is just after nine o'clock. He must be hungry.

Edruth leads us to a doorway, which opens as we approach, and we enter the building. The interior is decorated like an expensive office, perhaps in the headquarters of a bank, with sensible patterned carpet, expensive wallpaper, which has a crest of an animal with leaves and a square logo or something of the kind.

We enter a large lift and the doors close behind us. I look at Lucy.

"I'm not very good at emotional stuff," I say to her. "But you've always been there for me and I want you to know I am here for you." Lucy looks at me and I see tears in her eyes.

"It's not your fault. I just need to come to terms with this. You're lucky you have no feelings: Makes you the perfect person to survive the genocide of your own race."

Lucy is right about my feelings. I have seen people get really excited about a scenic view, or someone's achievement. It doesn't do anything for me. When I first met my wife I had to teach myself to appreciate her in the way she appreciated me. When I touched her face and stared into her eyes, she looked happy; contented. When she touched my face and looked into my eyes, I felt like she was looking at me – because she was. I had to tell myself this was a special moment between the two of us. It never came naturally. I did love her, a great deal, but the little things which told her how much I loved her, I had to fake.

I take Lucy's hand again and we stand in silence as the lift descends.

Leaving the lift, we enter a large hallway, which has the appearance of a church, with ornate stonework and columns along each side, sculpted with intricate designs of faces, vines and animals. At the end of the hallway is a large set of double doors. They are wooden and stand over twenty feet tall. A lone man awaits us at the doors. As we approach, he pulls on a handle and the huge doors open towards us, revealing a dark room beyond.

We enter the room and soft lighting comes on, illuminating the whole chamber, which is easily as large as St. Paul's Cathedral. Our footsteps echo as we walk on the stone tiles, towards the centre of the room. Ahead of us, five men and three women stand waiting. They are formally dressed in what appears to be suits. They wouldn't look out of place in a board room. I notice they all have trousers with the flap on the back. Is that the current fashion?

"Hello Nathan," one of the women says as we approach.

"Hello," I reply, my voice echoing around the chamber.

"Tragedy has struck your world," she continues.

"Clearly," I reply.

"Lucy can go with Edruth and join the other survivors," the woman says. I turn to Lucy, still holding her hand.

"Would you rather stay here?" I ask.

"I need to lie down," Lucy replies. She looks tired.

"The others are being cared for in luxury apartments," Edruth says. "You can have a room to yourself to lie down or you can join them in the lounge."

"I'll go to the apartments," Lucy says. She takes her hand from mine and touches my face. "Do you still want to die?" she asks. I feel awkward talking about it in front of these people.

"No. I'm not sure what I am feeling right now but dying has certainly dropped down the list."

"This could be the change you needed," Lucy says. Her hand leaves my face and I wonder whether she is now wishing she was dead instead.

"How about you?" I ask.

"Suicide is as alien to me as this world," she answers. "Despite feeling utterly distraught I could never take my own life."

"Go and lie down. I expect I'll be joining you later."

Edruth leads my sister back towards the huge doors, which open as they approach, and I see the last of my companions taken from me, however temporarily.

I turn to the council.

"Let us go somewhere more comfortable," the woman says. I follow as the eight council members lead Frank and myself across the stone cathedral-like floor towards a small door. One of the men opens the door and holds it to allow everyone to enter the room.

The room resembles an old library. All the walls are lined with bookshelves, filled with books. In the centre of the room is a square table on which a glass screen stands on a bracket. It looks as though it is designed to turn. The men and women of the council sit on the chairs around the table, so Frank and I join them.

"We are sorry for what has happened to your people," a man says to me. "But I understand you are of a frame of mind which inhibits a strong emotional response."

"It is true, I have been distracted." I admit. "Can we get to the point? What happened to Heather?"

The council members all look at the woman who had spoken to me in the large chamber.

"She is being debriefed," the woman answers.

"Debriefed? Or interrogated?"

"Debriefed. Heather has been released without charge," the woman explains. I sense Frank fidgeting next to me. He went to all that trouble of catching her and now they let her go. I turn to him in anticipation of what he is about to say.

"Released?" he questions.

"You were asked to find Heather," a man sitting on the opposite side from me says to Frank. "You did well. However, there was information in this case for which it was necessary to keep from you," he adds.

"Welcome to my world," I say quietly to Frank.

"I was hunting her based on evidence which showed her to be instrumental in the orbs' design."

"Yes, she was. However, she left the organisation and came to us. We were in the process of compiling evidence when she was kidnapped. We needed all but ourselves to believe she was a fleeing criminal so those who might hurt her would make themselves known."

"They didn't," I interject.

"We didn't know she had taken from them the final information needed to create the orbs," the woman says.

"So who kidnapped her?" I ask.

"We do not know. Someone who knew more about the case than we did," she answers.

"So, are you looking for them now?" I ask.

"We are looking for evidence to convict the people Heather was working for. It is they who completed the orbs and released them on your world."

"How many actual survivors are there?" I ask.

"So far, including you and your sister, we now have thirty-four humans on Periphera," a man sitting next to me says.

"So Earth is now full of dead bodies?" I'm numb to the concept and I realise that, at some point, it will sink in and I'll feel despair. However, right now, I don't feel anything.

"Yes," the woman answers. I see sadness in her eyes and a tear welling. She cares.

"How did an organisation make a weapon that killed a whole planet?" I ask.

"That is a question we are trying to answer now," the man opposite me says. "We knew Reeteh Steispeck was working on a weapon but we had no idea he had created a Baltron Phase.

"A what?" I question.

"A Baltron Phase. It turns off electrical activity in the brain. Up to now it has been purely theoretical."

An image of planes dropping from the sky enters my head as the significance of what has happened starts to become clearer.

"Did planes drop out of the sky?" I ask. I immediately wonder whether the question is puerile.

"Yes," the man answers. The council members seem to be finding it difficult to talk about the genocide. They shake their heads and stare at the table. One man has his head in his hands.

"There were seven billion people on Earth," I say. "That's a lot of bodies to clear up."

Silence.

"So humanity is now just thirty-four," I say.

"Yes," the woman confirms.

"Did you manage to get a mixture of races?"

"We could only save those nearest to our people who happened to be on Earth at the time: some Americans, a few English, a few Europeans. I'm not sure exactly who was rescued."

"No Africans? Chinese?"

"I haven't met the survivors," the woman admits. "I don't know which races survived."

"We will send teams to Earth to remove the bodies."

"Seven billion bodies? Really?"

"You seem to be a pragmatic man, Mr Glover," a man who has not spoken before says.

"Depends on the circumstances."

"We will ensure that the bodies most cared for by the survivors are treated according to their wishes. Thirty-four people will not restart the human race. Large parts of your world will remain as graves to the dead."

"Would you like to meet the other survivors?" the woman in charge asks.

"Not really," I reply. "Maybe later. I really just want to see Heather."

"You can see her in the morning," the woman assures me.

"So what happens now?" I ask. "What happens to Earth?"

"We are assembling a team who will plan the retrieval of all the human antiquities. We will preserve the cultures of the human race."

I find myself nodding before I speak. "Humanity is going to be a museum piece."

"Nathan, we are not the kind of people to make horrendous situations seem tolerable with false hope and assurances," the man opposite says. "Yes, humanity as you knew it will be recorded in our world in a kind of museum. We will salvage your art and antiquities; your literature and artefacts of historical significance. We will download the information from your Internet and attempt to document the lives of all who died today. Our priority now is the survivors. We need to ensure the history of the Earth is preserved, especially the history of the thirty-four survivors. We will salvage everything pertaining to your lives. The future generations of your race will be able to see where they came from."

"So much will be lost," I realise.

"We have drone devices circling the Earth, looking for any remnant Baltron Phase orbs. Once we are certain no more remain we will send teams to Earth to make the cities habitable again."

"Habitable for thirty-four people?"

"We must shut down the nuclear reactors and make the world safe. Once Earth is habitable you and your fellow humans will have the choice to move back or stay here with us. We will send colonies of our people to Earth to start a new civilisation."

"There's a lot to do," the chairwoman - as I now decide to call her - says. "It will take years."

"Your ways are different from ours. How will we continue to live as we were with colonies of your people living their lives on our planet?"

"For your race to succeed you will need to adapt. You cannot return to living in the manner in which you were used to. You have sixteen men and eighteen women. Twelve of those women are at an age where they can produce children. Our geneticists can work out how procreation can create the optimum number of babies and advance the race."

"It won't work," I state.

"Why do you think that?" the chairwoman asks.

"Because humans won't be manipulated."

"But for the survival of your race?"

"We're stubborn. I'm sure some of the women will be happy to have babies with twelve men but some won't want to. I don't want to have babies with those women."

"Even to help your race survive?" the chairwoman asks.

"A few days ago I wanted to leave my race. Now the race has left me. I don't feel as bad about it as I probably should."

"Do you have feelings for Heather?" The man next to me asks.

"Yes, I do," I admit.

"As we educate you, you will see why you must dispel those feelings."

"If he is having feelings for Heather he should be kept apart from her," a woman further down the table says. I shake my head and give her a stern stare.

"No," the chairwoman replies. "Nathan can go to Heather. She is one of us and will act appropriately. I would encourage her to explain our ways to Nathan. In the mean time Frank will join the search for Reetch Stcispeck."

"Is that the crime lord?" I ask.

"Yes," Frank replies.

"That sounds like a good plan. You search for the crime lord and I'll hang around with Heather."

"Mr Glover, despite the similarities in the appearances of your race and ours, I think you will find some stark differences," the chairwoman suggests.

"As you said, we need to adapt to a new way of life. Maybe your people will have some adapting to do as well," I suggest.

"I am certain we will."

The council escorts me out of the small room, into the cathedral-like chamber. I return to the lift, alone. The lift ascends to the top of the building and, when the doors open, I find a pretty young woman waiting for me.

Unlike the council, this woman is wearing a dress. Did humans copy Peripherans or vice versa? There are so many similarities.

"Mr Glover?" the woman asks.

"Yes."

"I am to show you to a room where you can sleep."

The young woman leads me along a corridor which is very bland in decor. The walls are painted white and the floor is a grey carpet. At the end of the corridor we turn into a second corridor and walk a few feet before stopping by a door. The woman opens the door by pressing a pad on the wall. Inside I see a single room with a bed.

"Get some sleep. If you need anything, press the button on the wall," the young woman says with a smile.

"How am I supposed to sleep when I am buzzing with adrenalin?" I ask.

"Lie down and relax. I can play music in the room for you if you wish."

"Beethoven's seventh would be nice," I say. The young woman nods her head and waits for me to enter the room before closing the door behind me. I feel like a prisoner. I turn and look at the door pad and consider opening it. If it is locked and doesn't open I will feel annoyed. Should I try it?

I decide to try and relax instead.

After a couple of minutes I hear Beethoven's seventh symphony playing through hidden speakers. Before the symphony ends, I fall asleep.

I am awoken by the voice of the young woman telling me it is the morning. I jump to my feet and find her standing in the doorway.

"It feels as though I only just fell asleep," I say to her. She smiles at me.

"You have a visitor," she says, stepping backwards into the corridor. I follow her out and find myself staring at the face of an angel. Heather's smile beams back at me. She holds her arms out to hug me, so I throw my arms around her and cling tightly to her warm body.

"I missed you," I say.

"I missed you too," Heather replies, pushing me back to look at my face. "I have been asked to educate you," she says.

"That sounds like fun. Educate me with what?"

"The ways of Periphera." Heather takes my arm and leads me along the corridor to the lifts. I take a moment to look at her clothing. She is now dressed as a Peripheran, with a dark green jacket – which might be leather, or a Peripheran equivalent – and black trousers, which have the now familiar flap on the back.

"What's with the flap on the back of your trousers?" I ask her. Heather stops and looks at me, then she twists around to show me the flap.

"Peripherans have a thing about showing their backsides. We tend to hide them. It's something we have done for centuries. We don't really feel dressed unless we have our backsides covered."

"Surely the trousers are already covering you butt," I quiz.

"Yes, but you can still see the shape of buttocks. Skirts and ananas cover that."

"Ananas?" I repeat. Sounds like bananas.

"That's what the flap is called. Anana."

"Okay, so do you find my trousers offensive?" I ask. Heather looks at my butt.

"No, but I wouldn't go out dressed like that myself." Heather smiles.

We ascend to the top floor, where the aircraft which brought me to the Asten building is waiting. I can hear its engines whining.

"Is it safe for you to leave? What if Reeteh whats-his-name comes looking for you?"

"The intelligence the council believes Reeteh Steispeck has no reason to come looking for me, since he achieved what he wanted."

"So where are we going first?" I ask.

"I think we should head out to the countryside. We can talk."

Chapter Twelve
That Which Cannot Happen

"I'm worried about Lucy," I say to Heather as we head out of the city in the aircraft.

"Really?" Heather asks. She seems genuinely surprised.

"She's my sister and she just lost her husband and all her friends. She's upset. Why does that surprise you?"

"Well," Heather starts. She picks up a small plastic device and waves it in front of me. "According to the information we have on you, you shouldn't be feeling anything."

"Information on me? How did you get that?"

"Apparently, when Frank discovered that you had met me, he started following you and, using our extensive resources, was able to build a profile on you."

"On a card?" It looks a credit card but a quarter of the size. It is grey with some white writing and a logo on it.

"This card transmits images and sounds directly to our brains. I just press my thumb over the logo and I see a menu in my mind. I use my mind to select from that menu." Heather seems to be staring into space as she talks. I assume she is seeing the images she is describing. "So, Nathan Glover the third. You suffer from clinical depression, not bipolar, but prone to bouts of anhedonia. Suicidal," she says. She turns her head and stares at me. "You did well at school though."

"Will that transmit to my brain?" I ask, holding my hand out to take the card.

"Does your brain extend down your spinal column?" Heather asks rhetorically.

"In some respects it does," I reply.

"This only works on Peripherans," Heather confirms. She finally passes the card to me.

"How do you feel right now?" she asks. I examine the card. There is no obvious chip or method of data storage.

"I am distracted," I reply. "Occasionally, I get a feeling of dread come over me and I have to remind myself that, technically my life ended and I can never return to it. This is a new beginning for me."

"We may be able to cure your depression," Heather says. I stop looking at the device and look at her. She is smiling at me, but not in a patronising way. She looks pleased.

"How?"

"You may have noticed that, as a race, we are using a much larger proportion of our brains cognitively than humans do. We know how the brain works. We know what to do to yours to rid you of depression."

"You want to mess with my brain?"

"No. I am just saying that we could, if you wanted us to."

We sit silently for a moment as I contemplate what that would mean to me. Being depressed has taken over my life and defined me. The Nathan I am is a Nathan whose abilities are those of a person with depression. If they take that part of me away I will be a different man. At first, this seems fantastic. However, being a tortured soul has made me good certain things. It has given me something to fight against. Without that, I may not be quite so good.

"It's something to think about," I say. I look out of the window at the view and see rolling fields stretching to the horizon.

The aircraft drops into a clearing and lands on a field of grass. Heather and I climb out onto the grass and simultaneously look up at the blue sky. The sun is bright and there are no clouds. I remind myself that the world I grew up in is lying stagnant, devoid of human life. It is hard to accept, especially since I am around people who look like humans.

"I haven't really taken it all in," I admit. "Your world looks like my world. Your people look like my people. I don't think I will accept what has happened until I return to my Earth and see it for real."

"Is that something you *want* to do, or *need* to?" Heather asks.

"Both, really."

Behind us, the aircraft rises into the sky. Heather and I walk along a track, which leads to a small woodland. It looks familiar. I turn my head side to side, examining the landscape.

"This place looks familiar," I say.

"It should do," Heather replies. "Salisbury is spread across these fields and hills. Look, you can see the five rivers." Heather points at the view down towards the rivers. I can imagine the cathedral sticking up amongst the buildings which exist in an alternate world. My world. "On Earth, this field is a housing estate," she adds.

"I know, Duke's Drive," I say.

"That's right," Heather says, looking at me. Ahead of us the track forks, with the right hand fork entering the trees and the left hand fork passing through some bushes. Heather stops walking and puts her arm across my chest to stop me.

"What?" I ask.

"See the bushes?"

"Yes."

"See the purple fruit on the taller bushes?"

"Yes."

"You need to stay well away from it. That fruit is poisonous to humans but to Peripherans it is a necessary part of our diet. I need to eat some."

"Okay, so you're making me a little worried. You're going to eat some poisonous fruit?" I look at the fruit on the bushes.

"It's not poisonous to my people. You know how I brought you to my world?" Heather asks. I turn and nod to her.

"The glowing angel wings. How could I forget?"

"The fruit helps maintain that ability," Heather explains.

"Purple fruit gives you glowing wings?"

"It's more complicated than that. Armaranos Fend is a quantum state of being created by our spinal columns. Once digested, the fruit gives off a kind of enzyme which the tissue in our spinal columns needs."

"Will the fruit be upset if you *don't* eat it?" I ask facetiously.

"No, but I would be foolish not to eat my fill whilst I need to. It's one of those things we do."

"Can I tag along if I promise not to eat the fruit?"

"No. You cannot go near the fruit. The aroma alone will render you unconscious. To eat it will kill you. You must follow the other track. I'll meet you where the tracks join, beyond the bushes."

"Okay. You enjoy the poisonous fruit. I'll see you on the other side." I pat Heather on the back and, for the first time, she doesn't flinch. I then walk backwards away from her. She waves at me as we separate, smiling all the while. I want to tell her that I love her but I stop myself.

I follow the track through some small trees, occasionally looking to see whether Heather is visible amongst the bushes. She is not and neither is the purple fruit. After two hundred metres I find myself in a clearing on the side of a hill. It looks familiar and I realise I am standing where, in my world, the valley descends to North Silestia House, where I first met Heather. How she has changed since that first meeting in the woods.

"Recognise the view?" Heather says from behind me. I turn and see her beautiful face smiling at me. I take her hand and hold it tightly.

"North Silestia is down there in my world," I say.

"Yes," Heather replies. We stand side by side and look at the view of the valley. For once I feel as though I can appreciate the beauty of the landscape. My depression used to make such views uninspiring. I got no emotional buzz from looking at beauty. Now, though, standing next to Heather everything looks fantastic. I can think of nowhere else I would want to be. I turn to Heather.

"You saved my life twice," I say.

"Twice?"

"You prevented my suicide and then saved me from the end of the world. Thank you." I hold her hand.

"You are most welcome," Heather replies. Her breath smells sweet.

"Er, is your breath toxic?" I ask. Heather laughs.

"I sucked on some berrinia. So you're safe."

"Berrinia?" I question.

"It's a berry which counteracts the aroma of the Fendura."

"Which means?"

"My breath is not toxic. It's the berrinia you can smell."

"Okay, just thought I should check."

"My people have been interacting with humans for a long time. We know how to protect you."

I want to remind her how her race wiped out my race but I stop myself. My expression gives me away and Heather notices.

"I'm sorry," she says. She seems genuinely concerned.

"Don't worry," I reply. "I understand what you meant."

I look at the valley again and imagine North Silestia at the bottom.

"There are only three dozen humans left and they are currently on a planet where there is deadly fruit. Will all your people protect us?" I ask.

"Of course," Heather replies. She sounds convincing.

We continue walking and follow the field along the top of the hill. In the distance I see the tops of the tall buildings in the Peripheran capital city, whose name I have forgotten. My sister is there, learning new things about a world she never knew existed. Heather and I walk through several fields of grass until we reach a field of crop.

"What crop is this?" I ask.

"Maize," Heather replies.

"Maize, like our maize? Human maize?"

"Yep. The very same." Heather slaps my back lightly. "Not toxic at all."

We walk along the side of the maize until we reach a field of blue flowers. I turn and look at Heather, wondering whether the flowers are safe.

"Don't worry," Heather says, "Not toxic. Just flowers." She loops her arm in mine and we walk through the field of flowers. As we walk I become aware of some trees ahead of us, with leaves which seem to be at least two feet wide. Below them, on the ground are some small objects scattered around. They look like large, pink, rubber pods.

"What's that?" I ask, pointing at the objects amongst the trees.

"That's what I brought you to see. The Morlillia, birthing field," Heather says.

"The what?" I look closely at the pods.

"It's where our children are born," Heather explains. I stop and look at her.

"Say that again. You give birth in a field?"

"We don't give birth like humans. We carry the child internally for nine months and then expel it."

"Expel it? That's giving birth."

"Not like you humans give birth. This is the fundamental reason why humans and Peripherans can't interbreed."

"Go on," I request.

"Inside out bodies the baby grows in a sac. We expel that sac, with the baby still inside it. As the baby and sac leave the body the sac remains attached to the womb. The womb is in two parts. There's the part where the baby has grown..."

"In the sac," I interject.

"Yes, and there's a part above that which fills with fluid. Once the sac is out of the body and starts pulling on the womb, the second part, the saclisora, opens and allows the fluid to drop out of the body into the sac, surrounding the baby. Then the sac disengages from the womb altogether. The clever part is that the top of the sac, once exposed to air, starts to shrink, sealing it. The baby then continues to grow for another six months."

"In a sac, in a field?" I feel my face screwing up at the thought.

"Yes."

"Why?"

"It allows the brain to fully form, giving us our ability to Armaranos Fend."

"The glowing angel wings?" I recall the words from the conversation earlier.

"Yes, glowing angel wings," Heather confirms.

"And it can't do that in the womb?"

"Do you know how big a baby is after fifteen months of gestation? The head wouldn't fit through a woman's pelvis."

"So, do you come and watch the baby everyday until it is born?"

"No, we never come back."

"Seriously? You leave the baby, in a sac, in a field and never come back to check on it?"

"We don't need to. We have elder women, called Sasmaidens, who watch the Morlillia. When a sac ruptures, they remove the baby and take it away."

"How do they know who the baby belongs to?"

114

"They don't need to. Our society isn't like yours. We don't raise our own young. The community raises them."

"Are you not curious about the welfare of your own baby?"

"No. It's just the way we are." Heather smiles at me. She is serious, though.

"I suppose you don't get to see the baby look up at you and take its first breath, like we do, so you don't bond with it."

"You can see now why we never breed with humans." Heather turns away from me and looks at the pods.

"So, how do you deal with the fact that your body has prepared itself to care for a baby?"

"You mean breast feeding?"

"Yes. Who does that, if you don't?"

"Our babies get their nutrients from certain plants."

"Like the purple fruit?"

"The fendura fruit is introduced later on."

"Okay, this might seem a strange question but why do your females have breasts if you don't breast feed babies?" I ask. Heather turns and smiles at me.

"Men like them," she says.

"Really?" I ask naively. She slaps my shoulder lightly, so I fake a laugh.

"No, silly. We used to be like humans but we have evolved further. Breasts are just a remnant from our past. A bit like your nipples? Do you really need them?"

"They tell me when it's cold," I say. I grin like a child.

Without warning Heather slaps me on the chest and shouts, "Catch me!" before running away. Like a gazelle, she jumps over a rock protruding from the ground. She is fast. I chase after her but cannot catch up. I stop breathing deeply. Heather returns, but when she reaches me she tackles me, pulling me to the ground. Once again, we find ourselves lying in each other's arms. Heather rolls onto her back and stares at the blue sky. I watch her chest rising and falling as she pants.

"What would happen if a human woman was impregnated by one of your men?" I ask. Heather turns onto her side and looks at me. I hope she doesn't guess what I am leading to.

"His genetic information would tell the baby to grow for fifteen months and the human woman's would tell it to grow for nine. I suppose it would grow somewhere between the two. The mother wouldn't be able to have a natural birth and the baby would probably die once out of the womb."

"Why?"

"It won't have a sac to keep growing in."

"So what if a human man impregnated one of your women?" I ask. I imagine Heather pregnant with my child, which is not hard since I have already seen her with a fake bump.

"I suppose that has a better chance, since we are prepared for a long gestation. The baby would probably need removing from the sac earlier, because its brain wouldn't have much more growing to do."

"Have any of your people ever bred with humans?" I ask.

"There was a story a long time ago about a man who impregnated a human woman. She died giving birth. Our society is very strict on this. Everyone accepts that we don't cross species."

As we lie on the grass, I become aware of footsteps coming along the path. I turn onto my side and see a pregnant woman heading towards the field, the Morlillia. Heather sits up and leans on my shoulder.

"She about to expel her baby?" I ask with a smile.

"Yes," Heather whispers.

"Why you whispering?" I ask.

"It's a private thing," Heather replies, watching the woman.

"Why you watching her then?" Heather's expression turns to worry. She pulls me onto my back and climbs on top of me to hold me down.

"What are you doing?" I ask.

"Shh," she replies. "Humans aren't allowed near the Morlillia when a woman is expelling."

"Do you have many human visitors?" I ask quietly.

"Only a privileged few."

I turn to look at the woman but Heather stops me, pulling my face back.

"Don't look," she commands. We lie still for a moment, with Heather's face hovering a few inches above mine. Her hair hangs down over my face like a tent. We stare at each other for a moment. Despite being from a different race, her eyes are very human in appearance. Her irises are green with streaks of hazel. As I stare into her pupils I remind myself that she is, technically, an alien – and that just makes her more attractive.

I know I am not allowed to look at the woman in the field of baby sac bags but I find the temptation hard to resist. Heather shakes her head and I wonder whether she can read my mind.

"Do you want to have children?" I ask.

"I've had children," Heather admits. I am surprised.

"What?"

"I've produced children. Two."

"When?"

"The first, when I was twenty-one, and the second at twenty-two. We are encouraged to have them at twenty-one."

"What if you don't have a boyfriend?" I ask. Heather looks at the woman in the mor-sacs-of-babies field. I try to look but her hand is still pressed against my face.

"Boyfriend?" she replies, now looking at me again. "You don't need a boyfriend. Obviously it makes it easier if you do have one. When you turn twenty-one, you'd automatically allow yourself to be impregnated by him. If you don't have a boyfriend, you go to a bordwar," Heather explains.

"A what?"

"A bordwar. It's where you go to get inseminated." The Peripheran attitude towards mating seems clinical.

"Did you have a boyfriend or did you do it at a borwar?" I ask.

"It's pronounced bordwar. I had a boyfriend. We produced two children." Heather has another quick look at the woman in the field. Then back at me. I like her lying on me. She is not heavy and I can feel the warmth of her body against mine.

"Where is he now?"

"We separated when I was twenty-three."

"Did you fall out?" I ask. I am enjoying being under the tent of Heather's hair.

"No, we just decided to separate."

"Do your people get married?"

"No, we don't have marriages. We live with our partners until we decide to part."

"What if you want to stay together?"

"Then we stay together."

"What if you want to show your devotion to your partner by tying the knot, with a ceremony?"

"We don't see the need for that. We are honest to each other. Every day we are together shows that we want each other. When we don't want to be with our partner we tell them and split up."

"What if the other person doesn't want to split up?" I question. This is all good research.

"Then they better keep their partner happy!" Heather smiles. I can still smell those berries on her breath.

"There goes my bucket list," I say, partly to myself.

"Your what?" Heather asks.

"It doesn't matter."

Heather slaps me gently on the cheek.

"Don't make promises to yourself you can't keep," she says.

118

"Okay, so can you read my mind?" I ask. That's one too many times she has anticipated my thoughts.

"Not at all. But I listen and I watch. You give off so many clues as to what you are thinking."

"And I thought I was good at reading body language."

"It's a useful skill." Heather admits.

"So why are you flirting with me, knowing we can never be lovers?"

"I'm taking your mind off the recent demise of your race and trying to give you hope for the future," Heather explains. I don't fully believe her.

"Yeah, I was hoping my future involved us being romantically attached."

"We will be friends and I will always be here for you," Heather states. "Remember, you saved my life as well."

"Well, in that case you must promise me that you will never get another boyfriend. I would hate to see you smooching up to some Peripheran guy."

Gripping my nose with her finger and thumb, Heather says, "I'm not promising anything." She rolls off me and sits up to look at the woman in the birthing pod sac field. As I sit up, Heather pulls me around so my back is towards the woman.

"Let's sneak off," she says, standing up. She pulls me up and leads me along the track, not giving me a chance to look back. I run along with her until we are amongst more trees. We stop and, as Heather checks that we are out of sight, I notice my shoe is untied. So I crouch down and tie it up.

"Where are you taking me next?" I ask.

"I'm hungry. Shall we eat?"

"I thought you would never ask. I haven't had any breakfast. What time is it?" I stand and look around. Ahead of us the path meanders along the side of a fast flowing river, beyond which a forest covers an entire hill. It looks familiar, like the Earth I know but with different features. I'm pretty certain that in my world there's a housing estate on that hill and the river runs under a main road. I turn and look back up the hill on which the Morlillia is situated.

"It's almost ten o'clock. You okay?" Heather asks.

"I'm trying to determine where in my world we would be now."

"The Morlillia, in your world, is a school."

"That's right," I recall. I turn and look at the woodland. "So that is a housing estate."

"Yes."

"Do you eat human food?" I ask, thinking about breakfast.

"Yes," Heather replies.

"I have so many questions," I tell her.

"The authorities gave me a house to stay in whilst they search for Reeteh Steispeck. Let's go there and eat. We can talk some more."

"That sounds like a good idea."

Chapter Thirteen
Periphera

Within minutes of requesting transport, Heather and I are picked up by an aircraft and carried to a large house in the centre of yet another forest. We land in front of the house in a small clearing. Unlike North Silestia, this house is new and its style is Peripheran - the corners of the walls are framed with ornate, twisting, stone branches, as though the house has grown out of the ground. It is a white house, with two storeys and six front facing windows. The entrance is built into the right-hand corner of the front wall and consists of a triangular porch, with plants growing up it.

The sun is high in the sky by the time we reach the house. I wonder whether it is just the planet which exists in a different reality or whether the whole universe is physically separate from the one I come from.

We are surrounded by trees, which all look familiar; like the trees on Earth.

"So they gave you a house in a forest? They obviously weren't worried about you having flashbacks about being kept prisoner in a house in a forest," I say, smiling.

"I chose this house," Heather replies. "I wanted to be able to talk to you uninterrupted. No one will bother us here," Heather explains, as we approach the front door. Our transport lifts into the air and disappears amongst the clouds.

"What were the other choices?" I ask.

"An apartment in Asten, the tower where the council is."

"The government building?" I recall.

"Asten's not a government building. The council is like a secret service. That's the equivalent of your MI5 building in London, but with a lot more secret stuff going on."

"Really?"

"Why do you think you can only access the building by air?" Heather looks at me for my response.

"I thought there was an entrance at street level as well," I admit.

"No. Just the rooftop." Heather swipes her hand across a small pad on the wall next to the huge front door.

"Hand scanner? Don't you have anything more high-tech than that?"

"That didn't scan my hand. It scanned my DNA. Most people have DNA in the sweat on their hands."

"What if you had someone else's DNA under your nails?"

"The device would know."

The door is big enough to be two doors. I hear a couple of clicks within the door and a moment later it opens a couple of inches. Heather pushes it open fully and we step into the house. A light comes on automatically.

"Quick tour?" Heather suggests.

"Okay."

She takes me on a whirlwind tour of the residence, which has a living room, dining room, kitchen, bathroom and four bedrooms. There is also a study, which has a wall of books, and an empty room with no furniture or windows. The whole house is just like those we have on Earth, with a few small differences.

"It's a nice house," I say to Heather as we head to the living room. The light comes on as we step through the doorway. The living room is sparsely furnished, with just two sofas and a coffee table. No television or stereo. "Do you know who lives here?"

"No. I suspect it is owned by the council."

"To hide witnesses?" I wonder. "Do you know what they have in store for me?" Will I get to go back to Earth or will I be given a residence on Periphera? Maybe I'll have to get a job and rent a house on Periphera.

"You actually have a choice," Heather replies.

"I do?"

"Yes. Temporarily, you can stay here with me until it is safe for me to return to my home, or you can move into an apartment in the tower."

"Oh, cool, a choice." I rub my hands together at the thought. "Is it really *my* choice though? What if you don't want me staying here with you?"

"I already told them I don't mind," Heather replies.

"Then it's a no brainer. I'm staying with you," I say, grinning.

"You do understand that we have separate bedrooms?"

"Of course." I sit down on one of two sofas, which are facing each other. They appear to be made from soft leather, with ornate wooden panels. The wood looks like mahogany.

My thoughts turn to my sister.

"So where is Lucy?"

"The other humans are being housed in apartments in Asten. Would you like to speak to her?"

"Yes, I would." I look at my watch and wonder whether time runs at the same speed on Periphera, or whether their position around the sun is the same as Earth. Is it autumn here as well? Seems cold enough.

Heather summons me with her finger, as she slips out of the room. I follow her into the hallway, where she stands by a screen. She presses her finger on the screen and a man's face appears.

"Heather?" the man says.

"Nathan would like to talk to Lucy."

"Diai," the man replies.

"Die?" I question. "That's a bit harsh."

"It means ok. D-I-A-I. Diai," Heather explains. I can see she is trying not to laugh. The screen goes blank and we wait. A minute or so later, I see Lucy on the screen. She is looking at a woman, who is standing by her side.

"Do I need to do anything?" Lucy asks the woman.

"No, just look at the screen and talk," the woman replies. Lucy looks at the screen and sees me. Her face lights up with delight. It's a reassuring sight.

"Hey, Nate. It's good to see you."

"How you doing sis?" I ask. Heather slips away, leaving me at the screen.

"I'm coping," Lucy replies.

"They treating you well?"

"Like a princess. I'm trying not to think about what happened. How are you doing?"

"I'm fine. I've been out with Heather learning about their weird ways."

"Heather's back?"

"Yes. They let her go. She's in protective custody as well. We all are."

"Did you hear how many humans are left?" Lucy asks.

"Just under three dozen," I reply.

"I still don't believe it. That can't be possible." I see her eyes wander as she recalls memories of the people she once knew.

"Try not to think about it, sis. So have they been teaching you about Periphera?"

"Not really. Just lots of questions. I don't even know where we are." Lucy looks around at the room she is in.

"You're in the capital city," I inform her. I forget what they call it."

"Verorlanden," Heather says from behind me, as she passes. She disappears into the kitchen.

"That's it, the capital city is Verorlanden," I say to Lucy.

"Where are you?" Lucy asks.

"I'm..." Heather is behind me again and I find her hand across my mouth. Her skin smells sweet.

"We're in a secret location." Heather says to Lucy. "We can't say where just in case someone is tapping this line." Heather removes her hand from my face and heads back into the kitchen.

"You two seem to be getting on well," Lucy notices. I look around to see whether Heather is nearby, she isn't.

"Not as well as I'd like. I think my chances of being her lover are remote," I say, recalling the conversation with Heather about human and Peripheran mating.

"Why?"

"They have some funny ways. Also, Peripherans NEVER have relations with humans."

"Never?"

"Never. It just doesn't happen."

"Knowing you, my little brother, that's not going to stop you trying." I smile at Lucy. I hear Heather cluttering about in the kitchen.

"She is perfect," I tell Lucy.

"Be realistic," Lucy replies. "Remember, some rules cannot be broken, even by the most charming suitor."

"I'm going to fight for her. I will never forgive myself if I don't try everything in my power to convince her."

"Do you think she feels the same about you?" Lucy asks.

"She likes me but she knows the rules, so she won't let herself give in. I need to find a way to get those rules relaxed."

"What if she is still not interested?"

"Well, at least that will be her decision."

"Don't get hurt," Lucy says. I can tell she is worried about my depression. She has a certain look of disappointment when she thinks about it."

"I have a lot occupying my mind right now, so I'll be fine," I assure her.

"So when will we get to meet up?" Lucy asks.

"I have no idea," I say. "How are *you* coping?"

"It's like I imagined everything. One minute I was in my garden with Jeremy and then I'm in another world and they tell me he is gone. I'm in denial at the moment. I think I need to see him before I can really accept what has happened."

"That might be tough," I suggest.

"I have to do it. If they'll let me," Lucy insists.

"Have you met any of the other human survivors?"

"Not yet."

"Me neither."

"Do you want to?" Lucy questions. "You never really liked people." She raises an eyebrow and smiles.

"No, I must admit I'm not eager to meet them."

Heather appears behind me.

"Ready to eat?" Heather asks.

"We're having a late breakfast," I say to Lucy.

"Enjoy it," Lucy replies. She smiles at me.

"Take care, sis. Bye," I reply.

"And you little bro." Lucy turns to look for the woman who helped her take my call. Heather presses her hand on the screen, making Lucy's image disappear. She holds my shoulders with both hands, reassuringly.

"Diai?" she says.

"Yes." I reply. Heather pats my shoulder.

"So what would you like to eat?" she asks.

"Something Peripheran," I reply, turning to look at her.

"You sure? We eat large spiders," she says, her eyes wide and her face grinning.

"What?"

"I'm just joking. Our food is mostly plant based, but we supplement those plants with the most amazing meats."

"So you eat the same as us?"

"Yes, and I'm pretty sure you asked me that earlier." She's right, I think I did.

"I fancy bacon," I suggest.

"Bacon is good. I'll order some."

"You not going to cook it?"

"This is a safe house. The cupboards are virtually empty. I'll get some bacon delivered."

"So what were you doing in the kitchen?"

"Looking for plates and cups." Heather presses her hand on the screen and the man's face appears again.

"Heather?" he asks.

"Sustenor," Heather says.

"What would you like?" the man asks. He looks miserable. Does he hate his job? Does he just sit there waiting to be called? How many other safe houses is he looking after?

"Bacon," Heather requests.

"Anything with the bacon?" he asks. Heather turns to me.

"Buttered bread and ketchup," I suggest.

"Buttered bread and ketchup," the man repeats. "Halven." Heather presses the screen to make the man's image disappear.

"Halven?" I question.

"Half an hour," Heather explains. She heads back into the living room, so I follow her. We each crash on a sofa.

"So how many times did you visit Earth?" I ask.

"As a scientist, I went there a lot."

"I notice that everyone here speaks English but you use some words of your own. Is English your primary language?"

"No, we speak Peripheran, but since England is our armarano, all people locally speak English as well. Those whose armarano is France will also speak French."

"Which do you prefer?"

"We tend to speak a mixture of both. There are some words we use which you don't have."

"Like armarano and morlillia."

"Yes."

"So, as a scientist, what was your job?" I lay out on the sofa, still looking at Heather.

"I worked in a lab doing neural mapping for the first part of my career. Then, two years ago, I was approached by Reeteh Steispeck to work on a project to create a neural switch."

"Reeteh Steispeck is the crime boss?"

"Yes. I knew he had questionable business ethics but he also owns a number of reputable businesses. I thought I was being hired to work for one of those. I didn't meet Reeteh until the team I worked with came up with something we realised would be catastrophic. We refused to do any more work and Reeteh visited us. He told us what might happen if we stopped working on the project."

"He threatened you?"

"Yes. The rest of the team continued, but at a very slow pace. They were in no hurry to finish the work."

"What did you do?" I ask.

"I was contacted by a man named Theo, who said he worked for the government and could get me out. I didn't believe him, but I didn't really have much in the way of choice. I never met him but he arranged for me to visit Asten, Verorlanden to meet with the council."

"When was this?"

"A year ago. I remember I was in protective custody in a house in Asten, Pelerush; that's America on Earth. Asten is the name for the secret service buildings around the world. I remember coming out of the building and seeing someone fire a weapon. I dived to the ground and crawled back to the doorway. A vehicle pulled up and a man told me to get in if I wanted to live. I jumped in and a bag was thrust over my head. I felt something penetrate my arm and then I fell unconscious. From then on, my memory is inconsistent. I remember being in

North Silestia, the doctor and his assistant. I remember a man visiting me once. He asked lots of questions. I remember going into the woods to play. That sounds ridiculous but I felt the need to play."

"You were like an adult with a child's mind when I met you," I recall.

"I remember that. I knew you wanted to kill yourself, so I kept your rope. It was quite selfish though. I wanted you to come and play and I knew you wouldn't if you were dead."

Heather looks at the door leading to the kitchen. "Would you like a drink?"

"Do you have anything resembling tea?"

"We have tea. You should assume that all human food and drink is available."

"Tea, then, please. Milk, no sugar."

"Keep me company while I make it," Heather says, jumping off the sofa. We head into the kitchen, which is huge. There is a breakfast bar along one wall and a variety of appliances set into a central worktop. I have to remind myself that this is an alien world. The close Peripheran-human relationship has made adjusting to their world easy. It's like an Englishman visiting the United States for the first time. It's not as different as one might expect. It's a shame the Peripheran-human relationship was so one-sided.

"So the bad guys found you in America, what is it called?"

"Pelerush," Heather says as she takes two ornate, tall mugs out of a cupboard. They are thin, white porcelain with mock branches rising up the sides, forming the handle. I can see trees play an important part in the lives of Peripherans, but not in the way hippies like trees.

"So what makes the council think Reeteh won't find you here?" I ask. Heather puts teabags in each cup and holds one of the cups under a pipe which is poking out of the wall over the sink. The pipe automatically dispenses boiling water.

"They're probably not looking for me. Last time, they needed the final part of the calculations to complete the Baltron Phase orbs. That was hidden in North Silestia House. They have now accomplished their aim, so they don't need me."

"So why are you being protected?" I ask, as Heather hands me the cup.

"See if there's still milk in there," she says, pointing at a small door under the end of the worktop. I open it and find a chilled cupboard, with milk and some fruit juice inside. I take the milk out and sniff the contents to check it's still fresh.

"I came here last night," Heather explains. "The milk was fresh then." I hand the milk to her and she pours some in both our drinks.

"I have to testify against Reeteh," Heather says, answering my question. "So the government wants to keep me safe whilst they hunt for him."

"You have to testify? So Reeteh *does* still have a reason to kill you." I take the teabag out and place it in the sink.

"Only if Reeteh is apprehended." Heather says as she finishes making her tea. She drops her teabag in the sink next to mine.

"Surely that's the whole point; to apprehend him and bring him to trial. If you are their key witness he will undoubtedly try to remove you from the equation. As safe as this place is, I think we should leave and go somewhere else. After all, we're just down the road from North Silestia and he found you there."

"That was different. I wasn't being protected by the government then."

"No, but you were when someone took you from Pelerush and stuck you in North Silestia."

"What do you suggest we do?"

"Do you know what happened to the other scientists you were working with? Are *they* going to testify?"

"I don't know."

"Why don't you ask the question?"

"What good will it do?"

"Ask the question," I insist. I leave the kitchen through the second door, which Heather had been using whilst I was talking to Lucy. I turn to see Heather following me. She places her hand on the screen and the now familiar face of grumpy man appears.

"Heather?" he asks for a third time tonight.

"I need some information," Heather states.

"Very well."

"I want to know what happened to each of the scientists in the team I was working with." The man looks at the screen and stares for a moment. I'm not sure whether it is the mention of Reeteh's name or the nature of the request which has unsettled him.

"I'll get that information and re-call you."

"Thank you," Heather says. She presses the screen and we return to the kitchen to finish our tea.

"I feel a little worried," Heather admits. She leans against the worktop. I place my tea on the floor and sit next to it, leaning against the cupboard. Heather slides down the opposite cupboard to join me.

"Déjà vu," I say, recalling our earlier floor conversation in my own kitchen.

"You are right," Heather says. "If I am to testify against Reeteh, I might not be safe."

"Is there anywhere else we could stay? Somewhere not connected with you or the council?"

"We could go to a hotel."

"Are your hotels like Earth hotels?"

"We grew alongside your race, remember."

We are distracted by the sound of a bell. Heather leaps up and leaves the kitchen. I follow her into the hallway, where a light is flashing on the screen. Heather places her hand on the screen and the man's face appears.

"Did you have anyone in particular you were curious about?" the man asks.

"No. I just want to know where they all are, right now."

The man pauses before saying, "None of them is alive today. It seems over the course of the last year they all died."

"How?" Heather asks. The man looks at something off-screen and then back at Heather.

"Some appear to have died from tragic accidents and a couple were killed by professional hits," the man explains.

"They were all killed by professional hits," I suggest. "They succeeded in making some look like accidents."

"Reeteh Steispeck?" Heather questions.

"I do not have such information," the man on the screen answers. "I have been asked to emphasize the importance of your testimony."

Heather and I look at each other. No words are spoken but I suspect we are thinking the same thoughts - Reeteh is leaving no loose ends.

"Could you pass a message to Frank..." Heather pauses. "What was his name? O'Toole."

"I'm not familiar with Frank O'Toole," the man admits.

"That might be his human alias," I say.

"His name is Frank. He brought me in," Heather explains.

"Frank Grihhe?" the man on the screen suggests.

"Yes, Frank Grihhe. Tell him to come to the house as soon as he can," Heather requests. She sounds worried. I am surprised she hadn't considered the threat before.

The grumpy man nods and the screen goes blank.

"Gry-hee? I query. That's Frank's surname?"

"G R I H H E," Heather spells out. "Grihhe."

"And you trust him?" I ask.

"I distrust him the least," she replies.

Chapter Fourteen
Frank

The main garden is at the rear of the house. Heather takes me on a tour of the plants, explaining what each is. I am impressed by her botanical knowledge. For my protection, she avoids the purple fendura fruit.

"I'm hungry," Heather says, as she sits on a bench built into a rockery. I sit next to her and hold her hand.

"Me too," I reply.

"Your hands are cold," she notices. "Are you warm enough?"

"I'm fine. Diai," I say.

"Diai means okay," Heather corrects me.

"I'm fine, okay," I repeat. "See, that works."

The sound of an engine takes our attention. We both stand up and Heather leads me through a passage, along the side of the house, which leads to a gate at the front. We peer through the gap between the gate and its post to see who is coming. A vehicle appears and pulls onto the driveway, coming to a halt by the front door.

The car - I assume it is a car - has one large ball underneath, on which it seems to sit and roll along. To stop the vehicle from tipping over, small jets of air burst out from each corner, blowing fallen leaves around on the ground.

The door opens in a similar manner to my Delorean, lifting upwards rather than opening out. With the sun behind him, the silhouetted figure of Frank climbs out of the vehicle.

"I miss my Delorean," I say quietly to Heather.

Frank looks straight at us.

"Paranoia can be a useful defence mechanism," he shouts to us. Heather opens the gate and waves at him.

"How did he know we were here?" I ask as we approach Frank. The door of his vehicle is still open and the engine is whining gently.

"What's wrong?" Frank asks.

"I don't feel safe," Heather replies. I look inside the vehicle and see an array of monitors and digital gauges across the dashboard. On one small screen a thermal imaging camera shows three figures standing next to the car.

"That's how he knew where we were," I say to myself. I head towards the rear of the vehicle to look for the engine.

"I have been asked to stay with you," Frank tells Heather. "You scared the council when you asked about the other scientists. They really need you to testify."

"And I will," Heather says, "but I must feel safe."

"Well, I cancelled your bacon and brought some of my own food," Frank says, reaching into the vehicle to pull out a small bag.

Under the corners of the vehicle I find the rear stabilising jets, which are blowing hot air at the ground.

"Don't get too close whilst it's running," Heather warns me. Although she is in conversation with Frank, she is keeping an eye on me, like a mother with a young child. Is that how she sees me? Am I like a child to her?

"How does it work?" I ask.

Frank answers, "the vehicle is sitting on a cushion of air over the ball. The small thrusters push it along."

"What pushes the ball if the vehicle is not actually attached to it?" I ask.

"The ball has technology which communicates with the vehicle. When the vehicle says, go forward, the ball goes forward in synchronization with the vehicle."

"Four wheels and a motor works for us," I say, looking at Frank across the vehicle.

"That's because you used fossil fuels. We don't," he replies.

He used past tense to describe the human method of fuelling. He is correct: humans no longer need fossil fuels, but it bothers me that he has already taken to using past tense to describe my race.

"What powers it then?" I ask, dismissing my concern about his use of past tense.

"Water," Frank replies as he walks down the side of the vehicle towards me.

"Do you extract the hydrogen from the water?"

"Something like that. I'm not an expert. I'll take you for a drive some time," Frank promises. He pats my shoulder and then heads towards the front door of the safe house. The vehicle's engine shuts down and the driver's door closes with no apparent control from Frank.

"What food did you bring?" I ask as we enter the house and make our way to the kitchen.

"Hungry?" Frank asks.

"Heather is," I say. I feel Heather's hands on my shoulders, which makes me feel contented.

"Anything will do," she says from behind me.

"I have rumplers," Franks says, grinning.

"Rumplers?" I question. I turn and look at Heather.

"I love rumplers," Heather says. The excitement in her voice is obvious.

"They are small pieces of beef, fried in herbs and spices, and battered," Frank explains.

"Very juicy," Heather adds.

"Diai," I say.

With two large plates of rumplers, more tea and what appears to be Danish pastries, the three of us settle in the living room for a late breakfast feast. Frank beats me to the sofa on which Heather has parked herself, leaving me with the sofa opposite them.

"So what else can you tell me about Periphera?" I ask Heather and Frank, who have left an acceptable distance between each other.

"What would you like to know?" Heather replies.

"Well, you know what humans were like, so what would be the significant differences? Apart from the morlillia stuff."

"Heather told you about that did she?" Frank says.

"Yes. So what else should I be aware of?"

"Our society is universally friendly," Frank states. "We greet everyone we see, even if we don't know them. Our historical records show that we have had the ability to armaranos fend for at least fourteen thousand years. We have ancient texts describing your Earth at that time. For the last two thousand years we have globally agreed to keep our existence secret from humanity. There was a scroll..."

"The Hybreen Scroll," Heather interjects.

"The Hybreen Scroll, which highlighted the problems our ancestors were having entering into a union with humanity."

"So, were you the angels mentioned in the bible?"

"We were misinterpreted as angels in your past. We were also assumed to be spacemen. We are neither."

"Did you build Stonehenge?"

"No, humans built Stonehenge," Frank answers. He frowns at my question. "It's just a stone circle. Give your ancestors some credit. They weren't idiots."

"So where does Periphera exist? Are we in a parallel universe?" I ask.

"Not really. The easiest way to describe it would be to suggest that all the dark matter your scientists believe makes up the missing mass of the universe, well that's us, except we're not dark matter. We're like a radio not quite tuned to the radio station. If you de-tune it enough you pick up another station."

"Does every planet have a Periphera twin?" I clarify.

"Well, since our de-tuned radio station," Frank looks at Heather, whose analogy he is using, "exists across the entire universe, every planet will have a twin. If we travelled from here to another planet we could fend into your universe."

"Can you travel to another planet?"

"We've been to Sarm," Frank states.

"Sarm?" I query.

"That's what we call Mars," he explains.

"We have no need to travel further," Heather states. "We manage the resources of this planet extremely well, so we don't have a population problem, we aren't running out of fuels, food, or any of the things which are needed to support our planet."

"Unlike my world was," I recall. I take a couple of rumplers from the table in front of me and throw one in my mouth. "I have a question, which might be a bit sensitive," I say after swallowing the chewed up rumpler.

"Yes?" Frank replies.

"If your people visit Earth at will, and you have been doing so for thousands of years, why, when my race was being wiped out, did only thirty-four humans get saved by your people?"

Heather and Frank look at each other.

"I was on Earth," Heather states. "I don't know the answer to that."

"I do," Frank admits. "When I was sent to find Heather, the Veronmovmen instructed all Peripherans to return to Periphera immediately. A global command was issued forbidding Peripherans from travelling to Earth until the Baltron Phase threat was dealt with. That's why there were only thirty-four Peripherans on Earth when the Baltron Phase was released. It is also the reason that most of those survivors were from your country. We knew Heather was being held in England and we had to find her before Reeteh."

"Shame you failed," I note.

"It is indeed," Frank says with a sigh.

"So what's going on inside your back when you armaranos fend?" I look at Heather. "Can I see you back? You were very protective of it before I knew who you were."

"There's really not much to see," Heather says, as she sits forwards and slips her jacket off. She unties her blouse and slips the shoulders off, turning to show me her back. I jump out of my seat and get a closer look. Heather's spine looks the same as a human spine; however, near the top of her back, between her shoulder blades, her skin is slightly translucent. I can see two bones in her back through the skin. The bones are horizontally placed against her spine.

"You have a couple of extra bones," I say. I want to touch her skin but I'm afraid she will object.

"They're not bones," Frank replies. "They are small lobes, attached to our spinal columns, which are extensions of our brains.

"It's like extra processing power, which activates the lobes and creates a quantum event," Heather explains.

"Always the scientist," I say to her. I force myself to touch her back. She doesn't flinch, so I run my finger along her translucent skin, across the lobes. I finger a heart shape and wonder whether she can tell what I did.

"Your skin is soft," I say to Heather. She turns and looks at me, pulling her top back over her shoulders.

"I'm sure Frank's skin is just as soft," she says.

"Yeah, I don't really care what Frank's skin is like," I say. "No offence, Frank."

"No offence taken," Frank replies. "More tea?"

"Yes please," Heather and I say simultaneously. Frank picks up our cups and leaves the room.

"You're coping well," Heather says once we are alone.

"I don't feel all that bad. Do you think that's normal?" I sit down next to Heather.

138

"Everyone deals with bad news in different ways," Heather reassures me.

"What do you think the chances are of Reeteh being caught?" I ask.

"I don't know." Heather eats a rumpler.

"Where is your real home?" I ask. "Do you have a family?"

"Family? Don't you remember what I said at the morlillia?"

"It seems odd to me not to grow up with your parents. Do you keep in touch with those who raised you?"

"Like all Peripherans, I was raised by my community. When we reach adulthood, we are encouraged to move away and find our life."

"Find your life?"

"Discover what we are good at and what we like doing and go to wherever those skills are needed."

"What were your skills?"

"Science. I picked it up quickly and studied physics."

"So, do you know more than Earth's physicists?" I ask. Heather nods her head.

"And you were happy keeping that knowledge to yourself?"

"Of course. Humanity had to evolve in its own way, making its own mistakes and finding its own place in the universe. You wouldn't benefit from us handing the universe to you on a plate. You would have just become part of our culture."

Frank comes back into the room with a tray of cups and sets them down on the table.

"So what is *your* job?" I ask him. Frank sits on the opposite sofa.

"I am an investigator," he answers.

"Like a detective?" I probe.

"Yes, like a detective. Most of my work is secret."

"Is there a lot of crime on Periphera?"

"We have criminals. All societies do."

"So this isn't a utopian society?" I question.

"We are closer to a utopian society than any of the countries of Earth ever were." Frank replies.

"Do you have poverty?" I ask. There must be something horrendously wrong with Periphera. It can't be *that* perfect.

"No, we don't. All our countries work together."

"So you don't have wars?"

"Not for over three hundred years," Frank seems pleased to announce.

"Just petty criminals," I suggest.

"Reeteh Steispeck's criminal activities revolve around business. People suffer at his hands, so we have to stop people like him."

"What about burglars and muggers?"

"We have those too. Not many, but it happens."

"Drug related?"

"Most crime on Earth is. We don't have any illegal drugs. We educate our children so they know to be careful what they ingest."

"Like the toxic fruit?"

"It's not toxic to us. *You* just need to be careful with those." Frank leans back and stretches his legs out to relax.

"You mentioned a prison island. Do you ever execute your criminals?" I ask. Heather doesn't seem to want to join in with this conversation.

"We don't execute anyone," Frank answers. "We restrict their movement and finances."

"Do you use money like we do?"

"We trade and use a global currency. We also exchange faraf."

"Sorry, what?"

"Faraf. It's a way of exchanging things. If your car breaks, I can fix it. If I need my lawn mowing, you can do it. No money changes hand."

"I see. But what if I can't do anything for you?" I question.

"You pay me."

"Does that work? Surely the government would object because you're not paying any tax."

"We don't exchange products, just services."

"Diai," I say, sceptically. I look at Heather and she smiles.

"You okay?" I ask.

"I'm fine," she replies. I turn to Frank.

"So, do you have high unemployment?"

"No, why would you assume so?"

"Because you don't need mechanics or grass cutters." I smile to show I am playing with him.

"Once you have settled in, we'll find you a job suitable for a human," Frank says, smiling. I anticipate the accompanying put-down but it doesn't come.

"That got you thinking didn't it," Frank says. He smiles and drinks some tea. I like Frank. He is interesting.

"So, do you have people doing menial jobs?" I ask.

"Like what?"

"I don't know, cleaning, factory work, dustbin collection?"

"You think those are menial?" Frank questions. He looks at Heather and then back at me.

"I wouldn't be able to do them," I state. The thought of doing something monotonous fills me with dread. I need my mind to be taxed.

"None of our cleaners or factory workers works full time," Frank states. "We are aware that people like you would not be able to do such work. So, to encourage everyone to do all jobs we give them time to do other things."

"Other things?"

"I pay you a full-time wage but you only work for me half the time. The other half you spend at a releeler," Frank explains.

"A what?"

"A releeler. It's a place where you go to tax your brain in a positive way, with puzzles, assault courses and the like. Most people are happy to clean offices every other day when the days in between are filled with releeler trips."

"Surely that's expensive for the employer," I suggest.

"They get reimbursed by the veronmovemen. The government."

"Where does that money come from?"

"It is in the government's interest to have everybody working: more productivity, more income, more tax to collect."

"But they give it away to those people."

"Not all jobs are subsidised in this way. The outlay is less than the reward."

"That's interesting," I say. I mean it. I wonder whether that could have worked on Earth.

Frank stays with Heather and me for most of the day. We go for a walk in the nearby woods and then watch a Peripheran movie, which is a bit dull. After a modest evening meal, Frank announces that he has to leave us.

"I thought you were protecting us," I state.

"I won't be far away and will come immediately if you call." He rummages through his jacket pocket and pulls out a small card-like object. He hands it to Heather. I assume it is literally his calling card.

Frank then leaves us.

Chapter Fifteen
Other Humans

Heather is keen to sleep, so we head for the same bedroom and lie on the double bed, fully clothed. We agree that staying in the same room is safest. Within minutes I am asleep.

I awake to find a ray of sunshine across my face. It feels good to be somewhere different. Heather is lying against my back, with her arm over my hip. I can feel her chest against my back as she breathes in and out. I lie still for a moment, hoping not to wake her.

The tranquil moment is ruined by the sound of a bell. Heather wakes up, jumps off the bed and runs out of the bedroom. I suspect there is an incoming call.

I sit up and scrutinize the room. The window is full-length, from ceiling to floor and has two a pair of white curtains across it which are not fully together, allowing the sun to shine into the room. The bed is made from wood and has a soft mattress. There is a small table in the corner and the opposite wall seems to have doors in it, although they are disguised to look like the wall.

I hear Heather talking downstairs, so I leave the bedroom and head for the bathroom.

When I return from the bathroom, Heather is sitting on the bed, waiting.

"Everything diai?" I ask.

"That was Frank," Heather tells me. "The council wants to see us. They want you to meet the other surviving humans."

I am quite apprehensive about meeting other humans. Lucy

had admitted to being in denial about the loss of her husband and I am not sure where my emotions currently lie. I don't really feel that bad. Every now and again a flash of something I'll miss pops into my head; like seeing my favourite bands live in concert or watching a good film. I remind myself that the music still exists, just not the bands; as do the films. Is it too soon to ask for a copy of every CD still remaining on Earth?

Heather reads the expression on my face.

"Does that not please you?"

"Not really. I grew to dislike people quite a lot. It made suicide seem an easy solution. If it wasn't for Lucy I would have done it long ago."

"And now?"

"And now the tables have turned. I outlived humanity. I don't really want to meet the other survivors."

"Do you understand how that will look to those survivors?" Heather asks. She looks serious.

"I haven't really given it much thought," I admit.

"You will look self-righteous. A person who thinks he's better than everyone else," Heather says.

"Don't hold back!" I say sarcastically.

"These people don't know your background. They don't know what trauma created the Nate standing before them and they won't give you time to explain yourself. You must meet them and pretend to be interested in the fate of your own race."

"I know. I'm just worried that they will see through me."

"I don't believe they will."

"You don't?"

"No. I think you've had a lot of practise making people think what you want them to think – like your sister. You use it as a way of hiding your depression."

"Lucy can see straight through me."

"She knows you better than anyone else," Heather states.

"True."

Heather is right and it surprises me to hear her nail me down so specifically. Her intelligence attracts me but I really underestimated her. She's not just hanging around with me; she's analysing me. She has an agenda.

"Is there anything going on that I should know about?" I ask.

"Like what?" Heather questions.

"Why have you let me into your life? I could be with the other humans right now but I have had the privilege of learning about your world and following you around. Why?"

"Well, I owe you my life, I like you and I think you have potential. You have no fear and you are intelligent. I feel safe having you with me."

"You want me as a sidekick?"

Heather steps forward and runs the palm of her hand down the side of my face. She leans close to me and whispers, "you always see the negative."

An hour later we are standing in a small room in the Asten building, waiting for a member of the council to see us. Before we meet the survivors, the council wants to brief me.

The room is sparsely decorated, with one wall of glass windows looking out across the city. In the centre of the room is a horseshoe shaped sofa. Unlike the stylish sofa in the safe house, this one is bright red and appears to be made from velvet. Heather and I stand in the centre of the room, waiting.

Edruth enters the room and smiles at both of us. She seems to be dressed in the same clothes as before.

"Hello," she says.

"Hello," Heather replies.

"Hello again," I say with a fake smile.

"You will be meeting the human survivors soon," Edruth starts. "Before you meet them, I need to ask you not to tell them anything about the time you have spent on Periphera. Everything Heather has shown you, told you, taught you please keep to yourself. Assimilating the other humans will take time and we will be introducing aspects of our world to them in a structured way. Please do not mention Reeteh Steispeck, the origin of the orbs, or Heather's involvement. The last thing you want is thirty three humans screaming for her head on a stick."

"That makes sense," I admit. I look at Heather for her opinion. She nods her head.

"What if they ask why I am not being kept with them?"

"Tell them you have been interacting with our people since before the genocide. It's not a lie. You just didn't know you were."

"Diai," I agree. I have a feeling that their use of the word 'okay' isn't as flexible as mine.

"I hope you find friends in those remaining," Edruth says as she heads for the door. She leaves Heather and me alone again.

"Did any of that sound unusual to you?" I ask Heather.

"In what way?"

"Do you think this room is bugged?"

"Undoubtedly."

"In that case, what she said was absolutely normal and does not concern me at all." I sit on the sofa and stare at the doorway. Heather sits beside me and her hand finds my knee.

"Nervous?" she asks. I look at her and see her smile, which disarms me.

"A little," I admit. Heather squeezes my knee.

"You don't have to do this. The moment you want to leave just say and we'll leave," she reassures me.

"Do you think any of them is a musician?" I ask.

"Possibly, why?"

"I love music. I can play the guitar but I'm not very good. I'd hate for humanity's future in music to rely on my ability to pick up where all those great musicians left off."

"You need to stop burdening yourself with issues which aren't important. Peripheran governments are putting together thousands of specialist teams who will go to Earth and preserve whatever they can."

"So they said. I would like to go back and see what it's like now."

"Why?" Heather asks.

"Closure, I suppose. As Lucy said, she doesn't know Jeremy is dead and she won't believe it until she sees for herself. I feel as though humanity is still there, getting along fine without me."

"The council is waiting for the all clear to be given before allowing anyone to visit Earth. When they do, I'll take you home."

"Diai," I say. I find myself smiling. That word still amuses me. I feel very relaxed in Heather's company, as though we have known each other for years, and I suspect she feels the same with me. At a time when our two worlds are undergoing immense change, we seem to have bonded. Either that or I am love-struck and blind and she is manipulating me.

"I should have a codeword," I suggest.

"A codeword?"

"To tell you that I want to leave, without the other person knowing."

"How about you tell me you are looking forward to a steak dinner," Heather suggests.

"Diai," I reply.

"You going to keep saying that?"

"It's your word."

"Well stop smirking every time you say it!" Heather slaps my arm and stands up. I lean back against the sofa and stretch my legs out. The door opens and a man enters the room. I determine that he is Peripheran, which is not hard to do since the back of his trousers have the anana over the backside. In his hand is a small metal case, which looks a little like a photographic camera case.

"Hello, Heather," the man says as he approaches. "My name is Emilio." He doesn't look at me.

"Hello Emilio," Heather replies. She turns to me. "This is Nate."

"We've met," I say. I put my hand out to shake and the man, although a little surprised by the action, complies. "You are one of the council."

"Yes, I am," Emilio confirms.

"We have a code phrase which means Nate wants to leave," Heather says to Emilio.

"You do?" he replies, with a surprised expression.

"Yes. If Nate says he is looking forward to a steak dinner, it means he wants to leave."

"Why do you feel the need for that?" Emilio asks.

"I am not great in the company of other people," I answer.

"Very well," Emilio acknowledges. "I will listen for that phrase and remove you from the room, should you invoke the request."

He opens the case and pulls out a small white bracelet, which seems to have two gemstones set in it.

"The council has issued all humans with one of these," he says, holding the bracelet.

"A bracelet?" I question. Emilio places the bracelet in my hand. It is light and feels like rubber. I pick at one of the gemstones to see whether he reacts.

"They are diamonds from Earth," Emilio says. "Not worth much to us but we thought you might like them as a token of your world."

"Thank you," I say politely. I am not sure whether I like the gift or whether I should feel insulted. Why not give me something that is worth a lot in this world, now that I have been forced to join their civilisation? I place the bracelet in my pocket and notice that doing so provokes the reaction I had anticipated with the gem picking. Why does putting the bracelet in my pocket agitate him? I pretend not to notice.

"You must wear the bracelet," Emilio commands. I turn to Heather to see what subliminal information her face is giving away. She frowns at me and then looks at Emilio. She doesn't know why I must wear the bracelet.

"Why?" I ask.

"Well, you may have noticed that our two races look identical. The bracelet will allow you to identify other humans."

Heather lets out a small puff of breath and I realise she doesn't agree with the reasoning.

"For me to identify other humans, or for you?" I question.

"For all of us." He places his hand on my shoulder and walks me towards the window, through which the entire city can be seen. "I am fully educated in human history. We are not Nazis. That bracelet is not like the marking of a prisoner of war. It is purely to allow everyone to know who is human and who is not." Heather joins us at the window.

"There are only thirty-four humans alive. Statistically, nearly all Peripherans will never meet a human. So why do we need to wear bracelets?" I ask.

Heather gives Emilio a stern stare.

"I don't make the rules," Emilio says. "Humans have a history of deception and I would assume that the Veronmovmen wants to protect our people."

"That's the government?" I question.

"Yes," Emilio states.

"Your government wants to protect your entire planet from thirty-four humans?"

"From small seeds large trees grow," Emilio quotes. I hate him for saying that. He walks back to the door and opens it. "I will bring the first human to you," he says.

"The first?" I query. "Am I not meeting them as a group?"

"One at a time," Emilio answers.

"Why? Why not put us all in one room and let us get to know each other?"

"It has been decided that you meet one to one," Emilio explains. He leaves the room before I can argue with him.

I feel Heather's hand on my shoulder. I turn and stare into her beautiful green eyes. She takes hold of my fingers on my right hand.

"Is your world as messed up as mine was?" I ask. "Am I being led to believe you all live in harmony but really you don't?"

"Everything you have seen is real." Heather replies. "There are some bad elements here but not as many as Earth had."

"And the bracelets."

"It *is* pretty," Heather says.

"Then you wear it." I hand the bracelet to Heather and, to my surprise, she attaches it to her wrist.

"That'll confuse them," she says, smiling.

"You are so beautiful," I say, without thinking. I try to keep eye contact, but it is something I am not good at. I have low self esteem and I worry she'll see me for who I really am – a man who never made much of his life and who wanted to kill himself instead of persevering. I can't stop myself from looking away but I immediately look back, hoping she gets the message. For the first time since we met, Heather blushes and looks away.

"Shall we sit back down?" she suggests.

"Diai," I reply. Heather looks at me and I assume it is to check I am not smirking. I manage to keep a straight face this time. We sit on the sofa, relatively close to each other, but not intimate, and wait for the first human to be brought to us.

"Are you certain you want me with you? I won't be offended if you want to be alone with them," Heather says.

"Hey, I spent my whole life with humans and they made me want to kill myself. You make me want to live, so stay."

Heather nods her head and looks expectantly at the door.

"I have to say that I don't feel as bad about the human race being wiped out as I probably should. Do you think I'm evil?" I ask.

"Firstly, there is no such thing as evil," Heather responds. "Secondly, the only living person you cared about was your sister, and she's fine. Besides, you might feel fine today and depressed tomorrow. Don't expect anything. No one in the history of mankind has been in the situation you are in."

"I suppose not."

The door opens and Emilio enters, along with a man who is wearing jeans and a blue checked shirt. He is portly and has no hair. I do a quick assessment of his clothing, the way he walks, the expression on his face and the quality of his watch and shoes and try to guess his occupation. He has a keychain on his belt which is attached to something in his pocket – probably keys. Could that be a crossover from his work? Is he a security guard?

Heather and I stand up and I feel her hand on my back. We step forward and meet the man in the centre of the room.

"Hello," I say, giving him a friendly smile. "Nate." I put my hand out to shake and the man reciprocates.

"Mike," he replies. His handshake is weak, despite his strong hands. He doesn't shake hands as part of his job. On his left wrist hangs the white diamond bracelet. A quick glance and I can see that he doesn't use his hands for work. They are too clean and soft. He has a tattoo on his right thumb, which appears to be a butterfly. He has a long term girlfriend, not a wife – no wedding ring, and he doesn't work in a job which would require him to remove rings for safety. The tattoo looks new, perhaps no more than a year old. He's probably still in the relationship. Her name might be something butterfly related, or sounding. Betty? No, too old-fashioned. Might be a type of butterfly, or she like butterflies. Now I am clutching at straws.

"How are you coping?" Mike asks.

"Coping?" I reply.

"With what happened."

"Fine," I reply. I feel Heather's hand pat my back and realise I should be more compassionate. "As fine as one can be under the circumstances. How about you? Did you lose your girlfriend or did she make it?"

Mike hesitates and his eyes look down and to the left as he brings images of his girlfriend into his mind. His eyes start to go red at the corners and I realise he lost her.

"I'm sorry," I say. I can't even reassure him by telling him that there are plenty more fish in the sea, because there aren't. The sea is almost empty, metaphorically speaking.

"What was her name?" I ask Mike.

"Tammy," he replies. He lifts his hand and shows me the tattoo. "She loved butterflies."

I'm not really sure what to say to Mike. I've never been very good at compassion, or small talk. It's even harder since everything in his life is now gone.

"Where are you from?" I ask.

"Exeter," he replies.

"Not too far then," I say.

"Did you lose anyone?" Mike asks me. I turn to Heather and then back to Mike. I consider telling him that I actually seem to have gained someone.

"Not recently," I reply. "How many of the other humans have you met?" I ask.

"Just three. A man who works in the tax office in Swindon, an old man who used to teach at a university and a woman who ran a chip shop. How about you?"

"None. You're the first. Were they all from England?"

"We rescued people whose armaranos was local to here. The other humans are scattered around the world," Emilio answers. He places a reassuring hand on Mike's back.

"What did the professor teach?" I ask.

"Professor?" Mike questions.

"The man who used to teach at the university."

"History, I think."

"Oh, right. Should be an interesting man to talk to," I suggest. Mike and I look at each other for a moment and I realise I have nothing more I want to ask him.

"What do you do?" he asks.

"Nothing," I reply. "I was on long term sick when it happened. How about you? Security?"

"Yes, how did you know?"

"Just a guess. Was it for a factory?"

"Yes. Night watchman and Leaders Foods."

"Are the Peripherans treating you well?"

"They've put me in a luxury hotel," Mike answers. He smiles. "Never been in a luxury hotel before."

"They want us to be comfortable," I say. I assume he doesn't know the luxury hotel is actually the Asten building. I turn to Heather and see she is almost crying. She is feeling the emotions I should be feeling. I feel disappointed in myself.

"I am looking forward to a steak dinner tonight," I say. Heather takes my hand and smiles at me.

"I can't eat," Mike says.

"Perhaps you can both catch up later," Emilio says. "We have a lot of introductions to make."

Emilio escorts Mike to the door.

"Bye Mike," I say.

"See you around," Mike replies.

Edruth enters the room, as Emilio and Mike leave. She closes the door behind her and walks briskly into the centre of the room.

"Good news," she says. For a moment I wonder if it has all been a misunderstanding and humanity is alive and well. "The Baltron Phase has neutralised and Earth is now safe to visit."

"Wow," I say, with some sarcasm. "I thought you were going to..." Heather stops me.

"When can we go there?" Heather asks.

"You can't. Reeteh Steispeck might be looking for you. We will be sending a preliminary team to North Silestia House to ascertain events leading up to the event."

"I want to go to Earth," I state. "I insist. And I want Heather to come with me."

"Not possible. You are an endangered species. Until Reeteh Steispeck is brought to justice you must stay here."

Heather steps behind me and, without warning, I see a flash of pink lightning light up the room. The light engulfs me and I feel my muscles tingle. I close my eyes because the light is so bright.

When I open my eyes I am shocked to see that I am suspended in the air over Salisbury Plain, with the ground at least a hundred metres below me.

Chapter Sixteen
Father Figure

My muscles are still tingling as I hang in the air. I can feel Heather pressed against my back, with her arms wrapped tightly around my waist under my armpits. Is she really strong enough to hold me in the air?

We start to descend slowly. Heather's head is pressed against my shoulder putting her face against mine. I look up and see her pink-lightning angel wings, crackling the air around them. They stretch at least four feet higher than our heads.

As we touch down on the grass, I step away and turn to look at Heather. Her energy wings dissipate gradually, from the tips down to Heather's back. She stands and stares at me awaiting my reaction.

"I have one question," I say. "Why didn't you do that before the party and leave me on Earth?"

"I tried," Heather admits. Her admission shocks me a little. I thought she had stayed with me because she wanted to.

"When we visited North Silestia I ate some fendura," Heather admits. "There was some in a bowl on the kitchen table but it took a while to take effect because of the drugs, which were stopping me fend. When I went to the bathroom at Lucy's house I tried but the effects of the medication were still inhibiting me. It was only by chance that my armaranos fend worked when the orbs appeared."

I look around at the barren landscape. The sun is shining and it is a nice day.

"What now?"

"I need to do some investigating of my own," Heather explains.

"We're in the middle of nowhere," I state.

"There's a road over there," Heather replies, pointing over the hill. "We might find a vehicle we can use."

"Okay, let's get walking."

We walk briskly across the grass until we reach the brow of the hill. I turn and check behind us to see whether Edruth has followed us but there is no sign of her. On the road further down the hill is a Land Rover. We run down to the vehicle and find it parked on the grass by the road. Lying on the ground next to the Land Rover is a dead man.

"You okay?" Heather asks, as we both stare at the corpse.

"I'm fine," I reply.

"We're going to drive into Salisbury and there will be a lot of these. I won't think less of you if you want to close your eyes," Heather reassures me.

"I really don't have a problem," I reply. I am surprised with myself. I have never seen a dead human before but the sight of the man doesn't bother me. He looks peaceful.

Heather jumps inside the Land Rover and starts the engine. I run around to the passenger side and climb aboard.

"We going to North Silestia House?" I ask.

"Yes," Heather replies. She drives the Landrover as fast as it will go.

"What about those orbs? What if more are released?" I question.

"You need to stay really close to me," Heather says.

"Do you need to feed up on fendura before you can transport us back?"

"No, I'm good for several trips." Heather looks at me and smiles. "You nervous?"

"I'm actually quite excited. We are in uncharted territory and I feel alive."

"I thought you might."

We drive for a few miles until we reach the edge of Salisbury. Heather stops the Land Rover next to a black Audi, which has come to a halt against the grass verge. The driver of the Audi is dead, lying on the floor next to the car.

"That's two people who were outside their vehicles," I notice.

"They probably saw the orbs and stopped to get a better look. Lucky for us, it means they turned their engines off."

"We climb into the Audi and Heather starts the engine. She floors the accelerator, making the tyres screech as we are thrust forwards.

We drive into Salisbury and pass the supermarket where I had met another, less attractive, Heather.

"Can we grab some food?" I ask. "I'm hungry."

"We need to be quick," Heather replies. She swings the Audi into the car park and drives up to the entrance doors. There are just a few cars in the car park- the orbs appeared at about the time the store was going to close. We climb out of the car and head into the supermarket.

As we pass through the security barriers I have to step over the body of a woman. Heather and I look down at her and I realise it is Heather Peavicante - the woman who wanted me to go out clubbing with her. She may have been waiting here for me, as a she said she would. I look at Heather.

"I recognise her," I say.

"Did you like her?" Heather asks.

"No," I admit.

"Then don't be distracted." Heather pulls me into the store, away from the dead woman. "Focus."

"Okay," I reply. By the tills, a manager lies dead. He is still holding a clipboard.

"Stay close to me!" Heather shouts as she runs up an aisle. She picks up a couple of small bottles of fizzy drinks as we pass a fridge containing drinks and sandwiches. We reach the bakery section. The fresh food has been standing around for a day and a half, so I avoid that counter and grab a packet of chocolate biscuits from a shelf.

"These will keep us going," I say to Heather. We run to the front of the shop, through the doors and into the car park.

Back in the Audi, we speed towards North Silestia House, eating biscuits and drinking fizzy orange along the way.

The grounds of the house are quiet. There are no vehicles or signs of occupancy. Heather parks the Audi next to the house and jumps out quickly, leaving the keys in the ignition. Without speaking, we run up to the front door and head inside.

In the kitchen I see the bowl of fendura Heather mentioned. It seems funny to now know the significance of that bowl of fruit. I might be dead if Heather had not eaten some. Whilst I look around the kitchen, clutching a couple of biscuits, Heather enters the room where we left the dead doctor and his assistant – I assume they are Peripherans.

"What are you looking for?" I ask.

"Clues I might have missed last time," Heather replies. She appears at the door. "If the orbs are released again I can only save you if you are standing next to me," she states. Realising the danger I could be in, I quickly join her.

"How were they killed?" I ask. I take a bite of a biscuit as Heather positions herself behind me. She looks at the bodies over my shoulder. It occurs to me that we are roughly the same height, give or take an inch. That means Heather is at least five feet, ten inches.

"Looks like a gunshot. Probably a Peripheran gun," she whispers.

"What's the difference?" I turn and look at Heather.

"Peripheran guns don't fire bullets," Heather explains. It feels strange standing so close to someone whilst having a conversation. We are in each other's intimate space.

"What do they fire?" I ask.

"Air."

"Really?" I check. "Guns that fire air?" I turn and look at the bodies. Their wounds look like regular gunshot wounds.

"They turn a minute piece of air into a quantum ball," Heather says.

"A quantum ball? You're making this up," I say. I know plenty about physics and I am sure quantum mechanics has never included turning air into a ball.

"It's a subatomic reaction which groups air particles," Heather explains. "The gun fires the ball of air particles at high speed. The quantum ball can only last a second, which is fine, because a second after being fired it is embedded in the target."

"That's pretty neat. I bet forensics examiners hate it. No bullet to analyse."

"Peripherans don't generally go around shooting each other."

"Oh yes, I forgot, your world is perfect." I smile.

A noise from upstairs takes our attention. Heather, like a mouse listening for predators, looks up at the ceiling.

"House moving?" I suggest.

"That sounded like someone dropping something," Heather disagrees.

We run out of the small room, through the kitchen towards the stairs. Heather runs up the stairs like a gazelle, missing two at a time. She stops half way to wait for me, realising the danger I might be in should the orbs appear. We continue together and slowly peer into the room which was Heather's bedroom. A man is sitting on Heather's bed. In his hands is a book. He looks at the door and sees us.

"Hello," he says, unsurprised by our entrance.

"I know you," Heather says as we enter the room. She pulls me to her side and then steps behind me, ready to armaranos fend if necessary.

159

"My name is Theo," the man answers. He places the book on the bed and looks directly at Heather.

"Theo?" I repeat. Heather mentioned him earlier. He helped her get to the council. "You can put a face to the name, now," I say to Heather.

"What are you doing here?" Heather asks.

"I thought you might return, so I decided to wait."

"Why?"

"My name is Theo Tandammbian. I rescued you from Reeteh Steispeck and brought you here."

Heather stares at Theo with a quizzical expression. "What was I wearing?"

"I dressed you in a maternity dress, complete with bump," he answers.

"Why did you bring me here?" I feel Heather move to my right hand side, still close to me.

"Purely selfish reasons," Theo replies. He looks at the floor as he thinks.

"Did you know about the baltron phase codes I had?" Heather asks. Theo looks up.

"No. I knew you needed to hide, so I kidnapped you and hid you here."

"Why?"

Ignoring Heather's question, Theo points at me.

"This gentleman. Do you have feelings for him?"

"We have bonded," Heather admits. I look at her and smile.

"We've bonded?" I check.

"I like you," Heather replies, without looking at me.

"I like you a lot," I state.

"You love each other?" Theo asks.

"Why do you ask?" Heather questions. Her face is stern. She didn't immediately say no, which might be promising.

"Peripherans and humans can never be lovers," Theo tells us.

"I know that," Heather replies. "Everyone knows that. What is your point?"

"My point is that not all Peripheran rules are just. If you love Nate you should be with him."

"How do you know my name?" I ask.

"I have people working for me," Theo replies. He stands up and approaches us.

"I broke a Peripheran rule," he says, staring straight at Heather.

"You loved a human?" Heather assumes.

"I watched the Sasmaiden take my child from the morlillia. Then I watched my child grow up. Twenty-five years later, my child needed my help, so I brought her here."

"What?" Heather says.

"He's your dad," I explain unnecessarily. Heather understands Theo. She is just having trouble comprehending his words.

"You are my daughter," Theo clarifies (also unnecessarily). "I spent a lot of time on Earth and I envied the bond humans have between parent and child. We never get to experience that. After your mother expelled you in morlillia I watched you. I waited. When you were born I followed you. For so many years I have wanted to tell you who I am."

As Theo talks, I watch his face. His eyes look like Heather's; deep set and big. Friendly; like Heather.

"I don't know what to say," Heather admits. "We don't raise our own children, so why would you think to do that?"

"As I said, I got the idea from watching humans."

I look at Heather and give her a wink. Maybe Theo's influence will work in my favour.

"So what now?" I ask.

"Well, I work for the Veronmovmen, so I was able to use certain resources to help you."

"Veronmovmen? The government?" I question.

"Yes," Theo states.

"I think someone at Asten is working for Reeteh," Heather admits.

"Really?" I question. She never said anything about that to me.

"I believe you are correct, but I don't know who it is," Theo replies. "I can tell you who it is not. Frank Grihhe is honest. So is Edruth. You can trust them. I hired Frank to watch you when it became apparent Reeteh was closing in. He never knew why he was watching you. I gave him enough information to bring you in if things got out of hand."

"Will you help us?" Heather asks.

"I'll get my people to do some searching." He returns to the bed and picks up the book. "It's important that you tell no one that you met me today."

"Why?" Heather questions.

"If someone in Asten is working for Reeteh, they might know I have been helping you."

Outside, a vehicle can be heard rolling along the gravel driveway.

"We must leave," Theo says. "That will be the investigating team." He runs out of the bedroom, so Heather and I follow him, jumping down the stairs, several at a time, until we reach the bottom. Theo's back lights up with pink lightning as his armaranos fend produces the electric angel wings. I feel Heather's arms wrap around my stomach and a second later there is another flash of pink lighting. My muscles tingle and I close my eyes in anticipation of the brightness which follows. When the lightning fades, I open my eyes and find myself back on Periphera, standing in the valley I had seen from above when Heather and I visited the morlillia.

Standing behind Theo are three men. I point at them but before Theo can turn around his chest explodes as a quantum ball of air pierces his back and disintegrates his internal organs before exiting through his ribcage, at which point it dissipates. I feel a gust of air hit my face gently as Theo falls to the ground.

"No!" Heather shouts. Her arms wrap around my stomach and I prepare myself for another armaranos fend.

"Heather," the man with the gun says. He looks a little like the late film actor, James Mason.

"Leave us alone," Heather demands.

"Listen to what I have to say," the man demands. He hands the gun to one of his colleagues.

"Who are you?" I ask. The man steps forward and holds his hand out to shake. He is standing over Theo.

"Reeteh Steispeck," he says. I don't shake his hand.

"Genocidal maniac," I say. His men are armed and I assume he wants Heather dead. We have no way of defending ourselves and, since he can also armaranos fend, no where to hide.

"I don't want to kill you, Heather," Reeteh says, trying to sound sincere. "You were my favourite scientist."

"You killed everyone on Earth!" Heather shouts at him.

"You believe that?" Reeteh questions. Heather says nothing. I can't see her face but I suspect she is scowling at him.

"I could kill you both now, but I don't believe there is really a need to do so. Please don't facilitate that need."

"By testifying against you?" Heather assumes.

"What is there to testify against? You don't know the whole story. It would be better for you to say nothing and live happily with your new human friend."

"And the alternative?" Heather asks. Her arms tighten around me.

"Well, I know where your safe house is, so you'll need to go into hiding somewhere else; live the rest of your life looking over your shoulder. Is that what you want?"

"What about the innocent people you killed?" Heather asks.

I'm not sure why she bothered to mention them. She is talking to the man who wanted to kill every human alive. I would be extremely surprised if he showed any remorse now.

"If you keep accusing me," Reeteh starts - he is quite well-spoken and has a gentle voice - "it could cost you your life."

"Are you suggesting you didn't," I say to Reeteh. I turn and look at Heather.

"I did not release the baltron phase," Reeteh states.

"Then who did?" I ask.

"That is a question I too am keen to answer," Reeteh replies. "If you leave me alone I can prove my innocence."

"Forgive me if I don't trust you," Heather says.

"I understand," Reeteh replies. "I wish to be open about my involvement." As he speaks, he rubs his top lip with his finger as though removing a spec of dirt. In reality, by putting his hand over his mouth he is subconsciously trying to stop lies coming out. When a person lies they often cover their mouth without knowing. There is no way Reeteh is stupid enough to believe we will actually keep quiet. So, we lied to him; he lied to us. What I don't understand is why he hasn't already killed us.

There is a flash of pink lightning and I feel my muscles tingle. I try to keep my eyes open this time to see what travelling from one world to another looks like but the glare from the angel wings is too bright and my eyes close involuntarily.

When I open them I am back in North Silestia House, standing at the foot of the staircase. I feel Heather's arms release and her hand takes hold of my arm.

"Quickly!" she shouts, pulling me towards the front door. As we approach the door, it flies open and the Peripheran equivalent of the S.A.S. bursts into the house. The soldiers are wearing full combat fatigues, with small Peripheran assault rifles and protective helmets. Heather throws her hands in the air and drops to her knees to let the armed men see she is not a threat, so I follow her lead and do the same.

"Reeteh Steispeck hereh Peripherano," Heather shouts. "Hurry!"

Without warning the first four soldiers release their glowing angel wings, filling the hallway with bright light. I put my arm across my face to shield my eyes and wait for the dark to return. When it does, I see Heather is now on her feet approaching the only man not in a combat uniform. He is wearing a grey suit, which looks expensive. In his hand is a small electronic device.

"Do you know Theo Tandammbian?" Heather asks. I step to her side. The man is staring at her, quizzically, squinting.

"Yes," the man replies. "Why do you ask?"

"He's dead. Reeteh just killed him," Heather informs him.

"How do you know Theo?" the man asks.

"We just met. What can you tell me about him?"

Before the man can answer, a flash of pink lightning takes our attention as one of the four soldiers returns from Periphera.

"He got away," the soldier says. "There was an aircraft waiting for him. We called for assistance. Base is tracking him. As soon as he lands we'll intercept him."

"Good," the suited man says.

"There was one casualty," the soldier continues, "a male in his fifties."

"Theo," Heather says. The suited man looks disappointed. I can think of a number of questions he might wish to ask us at this point but he seems to have no need to ask anything further.

Heather steps back and walks over to the staircase. She looks sad. As I step towards her she puts her hand up telling me to stop, so I do. The now familiar pink glow appears at her back and rises behind her as two glowing wings arc over her front, at which point the light becomes too bright to watch. The air crackles and then the light fades. Heather is gone. I am surprised to be left here by her. I turn to the suited man, who is talking to the soldier.

"What can you tell me?" I ask him. He looks at me with an accusing eye.

"Nothing. What can *you* tell me?" he replies. His voice is gruff, like a smoker. I wonder whether Peripherans smoke.

"Ditto," I say. I don't like his attitude, so I decide not to share anything with him. I'll wait to talk to Frank instead. "When Heather returns, tell her I went home," I say as I head for the front door.

To my surprise, no one stops me as I leave North Silestia House and jump into the Audi. I drive home, passing a number of crashed cars along the way, in which the drivers are dead. At home, I see my neighbour lying in the street with his wife. Their dog is running around. If I was a different, more caring, person, I might take the dog into my care and look after it on their behalf. But I am not, and right now I couldn't care less about the welfare of their dog.

Chapter Seventeen
Pieces of the Puzzle

Back in my own home, the only human alive on Earth, I put the kettle on to make some tea - and nothing happens. The power is out. Through the kitchen window I see the neighbour's dog run across my lawn. My mind turns to all the things which won't happen now that humanity is gone. The power is already off; no one will cut the grass; bodies will decay; food will rot; the houses will smell; and animals in captivity will die. I am sure there are many more things but those are the ones which come to mind.

Under my sink, I keep a small camping gas cooker. It is fuelled by a small gas canister, which I have rarely used. Within minutes, I have a saucepan of boiling water. I wipe my face and see blood on my fingers. Not my blood; Theo's. I only knew him for a few minutes - the last few minutes of his life. As I wash my face in the sink I think about his death. I have never seen a man killed before; except for the people at the party, but they just looked like they were falling asleep. Theo died in a graphic way, standing just a couple of feet in front of me; shot in the chest by a gun which fires air.

I dry my face, pick up my tea and head into the living room to relax on the sofa.

The Baltron Phase orbs didn't kill the animals but clearly the animals know something is wrong. There is not a sound coming through the open window. Everything is silent.

I have no television, no music, no one to telephone. At least Lucy is safe on Periphera. I hope she is safe. Would Reeteh go after her? He probably doesn't even know she survived, unless someone at the council is working for him – as Heather suspects. I wonder what led her to think so.

I feel restless. The idea of having the whole planet to myself might seem a peaceful concept, but in reality nothing seems different. I am still alone in my house, dwelling on a whole variety of issues. It's just that the issues have changed from what they were before. I think about Heather and I wonder what she is thinking, having had her own father admit he kidnapped her. The nuclear family is an alien concept to Peripherans. Not only does Heather have to come to terms with the death of Theo, but she has to accept that he saw her as his daughter. Will she be able to accept he was her father? His death has made that unlikely.

The thought occurs to me that I am reliant upon the Peripherans. If no one comes for me I will be stranded on Earth, and will have to forage for food. I could move in to the supermarket and live off the tinned food once the fresh food has run out. Once the tinned food runs out I will need to find my own.

I glance at the television, sitting in the corner of the room. I never got around to buying a flat screen television. I wasn't in any hurry because I didn't watch it often: just the occasional film or documentary. I am going to miss music though.

After drinking the best cup of tea I have ever had, I fall asleep.

Half way through a dream, in which I am a rock star, I am awoken by a bright light shining across my face. I open my eyes and see Heather's friendly face looking at me.

"Hello, sleepy," she says, with a solemn attempt at a smile. She looks as though she has been crying. Her eyes are red and somewhat bloodshot. I sit up and pat the sofa next to me.

"Hi. Sit down," I request. I am not sure what frame of mind she is in.

Heather sits next to me on the sofa and places her hand on my thigh. "My mind is a mess," she admits. I look at her and try to give her a reassuring smile, although I'm not sure I have had enough practice at this kind of thing. I place my hand on hers. She is my only friend in the world - in two worlds. That is if you disregard my sister. I don't know whether I am falling in love with Heather or whether I am just clinging to her because she is all I have. Either way, I feel excited to be with her.

"Do you think Theo was your father?" I ask.

"I see no reason why he would lie." Heather wipes her eyes.

"Where did you go when you left me at North Silestia?"

Heather looks at me and I see guilt in her eyes.

"I didn't mean to leave you like that," she explains. "I needed to see Theo. I checked his pockets for identification and clues as to who he was. He had nothing on him. The investigators took him to Verorlanden. They will test his DNA to see whether he is my biological father. I contacted Frank and told him what happened. Since we don't know whether Reeteh has a mole in the council, Frank is keeping everything to himself. He will let us know what the DNA tests reveal."

"If he *was* your father, how does that make you feel?"

"I don't know. It's not a Peripheran concept. We don't raise our biological offspring. Babies come into our community and we all take a part in raising them. When I was growing up I had a hundred fathers. All the men in my village raised me, along with all the women. To have just one father and mother seems narrow-minded. Just think how much knowledge you miss out on by relying on just two parents."

"Yes, but we go to school to learn as well," I defend.

"I have seen how human schools work. They didn't teach you about life. They followed a curriculum." There's that past tense again.

"Do you think that is why Periphera is so far advanced technologically? Because everyone raises the children?"

"I think so. One man in my village told me to always try to be the best at everything I do but never, ever, believe I am the best because there is always someone better. A woman told me what expelling a child was like. Her experience was totally different from the experiences of another woman. A man named Gared taught me about science. Another taught me about wildlife and took me out to the woods to see the animals."

"You went into the woods with a strange man?" I laugh to show how that might seem creepy.

"I was ten and we had other children with us. His enthusiasm for the world of the wild animal was infectious. I went home and drew pictures of the forest."

"I suppose it was the guy who taught you science who had the biggest affect on you," I say, knowing Heather is a scientist.

"Yes. Gared was amazing. He taught me how armaranos fend works and encouraged me to ask questions about the universe."

"Do you still have contact with these people?"

"When I go back to my village they are there."

"So who did you live with?"

"We have houses in which children live, run by sasmaidens. Each day, adults and older children visit the homes and play with the children, or teach them the sciences, languages or mathematics.

"I remember covering a lot of subjects. There was a really old man, who used to come in every day and tell us about his sea-faring voyages. We would also learn about Earth and the humans."

"So you don't have schools?"

"The whole village is a school."

"It's an interesting concept," I admit. "How do you stop children going to Earth unsupervised?"

"We don't. The ability to armaranos fend doesn't work until puberty, by which time, we have learnt and understand the rules about visiting Earth."

I nod as I consider what Heather is saying.

"So what now?" I ask.

"I have Theo's address. I want to go and have a look at his home."

"Can I come?" I'm not sure whether Heather has visited me to say goodbye or whether I am invited to join her.

"I *need* you to come with me," Heather replies. I feel her hand tighten on my knee. "You're human and it seems Theo was heavily influenced by your culture. I may need your opinion on what I find in his home."

"What if you don't like it?" I ask.

"I have an open mind," Heather replies. I want to tell her how closed her mind is because of her feelings about human-Peripheran relationships, but I stop myself.

"Diai," I say, instead.

We leave and head outside. I glance at the Audi, parked on my driveway and I am reminded of my Delorean, which I left at Lucy's house. I must make a point of getting that back.

Theo's home is a large house in the centre of Verorlanden, surrounded by large white skyscrapers and high-rise buildings. This is the first time I have set foot in the centre of the city, which has roads criss-crossing between the buildings and a surprising number of trees and grassed areas. There is an even balance between nature and the buildings. There is a lot of traffic on the roads and I am intrigued by the Peripheran cars, which all have the same basic feature of a large ball under the body of the car. The city is crowded with people, who all look happy. As they pass each other they smile. It looks tiring.

Heather stops walking at the entrance to Theo's home.

"You okay?" she asks me. I realise she has been watching me. I must look like a kid in a sweet shop.

"Yeah, I'm fine," I reply. "This place is amazing."

"Shall we go in?" Heather suggests, pointing at the door. I look at the house, which has two guards posted at the front door. There is no front garden, but the house seems cosy, despite being in the middle of the city. It has high windows on the ground level, so passers by cannot see inside, and ornate woodwork across the front. The windows have wooden shutters, which are all closed.

We approach the guards at the door and Heather pulls out a small plastic-looking card. She shows it to a guard and he nods his head. Heather turns and points at me and the guard smiles. He looks at my trousers and then my face.

"I know who you are," he says, as he steps aside to let us through.

Heather pushes the door open and we enter Theo's home, which is dark.

"What's on your card?" I ask Heather as she places it in her pocket. She takes it out again and hands it to me. A pattern of coloured squares takes up the front of the card. The reverse is blank.

"It's just coloured squares," I say as we stand by the open front door. Heather finds a light switch and turns on the lights, then closes the front door.

"It's an identity code," she informs me.

"And the guard could read it?"

"No, but the camera he was wearing could. It automatically confirms my credentials."

"And he knew who I was?"

"Apparently. You must now be famous."

"I doubt that. It's probably my trousers. I need to get some Peripheran slacks." We head along the corridor, which is carpeted and has an expensive look to it. There are oil paintings on the wall and the wall lights look like they are made from silver. They remind me of Victorian silverware. Crystal shades cover whatever is giving off the light - I don't know whether they have light bulbs or some Peripheran equivalent. The wallpaper reminds me of William Morris' trademark pattern and a small mahogany table is accompanied by two elegant Georgian style chairs.

"Looks like Theo was wealthy," I say as we head through a door into a study. "Do you use money on Periphera?"

"Yes," Heather replies, with a curt tone of voice. I think she wants me to shut up because she is staring intently at Theo's desk, which is covered in books and paperwork.

The study looks very English. There is a large desk in the centre of the room, with a wall of books along the side. A small window looks out across a walled garden, beyond which the rest of the city can be seen. I browse the books to see whether Theo collected anything human.

"What are we looking for?" I ask Heather.

"We're learning about Theo. I want to know why he felt the need to be my father."

"Maybe because he *was* your father," I suggest. I turn and smile at Heather but she has her back to me as she sifts through the work on Theo's desk.

"We don't have fathers," Heather replies without turning around.

"Or human lovers," I say quietly to myself but just loud enough for Heather to hear.

The books on the shelves are a mixture of Peripheran and English. Some of the Peripheran books are written in the Peripheran language, which looks very ornate, with curly letters. They use the same alphabet as the English language – well, as all languages which use that alphabet. I can't remember what it is called but know that seven years ago I did. I have forgotten so much.

"Is this the Peripheran language?" I ask Heather, just to be sure. I hold up a book which has large writing across the cover.

Heather turns and looks at it briefly and then resumes her sifting through the desk contents. Theo kept an untidy desk.

"Yes," she replies.

"I take it you read it from left to right," I check.

"All Peripherans are taught to read left-to-right and right-to-left. That way left-handed people can write their text from right to left with ease and it still makes sense."

"Wouldn't that be like mirror writing?"

"Only if you actually reverse the characters. Try writing English in that way; you can still read it given some practice. We also have quite a few words in our language which are spelt the same backwards as forwards."

"Palindromes. Really?" I am surprised.

"Remember Skereks?" Heather asks.

"Skereks?"

"It's what we call London. Skereks. The word reads the same backwards."

I try to imagine what English would look like backwards.

.yaw siht hsilgne gnitirw yrT

"In my world left-handed people just have to put up with writing like everyone else. In fact, in Victorian times, left-handed children were punished for trying to use the wrong hand."

"Harsh," Heather says, crouching down to pull open the desk drawers. Harsh is one of *my* words. I know I overuse it. Is she using it to make me feel comfortable?

Theo's bookshelf contains a lot of factual books from Earth; mostly historical. There are some science books as well, like Hawking's 'A brief history of time'. As I scan the spines of the books I find a large black book with Heather's name on the spine. I pull it out and lay it on the nearby chair. Inside, the book records Heather's life, from birth to the present, with photographs and text, written in Peripheran.

"You should see this," I say to Heather.

She drops the paperwork she is holding and wanders over to me.

"What is it?"

"Well, Heather," I start. "This is your life!" I say, trying to sound like the Irish man who presented the programme, *This is your life*, on British TV. What was his name?

Heather flicks through the book in silence.

"What does it say?" I ask.

"It's telling my life story," Heather replies, her voice soft as she tries to hide her emotion.

"Is that your surname? Lani Tasston?"

"Lani is my middle name." Heather looks at me. "We have similar name structures to you. Tasston is my surname."

"Heather Lani Tasston. Weird surname. What does it mean?"

"It relates to the day I was born. All people with the surname Tasston were born on the same day."

"So is Tasston a day of the week here?"

"No, it's just one day, every twenty years."

"Why is that?"

"Twenty years is roughly a generation, so each generation gets to name children Tasston."

"There must be a lot of people with the same surname," I realise. I start doing calculations in my head.

"It's also regional and will differ across the world. You have a lot of people with the same surname on Earth. They soon spread out."

"So, Theo's surname?"

"Tandammbian."

"Means the day he was born?"

"Yep."

"So, statistically, you have three hundred and sixty-five surnames?"

"Each year. So there are three hundred and sixty-five times twenty."

"Seven thousand three hundred," I calculate. I liked maths at school.

"You did that quickly," Heather commends. I must admit I haven't been able to do sums like that in my head for a while.

"I have a gift for numbers. If there were sixty million people in your equivalent of England, that would mean you have eight thousand two hundred and nineteen people with each surname."

"Impressive."

"Thanks." I tap the book about Heather. "He really did follow you all your life."

"Yes, he did." Heather closes the book.

"How does that make you feel?" I ask. Heather stares into my eyes, deep in thought.

"Somewhat strange," she finally replies. "I don't understand what benefit he got from knowing what happened to me."

"He spent too much time on Earth and realised that humans love their children. He wanted some of that for himself."

"He never got it."

"No. Maybe the Peripheran in him stopped him from revealing himself to you."

Outside the study a door slams. A moment later, a flustered Frank enters the room, in a hurry. He swings the door open so fast it hits the wall, startling me and Heather.

"We found the complex where they built the orbs," Frank declares.

Chapter Eighteen
The Baltron Phase

Pelerush is what the Peripherans call North America.

Within two hours of leaving Theo's study, Heather, Frank and myself touch down in an airport just outside Menanem; their version of Boston. The supersonic aircraft we travelled on made Concorde look like a biplane by comparison. I would have quizzed Heather about its propulsion, except I slept most of the way.

As we leave the airport I realise I have lost track of the time. If my reasoning is correct, it is now Monday morning, although in Menanem it is still the middle of the night, since they are five hours behind Mistep-hoak, or Britain as I like to call it.

"Did you sleep during the flight?" Heather asks as we climb out of the aircraft and into a bus-sized ball-vehicle, which has two balls.

"Yes, most of the way," I reply. "I see you did."

"I was so tired," Heather admits.

"It's Monday morning now, right?" I check.

"On Earth, in Britain, yes." Heather straps herself into the seat next to me and helps me find my straps. The bus has twelve seats in the back, with one at the front for the driver, who is positioned centrally to the dashboard. Frank and five other men and women join us on the bus. Frank introduces them as investigators.

"I am leading this investigation," Frank announces. "My colleagues are here to assist me."

Heather nods as she looks at the investigators. They smile

but remain silent. Three of them have small laptop sized devices, which they are controlling with their fingers. I have no idea what they are for.

"We need Heather to assess the state of the Baltron Phase," Frank informs us as we speed along a wide road, passing other vehicles. The bus is fast. I wonder what their Highway Code rules are.

"How did you find it?" Heather asks.

"Sources close to Reeteh leaked its location to the council," Frank replies. "When you worked on it, were you anywhere near Menanem?"

"Not at all. I was in Pelerush but further down the coast, near Renner," Heather replies.

"The other scientists are all dead, so we are bringing in some outside help. Your immediate task is to ensure the Baltron Phase is disabled." Frank stares at Heather for a moment. I wonder whether he blames her for her part in the genocide of my race. "Can you do that?" he asks.

"With ease," Heather replies. "The codes I took to North Silestia control the subatomic differentiator."

"The what?" Frank questions.

"It's a small box, which acts like the brain of the machine. Without it, the orbs collapse into themselves within milliseconds of being released."

"Did you design it?"

Heather pauses before answering. "Yes, I did," she admits.

"You had no idea what it was going to be used for?" Frank probes.

"No."

"Did you not wonder?" Frank looks stern, like a hard-nosed police detective of the nineteen seventies.

"Reeteh hinted that I was making a brain for a propulsion system. When I realised what it could do I stopped working," Heather explains.

Frank nods his head, silent. He turns to one of the investigators. They, in turn, look at Heather but say nothing.

"And the codes?" Frank asks.

"I took them with me."

"Why didn't you destroy them?"

"I didn't have a chance. I destroyed all my written work, but the baltron - the brain - was already assembled, so I took its control unit with me. I had planned to hand it over to Asten, but Theo found me first."

"And now Reeteh is tidying up the loose ends," Frank states. "What we don't know is why he didn't kill you when he shot Theo. There must be something from you he still wants."

The bus stops next to a field and the driver opens the doors, to let us out. As I step onto the grass, I look around and see nothing but fields.

"Is it underground?" I ask. Heather says nothing. She seems distracted, possibly by the guilt she must be feeling for her part in creating the Baltron Phase.

"It's on Earth," Frank answers. He steps back and releases his electric angel wings. With a flash of pink light, he is gone. The five investigators follow suit and disappear, leaving Heather and I alone.

"You okay?" I ask her. I take hold of her hand and rub it reassuringly.

"It's all starting to come back clearly," Heather recalls. "I killed the human race."

"No, you didn't. Reeteh killed the human race. He manipulated you to get you to make something he could use. You didn't do anything wrong. I pull her towards me and hug her."

"How can you say that? Your entire race is gone. How can you stand to be near me?" Heather pushes me away.

"If I thought you did it because you hated humans I would

shoot you myself. But you didn't. The only thing you are guilty of is being a bit gullible and that's normal."

"A bit gullible?" Heather questions. "A bit gullible doesn't get a race of people killed."

"Don't blame yourself." I hug Heather and hold her tightly to stop her pushing me away again. "You built a hammer and Reeteh buried it in someone else's head. It wasn't your fault."

There is a flash of light and I feel my hair standing on end. I turn and find Frank standing nearby.

"You two coming?" he asks.

Heather steps behind me and puts her arms around my waist. A moment later there is the now familiar flash of light and I find myself standing next to a building, a few miles from the outskirts of Boston, Massachusetts.

In the distance I can see the city's skyline of skyscrapers. Black smoke rises from some of the buildings, darkening the sky.

"This way," Frank says, running into the large building, which looks like an aircraft hangar. Two of the men from the bus are standing by the door. They follow Frank inside. As Heather and I approach the building there is a blinding light and I feel the hair stand up on the back of my neck. At first I am worried that the orbs have been released again, but a second later I see a dozen Peripheran soldiers materialise from the light. They stand silently, awaiting orders.

Heather stops and looks at the soldiers.

"We going in?" I ask.

"Yes."

Heather heads into the dark building. We follow a corridor of corrugated steel through a metal door, which Frank has left open. Inside is a large machine, which looks like something from a science fiction film. It has vents, cables and pipes all over it, with a large glass dome at the top. Inside the glass dome is a liquid, which looks like water. The whole machine is about sixty feet high. At the top, extending from the glass dome, are conduits and more cables. At the base is a control panel, which looks as though it has a panel of lights across it. None of the lights is illuminated, so I assume the machine is turned off.

"Wow," I say, to myself.

"Don't," Heather replies. "It doesn't deserve your respect."

"Which bit did you build?" I ask.

Heather approaches the machine and presses a button on the control panel. Frank and the five investigators uniformly step back. I smile because they have nothing to worry about. The orbs only kill humans. Then it occurs to me that there is one person present who should be worried – me!

A drawer next to the control panel opens. Heather takes hold of a handle on the side of the drawer and pulls it out of the machine. It is a metal box about the size of a shoe box.

"This is the baltron," Heather says.

"Which bit did you hide in North Silestia?" Frank asks.

"The control unit. It's a small component inside."

Frank steps closer and takes the box from Heather. As he examines it he looks at Heather.

"You had the component with you when Theo kidnapped you?"

"Yes."

"So why didn't he destroy it?" Frank asks.

"Maybe he didn't know I had it," Heather speculates. "It was in my pocket."

"He changed your clothing." Frank argues, "He must have found it."

"What are you implying?" I ask. It seems as though Frank suspects Theo to have been dishonest.

"I'm not implying anything. I'm just gathering facts and trying to understand how they fit together." Frank hands the baltron back to Heather.

"Make sure this thing is disabled. Then we will destroy it," he says, turning to leave the room. The five investigators leave with him.

"Do you think they are really investigators?" I ask Heather. She looks at them as they leave.

"I don't see why they would not be," she replies. Her voice seems monotone, as though she is fed up.

"You ok? Diai?" I ask. Heather looks at me and for the first time she has lost that spark of energy which attracted me to her. "This wasn't your fault," I say, anticipating her response.

"I don't like to make mistakes," Heather explains. "And yet, I made the biggest mistake and cost a race of people their lives."

"I disagree," I say, trying to sound confident. "If you lean on a button that sets off a bomb and kills people, you can be angry with yourself for making the mistake of not looking where you lean. But that's not what happened. You were manipulated by a clever criminal, who hired you under false pretences. When you realised something was wrong, you quit. It's really not your fault." I step forward and wrap my arms around her. I feel her arms gently wrap around me and for a moment I feel content.

We are interrupted by Frank, who steps into the room.

"We're going to set some charges and blow this building up," Frank shouts across the room. "You might like to get out of here and work on the baltron in the bus."

Heather and I head over to Frank, who is having trouble keeping his eyes off the baltron.

"You know what to do with that?" he asks Heather.

"Yes," she replies, bluntly. "Once I have disabled it we can blow it up with the whole building."

"That sounds like a good idea," Frank agrees.

"Could we not just blow it up?" I suggest. "Does it *need* disabling first?"

"It would be safer to disable it first," Heather replies.

Heather transports us to Periphera, where the bus awaits, solitary amongst a field of grass. We make our way to the back of the bus and sit down. The five investigators join us and chat amongst themselves, quietly. Heather takes the cover off the baltron and carefully removes a small, glass, jam-jar sized object.

"This bowl alone," Heather says to me, "is volatile if dropped."

"Which is the part you carried to North Silestia?" I ask. Heather points at a small box, which looks like it is made from grey plastic.

"What are you going to do with this?" I ask.

In answer to my question, Heather disconnects a part of the device from the bowl and pulls a pin out of the top of the glass, where a metal lid is attached. She pulls the lid off, slips the bowl out of its housing and turns it upside down, holding it away from us. A blue liquid tips onto the floor of the bus. I jump up, watching Heather's face to see whether I should be concerned.

"It's safe to do that, is it?" I question.

"Without the ferval liquid, the bowl becomes harmless," Heather explains. "It's only when it is complete that it is volatile." Heather drops the bowl back into the case and presses a couple of buttons on a small control panel inside. A circuit board type of component unclips itself and Heather removes it from the case.

"It's disabled now," Heather says.

"What now?"

"We put it back in the hangar and let the explosives do their job." Heather stands up and vacates the bus. As I follow, we meet Frank outside.

"It's disabled," Heather says, waving the circuit board component in front of Frank.

"Good," Frank replies. He looks at the component, without touching it.

"I'm going to take this back inside and place it on the floor next to the phase," Heather says.

"Very well," Frank replies.

Heather steps away and disappears in a flash of pink light.

"How are you coping?" Frank asks.

"I'm fine," I reply. For the first time in a long while, I have told someone I am fine and actually meant it.

"And Heather?"

"She has a lot of guilt. I've been trying to tell her it wasn't her fault."

"The investigation will clear her of wrong-doing. It is my intention to keep you and Heather with me as we move closer to Reeteh," Frank confides.

"Why?"

"It will be good for Heather to seek justice for Reeteh's crime and it may make her accept that she should hold no guilt. Don't misunderstand me. If the evidence was leading towards Heather being crooked, I would have no hesitation in arresting her. However, it doesn't, so I want to make sure she comes out of this unhurt."

"That's nice," I say.

There is a flash of the familiar pink light as a soldier appears. He runs up to us.

"Mr Grihhe?" the soldier asks as he approaches.

"Yes," Frank replies. His voice is loud and authoritative.

"We have a problem inside," the soldier says. Frank steps away and uses his armaranos fend to travel to Earth, leaving me with the soldier.

"Take me to Earth," I demand. The soldier looks at me but says nothing. "Please," I add. The soldier steps close to me so I turn my back to allow him to transport me to Earth. I feel his arms around me and then the world turns a bright pink.

We appear outside the hangar, so I run inside to the room where the baltron phase has been rigged with explosives. Sitting on the floor in front of the baltron phase is Heather. She is clinging to the unit she disabled whilst on the bus.

"What's going on?" I ask Frank, who is standing with one of the investigators. I approach Heather and see that she is crying.

"She has a grenade," Frank answers.

"Why?" I ask. As I get closer I notice the grenade sitting on Heather's lap. She has a second grenade in her left hand.

"I'm sorry Nate," Heather says, through the tears. "I can't leave. I made this thing and killed your race. I can't live with that." She looks away for a moment and then back at me.

"Heather, you can't do this. This is the kind of thing *I* do. Remember, in the woods. You stopped me from killing myself. If you die now that will all have been for nothing." I feel Frank standing at my side.

"We must leave," Frank says quietly into my ear.

"I'm not leaving," I reply without looking at him.

"You *must* leave," Heather says. She looks up at the baltron phase machine.

"Dharahd," Frank shouts. I turn my head and see him signalling to the investigators. As the investigators leave, three soldiers run towards us. I turn and crouch down to Heather. She touches my face.

"Go, Nate. Start a new life on Periphera. We have so much for you to learn," she says.

"It doesn't work that way, Heather," I reply. I decide to try to be stern. "You don't understand."

"You're right, I don't understand. Theo was my father. He lived with a human woman and followed me as his daughter. We don't do that. Peripherans don't have daughters."

"He proved that Peripherans and humans can love each other and that it's ok to love your children," I argue.

"I don't believe that," Heather says, her eyes red from tears. She lifts the grenade and presses it against her forehead. I try to leap forward and stop her but I find myself restrained by the three soldiers, who pull me back.

"We must leave," Frank says.

"No!" I shout. "I'm not leaving Heather."

Frank grasps my face with his hands and stares at me with a menacing expression and determined authority.

"You are one of thirty-four surviving humans. You cannot die in here with Heather," he states.

"Heather cannot die," I reply. I realise I have no choice. They are going to drag me out of here and let Heather blow herself up.

"Heather has made her choice," Frank says.

I try to look at Heather but the soldiers' grip is strong and I cannot move. I catch a glimpse of her legs as the soldiers drag me out of the hangar.

Outside, it has started to rain. The investigators are waiting at the end of the lane which joins the hangar to the nearest road. The soldiers, with Frank's help, lift me off the ground and run as fast as they can away from the hangar, towards the investigators. Half way down the lane I manage to wriggle a leg free, so I use it to alter my centre of gravity and wriggle out of the soldiers' grip. I fall to the floor and quickly roll to the edge of the dirt track. As I stand up, the soldiers grab me again. Before they can pull me away, the hangar explodes. A huge white, blinding light balloons out of the building disintegrating everything within a hundred metres of the complex. I feel the heat on my face and the shockwave knocks me onto the floor, along with the soldiers and Frank.

At that moment, I feel my life drain from me. My reason to live is exhausted and the woman I love gone. I am alone. My thoughts briefly turn to my sister, Lucy, but I find her image repulsive. I want to die. I close my eyes and lie still. After a few seconds I realise rain is falling on my face. I don't care.

"Nate?" Frank says. I feel his hands on my face, cupping my cheeks as though my face is a bowl. "I'm sorry, Nate."

I open my eyes and look at Frank.

"Help me catch Reeteh," he says. "After that, you can do what you want. I need your help to catch him. Stick with me."

Chapter Nineteen
Tammat, Tammat

Frank transports me back to Periphera, where the investigators are waiting on the bus. An aircraft resembling a large helicopter, but without blades, hovers overhead. It lands in the field to collect the soldiers.

"You with me?" Frank asks. I look at him but find it difficult to acknowledge his existence. "We're not going back on the bus," he adds. He lowers me to the ground, where I sit and watch as he approaches the bus and waves at the investigators. I wonder what the point of them coming along was, when they said and did nothing. As the bus-load of investigators leaves, the soldiers disappear into the sky, leaving Frank and I alone.

Frank walks back to me and sits on the floor opposite me. It was raining on Earth but here the sun is shining.

"I want to take you somewhere to teach you some things which will help us when we confront Reeteh." he says.

"I don't see what I can do," I reply. It seems to me that Heather was the one person who could help catch Reeteh. I have nothing to bring to the table.

"Do you trust me?" Frank asks.

"I did, until you let Heather die."

"Peripherans have a different outlook on life from humans; different beliefs about death. One day you will understand why I did not stop Heather. Now is not the time to explain." Frank pats me on the knee. "In the mean time, I'm going to take you to a place away from all this."

"Why bother? Just take me to my sister."

"I was hoping you would work with me to track Reeteh," Frank says.

"I'm not really in the mood."

"There is one lead I have not followed. Theo's human wife. I believe Reeteh kidnapped Theo's wife to get him to give up Heather's location at North Silestia. With Theo dead, what happened to his wife?"

"Maybe she was on Earth when the orbs were released," I suggest.

"She lived in Devon," Frank discloses.

"So she's dead."

"Not necessarily."

"How so?"

"Theo's Devon home was built on the same site as a Peripheran building he also owned. He moved her between the two."

"But surely Reeteh will have killed her by now. He killed Theo."

"The Devon house was secret. I only know it exists because Theo and I were friends. Earlier, when I quizzed Heather about Theo not finding the component she carried, I wanted to know what my friend had been doing. He assigned me to watch Heather but didn't tell me why. I need to know what else he was involved in. I had no idea Heather was his daughter."

"Yes, he mentioned that," I recall.

"I can now understand why he wanted me to bring her back. She was safer with me."

"Really? So where is she now? Where is Theo? Where is the human race? You're not doing a very good job. It seems to me that you don't need me at all. You're clutching at straws."

Frank smiles before saying, "I don't really need you, but *you* need me."

"How do I need you?"

"I'm keeping you motivated and giving you a reason to live."

"I don't want a reason to live. The only reason I had to live just blew herself up."

"Let's make a deal. You come to my New York home with me and rest. Tomorrow we'll fly back to Mistep-Hoak and visit Theo's Devon home."

"I can't stop thinking about Heather." I feel tears forming in my eyes. Frank slaps my shoulder.

"I understand. The quicker we get to New York, the quicker I can help you get over that."

Frank seems totally unaffected by Heather's death. Are all Peripherans this cold? These are the people who give birth in a field and let strangers raise their children, so maybe Heather's death really isn't a big deal to Frank.

After half an hour of waiting, an aircraft comes to collect me and Frank. It flies us to the Peripheran equivalent of New York – which is called Tammat. It is also a city, similar in design to Verorlanden - the capital city of the Peripheran version of Britain.

We land on the island, which I know as Manhattan, amongst buildings which are considerably shorter than the skyscrapers of New York. Frank escorts me to a small, two-seater vehicle, which is an attractive metallic dark red in colour. It is like the ball car Frank drove to the hideaway house.

We climb into the vehicle and I feel a little uneasy as it wobbles with the change in centre of gravity as we sit down. I sit beside him, amongst an array of lights and displays.

"Are all cars this technical?" I ask.

"It looks technical, but it's all pretty straight forward," Frank replies. He presses some buttons and the car's engine hums a little louder. Then Frank pushes the vehicle forward, steering with a kind of handlebar.

We drive uptown, through a Peripheran city equally as busy as New York.

We reach a large building which seems to be located in Central Park, except on Periphera there is no central park. It's all buildings. The building we approach is shorter than the others and has no windows. A large door looks like it is designed to take deliveries because it would fit a lorry through it.

Frank parks the car and we get out.

"Huruh," a female stranger says to Frank as she passes.

"Huruh," Frank replies, smiling.

"Who was that?" I ask.

"I have no idea," Frank replies.

"Why did you say huruh?"

"Peripherans always say hello to strangers on the street when they arrive."

"When they arrive?"

"If you step out of a doorway onto a busy street, people will greet you. That's what we do. We got out of the vehicle and she said hello. Now we are on the street people will ignore us."

"Diai," I say. It seems a bit weird, but nice.

Frank opens the large door, to reveal a courtyard, which is dark. He waves his hand over a screen by the door and the courtyard's lights come on. I step inside as Frank heads back to the vehicle. He drives it into the courtyard, so I close the door behind him. It latches itself and locks with a clunk.

"This is *my* secret home," Frank says as he gets out of the vehicle.

"Secret?" I query.

"I don't let too many people know I own it. It's a good place to lie low."

Frank opens a small door which leads to a set of stairs. We head up to a kitchen which looks similar to the kitchen in the hideaway house.

Frank cooks a Peripheran meal for us, despite me telling him I am not hungry. He over estimates how much food we need and there is a lot of leftovers. I have lost my appetite because I cannot stop thinking about Heather, so I just nibble at a piece of meat and drink some wine.

After the meal, Frank stores the leftovers in a fridge and disappears into the living room.

"Come in here," he shouts through the doorway. I follow him in, taking my wine with me.

The living room is dark, so Frank turns on a small light, which is sitting on a side table next to a long sofa. (I recall the lights in Heather's safe house coming on as soon as we entered the room.) I look up at the ceiling and see several lights, which are off.

"A lot of your Peripheran stuff is like human stuff," I tell Frank.

"We evolved alongside you."

"So Heather kept saying," I recall.

Frank picks up a shoebox-sized case from the lamp table. He sits on the sofa and places the case on his lap.

"Do you know how to use a gun?" he asks. I lean forward and look at the case as Frank undoes the latches on it. He takes out a Peripheran pistol.

Frank hands the gun to me.

"I've fired air rifles," I reply.

Frank takes another gun out of the case.

"These fire balls of air," he says as he unclips the top of the gun. "Pull the clip back and press the button in the top." He does that to his gun and it makes a whooshing sound, like a small water jet. I pull the clip on the top of my gun and press the button inside. My gun makes the same whooshing sound.

"Before we proceed," Franks says, staring at me with a serious expression. "I need to be certain you will not shoot yourself with that thing."

"I'm very good at lying," I reply. "Would you like me to tell you it has not already crossed my mind?"

"I'd like you not to shoot yourself in my house," Frank replies.

We are interrupted by a ringing sound, like an old servant's bell in an Edwardian house.

"That will be my guest," Frank says, jumping to his feet. He grabs my arm and pulls me out of the room. We head down the stairs to the courtyard, which I notice is covered with a glass roof.

Frank opens the large door to reveal a shadowy figure standing on the pavement. I hadn't noticed it get dark outside. The person is wearing a large hooded overcoat, so I cannot see whether it is a man or a woman.

"You made good time," Frank says to the figure as they step through the door. Frank shuts the door behind them.

"I caught a lift," the woman replies. I immediately recognise her voice and, as she pulls her hood down, I am shocked to see Heather, alive and well. Without saying a word, I throw my arms around her and squeeze her tightly.

"You're still alive then," Heather says to me. I pull myself back and look into her eyes.

"You faked your death?"

"Yes," Heather says, smiling.

"Come upstairs and have some food," Frank interrupts. We can explain everything to Nate in comfort."

We head up to the kitchen and Frank dishes out the spare food for Heather. I cannot stop looking at her. Heather and I sit down at the table whilst Frank opens the wine. Heather starts eating.

"Now you understand why I made so much food," Frank says, offering me some more wine. I gladly take it and drink a large mouthful, whilst watching Heather eat, out of the corner of my eye.

"So, I assume the faked death was to make Reeteh think you were out of the picture," I say to Heather. She shakes her head, not wanting to speak with her mouth full of food.

"Not Reeteh; the council," Frank answers. "The investigators on the bus were assigned by the council," he explains. "I wanted them to think Heather had died with the baltron phase. They were really only there to observe."

"So now Reeteh and the dodgy council member think Heather is dead. That gets them off her back but how does that help us?"

"Their attention will now be focussed on me. So I am going to give you everything I have and let you two continue with the investigation. You can work from here. In the mean time, I am going to lead the council on a plastee vorov - a wild goose chase."

"Plastee vorov?"

"A plastee is like a goose. Vorov means to chase," Heather explains.

"So when did you come up with this plan and why did you keep it from me?" I ask.

"After Heather left you at North Silestia, following Theo's death, she visited me. We put our heads together and came up with this plan. We only left you out because you weren't there at its conception. After that we were concerned the council would hear us talk about it, so we kept it secret."

"And you couldn't tell me as soon as we got to New York, or whatever this city is called on Periphera?"

"I wanted to wait until I knew Heather was safe."

The thought of shooting myself with Frank's gun had already crossed my mind. I wonder whether he had considered that. My emotions are all over the place at the moment. I have gone from excitement to despair, to happiness in a short space of time. This cannot be good for my mind.

"So what now?" I ask.

"Tomorrow, you visit Theo's secret home and track his human wife.

"Did he actually marry her? Is that allowed?" I ask.

"He attained a human identity and married her on Earth," Frank explains. He leaves the kitchen for a moment. Whilst he is gone I smile at Heather.

"You going to keep grinning at me all night?" Heather asks.

"You would not believe how pleased I am to see you," I say to her. "You really messed with my head."

"I'm sorry," Heather apologises. "I was worried how you might react and I feared I would get here and find you dead. Frank assured me he would keep you with him."

"Your timing was perfect. Once again, you stopped me ending it all." I find it hard to say the words, 'killing myself' aloud.

"I would miss you," Heather tells me; an odd choice of phrase.

"I love you," I say.

Heather looks away for a second and I assume she is thinking of a gentle let down for me.

"You hardly know me," she says. She then takes hold of my hand. "I love you as a friend."

"I know Peripherans and humans don't fall in love, but your father proved that it can happen. He married a human." I turn and look at Frank, who is standing in the doorway. He comes back into the room, carrying some paperwork, which he places on the table.

"I don't understand my own feelings," Heather admits. She pushes the plate of food away from her.

"Do they conflict with Peripheran rules?"

"Don't take this the wrong way, but loving a human is so wrong, we are taught it is akin to bestiality."

"I think you are in love with me, but you are suppressing it," I suggest.

Frank leans against the table, placing both hands down on the table-top. He looks at me and then Heather.

"Heather, the world the humans lived in has gone. Humanity died and the few remaining survivors now live with us. They can no longer live in the manner they are accustomed. We, as Peripherans, would be naive to believe it was only the human world which has changed. We have to accommodate those humans and let them become part of our world. Our attitudes must change. I notice you are wearing Nate's humanity band. Whether you admit it to yourself or not, you and Nate have bonded intimately. He clearly loves you and, in my opinion, it would be acceptable for you to love him, given the circumstances."

I am surprised at Frank's speech. I look at Heather and see she is looking at the humanity band. She takes it off and places it on the table.

"If humanity is to become part of our world, there should be no place for these bands," she says.

I take hold of Heather's hand and, for the first time in years, I feel my heart race with excitement. Heather's fingers grip mine and she pulls me towards her. Just as I think we are about to kiss, she stops.

"I need time," she says quietly, staring into my eyes. I sit back and let go of her hand. I find myself nodding.

"Okay. Diai," I reluctantly say. She is worth waiting for.

"This is very moving," Frank interjects, "but I think we should do some work." He drags the paperwork to the middle of the table and spreads it out. Amongst the papers is a picture of a woman.

"Is that Theo's wife?" I ask, picking up the photo.

"Yes, it is. Her name is Tina Hoffeum-Howe," Frank says as he pulls out a chair and sits down.

"Hoffeum?" I question.

"It's a Peripheran term, which means sanctuary," Frank

explains. "She changed her name after she met Theo. Before that, she was Tina Howe."

"And you think she was kidnapped by Reeteh?"

"Possibly. My intelligence tells me Reeteh is looking for someone. It's not Heather, because he could have killed her when he killed Theo."

"What do you think?" I ask Heather.

"I don't know. Reeteh never gave much away."

"I want you two to read through all this and get your heads into the investigation. Stay here tomorrow and relax. Then come back to Mistep-Hoak and find Tina. I'm going ahead to Verorlanden. I have a fox to snare."

"A fox?" I question.

"Someone cunning."

"A council member," Heather says before I can say the words.

Frank taps the pile of papers with his finger.

"Direct your attention here."

Chapter Twenty
Guns

Alone with Heather, sitting on the sofa, I start to analyse my life. Heather is reading the paperwork Frank left with us. She has a small plastic device which is transmitting images into her mind. She looks strange sitting there with her eyes closed, receiving the images transmitted by the small box.

I knew I liked Heather but thinking she was dead made me feel the way I felt when I found out about the accident which killed my wife and son. It's like your heart suddenly becomes so heavy it falls through your chest and into your stomach and makes you want to vomit. Then numbness clouds your mind and you just want to die. At least, that's how it felt to me. Everyone is different.

Frank left for Verorlanden, leaving Heather and I three thousand miles away from the council and Reeteh in the Peripheran equivalent of New York. One day, I hope to quiz Frank about his job and the covert things he has done whilst investigating. I wonder whether any of the human governments were working with Peripherans on secret stuff.

Heather thrusts a photograph in front of me.

"Recognise this person?" she asks. The photo shows a dark doorway with a shadowy person standing just inside the building. They are out of focus and impossible to identify. I turn and look at Heather.

"From that? Not even if it was my mother."

"According to this file, that is the only photograph of the informant working for the council."

"Who do *you* think it is?" I ask.

"I have no clue. My interaction with the council was brief until I met you. I don't know much about any of them." Heather puts the photo back in the file.

"Who do you think is the bigger threat, Reeteh, or that person?" I ask.

"Depends who has the control. Does Reeteh work for them or are they Reeteh's puppet? I would suggest that, if we take Reeteh out, this person will replace him," Heather says, tapping the file with her finger. "So the council member is worse," Heather answers. I agree with her.

I lean forward and pull Frank's gun box off the small table and drop it on my lap.

"What's that?" Heather asks.

"Guns." I open the box and take a pistol out.

"Did Frank show you how to use them?"

"No. Luckily, you turned up just as he was showing them to me."

"Luckily?" Heather looks confused.

"I thought you were dead." I raise an eyebrow to give her a hint of what I am implying.

"I see." Heather stares at me for a moment, possibly trying to read my face. "And now?"

"And now I am happier."

"Happier? Not happy?" Heather leans forward and picks up a gun.

"Happiness is on the horizon, and I hope I am heading towards it," I answer. Heather presses the button in the top of her gun and it makes the brief whooshing sound.

"What *is* that noise?" I ask.

"It's the fuel cell depositing energy in the..." Heather pauses. "It's charging up."

"So, as a scientist, do you understand how it all works?" I ask.

"Yes. I built one once." Heather smiles as she pulls a small slide switch on the side of the gun. She aims the gun at opposite wall. "You can set distance with the dial on the back. Each click is..." Heather stops and thinks. "Each click is about two feet. We don't use feet as a measurement."

"So, what is it set for?"

Heather turns the dial on the back to the left until it will go no further.

"That is the minimum distance, two feet. Each click adds two feet to the range of the weapon. She turns the dial to the right - it reminds me of the dial on the top of a digital camera - and then aims the gun at the wall. She pulls the trigger and the gun makes a plopping kind of sound as a blur of air fires out the end of the gun and flies across the room. It dissipates just before it reaches the opposite wall.

"You want to go and shoot something?" Heather asks.

"I'd love to," I reply.

We head down to the courtyard, where Heather sets up a target made from a sheet of paper. She draws a cross in the centre and then a series of circles starting from the smallest at the centre with larger circles around it. We have a gun each.

"Ready?" she asks.

"Yes," I reply. Heather takes my gun from me and holds it up. She turns the dial to the left setting it at the minimum distance.

"Get used to firing this at minimum distance and work your way back."

"Show me," I say. Heather hands my gun back to me and raises hers. She stands so the gun is a couple of feet away from the target and pulls the trigger. The air bullet hits the paper and makes a small hole in the centre of the cross. Heather steps back and adjusts the dial on the gun. She aims it at the paper and fires another air bullet into the paper, almost exactly into the first hole she made.

"You see?" she asks. I nod my head.

"How far back can you go?"

"These have a range of a hundred feet."

"Could you hit the target from back there?" I ask, pointing at the door leading out to the street.

"You want me to show off?" Heather spins the gun on her finger and blows in the end of the barrel. She then stands with her hands on her hips, smiling.

"Yes, I do," I reply.

Heather walks over to the door. She sets the dial on the gun and then looks at me.

"Get out of the way then," she commands. I step aside and watch as she aims the gun at the paper, from a distance of about sixty feet. She pulls the trigger and the air bullet fires from the gun, almost silently, apart from the brief popping sound. The paper makes a cracking sound as the air hits it. I step closer and see Heather's third shot has hit close to the first two. Heather joins me at the paper.

"Your turn," she says, stepping aside. I check my gun is set to minimum and then aim it at the paper. I pull the trigger and fire an air bullet, which hits the paper near the centre. Heather watches intently but says nothing. I step back and adjust the dial on my gun. At four feet I hit the target near the first shot. I work my way back until I am about fifty feet away. I adjust the dial and aim at the target. Heather comes and stands beside me.

"If you can hit the paper at this distance it would be a kill shot on a person, if the paper was his head," Heather says. I pull the trigger and listen for the paper to crack. It does but from this distance I cannot see where I hit. We both approach the paper and I see the hole I made in the cross. I am pleased to see it close to the centre.

"You're a natural," Heather says, patting me on the back.

"Don't touch my back," I say, mimicking her from that moment in my kitchen. I smile and take her hand. "Just kidding." I look at the holes in the paper. "That was pure luck," I say.

We keep shooting at the target for an hour, by which time I feel comfortable using the gun.

"They're quite nifty weapons," I say to Heather as we take a break.

"Nifty?"

"Neat; handy."

"The advantage of these guns is that there is no ricochet and no stray bullets. You can shoot them into a crowd and only hit the person you intended to hit."

"Shoot into a crowd?" I question. "You'd do that?"

"No, I was just using it as an example," Heather defends.

We retire to the living area upstairs and make some tea. Afterwards, we head to the bedroom to sleep, which I am a little disappointed to find has two single beds.

The following morning, I am awoken by Heather, who has her hand over my mouth and has placed a pistol on my chest. She is fully dressed.

"There is someone in the courtyard," she whispers. She takes her hand off my mouth.

"Who?" I ask quietly.

"Two men."

"How do you know?"

"Frank installed cameras. There is a monitor in the study." The sound of a door being shaken takes our attention and I realise the two men are trying to come up stairs.

"I locked the door last night," Heather says.

I sit up and take the pistol off my chest. Heather heads over to the door and peers through to the hallway, holding her gun against the door. I quietly get dressed and then arm my gun. I set the dial to a distance of ten feet and join Heather at the door.

"What do we do?" I whisper.

"They have guns," Heather replies.

"Should we hide and wait until they leave?" I suggest. Heather looks at me.

"There is nowhere to hide. Just because they can't see us doesn't mean they can't find us. Peripheran technology makes finding people very easy."

"So they know we're up here?"

"I expect so."

"Would we go to prison if we just went down there and shot them?"

"What if they are friends of Frank?"

"Then they are stupid. Why break into a place where we are hiding, armed?"

The sound of the door being forced open takes our attention; then footsteps on the stairs. Frank's friends wouldn't break in.

I look around the room and consider our options. We are going to need to defend this room.

"Get away from the door," I command Heather.

"What are you doing?" she asks. I pull her away from the door.

"Just stay out of their way."

I look at the window, which doesn't have curtains.

"Do you not have curtains on Periphera?" I ask. Heather presses a button on the wall and the glass in the window turns black, darkening the room. I go back to the door and open it wide. The footsteps are heading across the lower landing. Our room is on the floor above, so they have another set of stairs to climb before they reach us.

"If we lie down we will have the element of surprise," I say quietly as I lie on the floor and aim my gun along the hallway, waiting. Heather comes back to the doorway and lies down on the floor next to me.

"We have two guns. We might as well use them both," she whispers.

"What distance is yours set at?" I ask. Heather looks at her gun.

"Thirty feet."

"Thirty?" I turn the dial on my gun to the right until it clicks to thirty feet.

The footsteps head up the second staircase, which is just beyond the door at the end of the hallway. The door handle turns and then stops.

If they have something like thermal imaging cameras, they will see we are lying on the floor. If they have sensitive microphones, they may have heard us talk about the guns. If they have some other, Peripheran technology they might be watching us on small screens, laughing.

The door opens and the first of the two men steps into the hallway. The light from the staircase behind him turns him into a silhouette. His gun is aimed at the floor, so he is obviously not expecting to see us in the hallway. I hope the darkness of our room will make him think the door is closed.

The second man steps into the hallway. He waves his hand and the light in the hallway comes on, illuminating both intruders. Heather fires her gun first, hitting the first man in the chest. I pull my trigger and shoot the second man in the chest before he can raise his gun. They both fall to the floor. I jump up to approach them, but Heather stops me.

"He is still holding his gun," Heather says, pointing at the second man. I raise my gun and shoot at the man's hand, hitting his gun.

Heather runs over to the first man and kicks his gun away. I do the same to the second man's gun.

"This one is dead," Heather says. I turn and look at the man she shot. His eyes are staring into nowhere and the hole in his chest is bleeding. It looks as though Heather shot him through the heart. I turn to the man I shot and see he is struggling to breathe. Blood is coming out of his mouth.

"Should we interrogate him?" I ask Heather.

"You shot him through the lung. He can hardly breathe. I don't think we'll get him to talk."

"What do we do with him?" The idea of killing a man who is no longer a threat seems wrong. On the other hand, leaving him to die slowly is also wrong. I have always considered myself to be a man of high morals, despite my dislike of humanity. However, this is one of those areas where doing nothing might be just as bad as killing him.

Heather takes a small device out of her pocket and holds it to her ear.

"Cell phone?" I ask. Heather nods.

"Don't you have the technology to implant those in your head?"

"Just because we can, doesn't mean we should. We also have the technology to make flying cars. Doesn't mean we should let the general public have them."

"Frank. Look at this," Heather says. She then aims the device at the dying man and then the dead man. After a few seconds she puts the device back to her ear. I don't know what Frank is saying to her but I hope he is telling her what to do. I would rather kill the man because someone in authority told me to, rather than make my own judgment and be wrong.

Heather puts the phone back in her pocket and aims her gun at the man's head. She adjusts the dial on the gun and pauses.

"I can't do it," she says.

"What did Frank say?" I ask.

"He recognised them," Heather says. "They are Reeteh's hitmen."

The hitman stops breathing and his mouth fills with blood. I assume he has died.

"Not anymore," I say. Heather presses the button on the top of her gun to switch it off, so I do the same to mine. We leave the men on the landing and head downstairs to the kitchen, where Heather fills two glasses with water.

"Have a drink," she says, picking up a glass. My thoughts turn to the two dead bodies we left on the landing above. "Are you hungry?"

"Not really. I was never a breakfast eater."

Heather rummages through the cupboards for food.

"We need to leave," she says. "Somehow, Reeteh knows we are here, so we need to get out before he sends someone else."

"Two questions," I say; my mind full of questions. Two seem appropriate to mention. "How did he find us and why does he now want us dead?"

"He wants *you* dead. He couldn't have known I was here," Heather disputes.

"Unless Frank told him," I suggest.

"Frank is not dirty," Heather states.

"So how did they know we were here?" I ask. Heather looks past my shoulder at the table where she had eaten last night. Sitting on the table is the bracelet she wore, which I was given. I turn and see the bracelet.

"You think that has a tracking device?" I say.

"It would make sense," Heather replies as she reaches forward and picks up the bracelet.

"But *you* were wearing that. That means they tracked you as you came here after faking your death."

"Yes, but they thought they were tracking you," Heather says. She examines the bracelet.

"Not if those investigators saw you wearing it at the baltron phase and reported that back to Reeteh. Once it started to move they knew you were still alive."

"Either way, it led them here," Heather says.

"The man who gave it to me, Emilio, do you think he is Reeteh's man?"

"Could be. He is a member of the council," Heather agrees.

"Should we tell Frank?"

"He saw the hitmen. He will work out how they found this place. We should stick to what he asked us to do. Follow the evidence to Reeteh."

"So, do you have any idea where we should start? That file of paperwork seemed to be heading nowhere."

"Frank gave one lead for us to follow," Heather says. She puts some biscuit-like food into a bag and slings it over her shoulder. "I'll get the file."

"Theo's human wife?" I ask, following Heather into the living room, where the file is sitting on the table. Heather picks it up and turns to me.

"Yes. She lived in Devon. Frank wanted us to go back and find the house." Heather stares at me for a moment and I wonder what she is thinking.

"You okay?" I ask.

"I'm fine. We need to leave."

I head back into the kitchen, with Heather following. A thought enters my head, so turn to her.

"If all the orbs started in the baltron phase just outside Boston, how come they managed to wipe out everyone on Earth in an hour and yet when we saw them they were travelling slowly? Surely they would need to travel pretty fast to cover the entire planet in an hour."

"A core number of large orbs were released from the baltron phase. They moved very fast and would have ascended high into the air. Then they replicated to form more orbs. Those replicated orbs dropped to Earth and floated around, being pulled towards the quantum signatures of human brains."

"They were programmed to seek the signatures of human brains?" I question.

"Yes."

I pick up the bracelet and put it in my pocket.

"What are you doing with that?" Heather asks.

"I thought I would send it on a journey, to lead Emilio away from us."

"We don't know for definite that Emilio is the informant," Heather corrects me.

"No, but I am willing to put money on it," I say.

"So what do you propose to do with the bracelet?"

"I thought we could put it on a ship heading away from here. Do you have ships on Periphera?"

Heather smiles.

"Yes we do. If we head down to the harbour we can put it on a ship heading south."

"Sounds perfect. Is south here the same as south on Earth?"

"Yes, but we don't call it south. We also don't use northern and southern hemispheres on our maps. We assume the Earth to rotate top to bottom so your north and south poles are actually on the left and right-hand sides of our maps."

"Wow, why?"

"Periphera's rotation like a round wheel makes sense visually."

"I suppose so. I'd like to see what those maps look like one day. So what do we do about the bodies upstairs?" I ask.

"Frank will sort those out."

I am surprised at Heather's ability to shoot and kill a man and yet remain unperturbed by the event. Even with the negative feelings my depression has given me I still feel shocked to have gone through that episode. I have to keep reminding myself that those two men were hitmen, sent to kill us. We killed them in self-defence. Also, they worked for the man who killed everyone on Earth.

Chapter Twenty-One
Breathing Space

With the bracelet safely stowed on a water-going vessel (which looked more like a spaceship than a boat) Heather and I head to Tammat Aerodrome – they don't call them airports. Sitting on the aircraft, waiting to take off I lean back and close my eyes. Heather got the window seat.

"How are you coping?" she asks.

"Coping? I'm fine, why?" I ask, keeping my eyes closed.

"Just checking you're okay."

"You think I'm going to flip out?" I question, my eyes now open. I look at Heather.

"Flip out?" Heather frowns.

"Go mad and do something stupid."

"No, I don't think that at all. I just want to make sure you're okay."

"I'm fine. How are *you* coping?" I ask. Heather stares at me. She doesn't like my attitude, so I smile to disarm her. It doesn't work.

"Do you know where in Devon the house is?" I ask. Heather pulls the small plastic cell phone type object out of her pocket and presses a button on it. She closes her eyes for a moment as she watches the projected information in her head. I see her eyes move under her eyelids as she looks at the information. Then she opens her eyes.

"Near a town called Tavistock," she states.

"How long before we get to England, I mean Mistep-Hoak?" I ask.

"Couple of hours," Heather replies. I look down the centre aisle at the other passengers on the aircraft. There seems to be around a hundred seats, in four rows, with an aisle down the centre. The man opposite me sees me looking and smiles.

"Huruh," I say to him.

"Huruh," he replies with a smile.

"I'm going home," I say to him. He takes a moment to contemplate his response and, at first, I wonder why. Then I realise I am speaking English to him. Why would a Peripheran speak English to another Peripheran unnecessarily?

"Mistep-Hoak?" the man asks.

"Yes, I'm from Mistep-Hoak," I reply. I notice his accent is similar to Scandinavian. I think about Heather's accent and recall that she sounds English. What is the natural Peripheran accent? "And you?"

"I'm visiting," the man divulges. "Awful what happened to Earth," he adds. I wonder whether he has realised I am human or whether he just feels the need to mention it.

"Yes," I reply. I am not sure what else to say. Should I let him know I am human? I feel Heather's hand on my knee, so I turn and look at her. She smiles at the man and then me.

"Am I acting out of place?" I ask her quietly.

"No, you're doing fine. He probably wonders why you're speaking to him in English but he seems happy to talk."

"Every Peripheran you have spoken to, you've used English," I recall.

"That's because you have been with me and they know who you are. It would be rude to speak in Peripheran with you around."

"I'd like to learn Peripheran one day," I say to my new best friend.

"If you would like, I will teach you," Heather proposes.

"I would like that very much," I reply. I cannot stop myself from smiling.

"Would you like to have a look at the file?" Heather asks. I look down at the file and the small device she is holding. The writing on the file is Peripheran.

"Maybe later." I lean back and look up at the ceiling. The shape of the cabin is similar to a human airliner. "Do you think it's a bit weird that Frank has asked us to get involved in his investigation?" I ask. Why would a specially trained investigator ask two untrained civilians to help him with a case? He must have colleagues who are trained to help."

"I suppose it's unusual," Heather admits. "What are you thinking?"

"I'm not sure. Frank has placed a lot of trust in us and I'm not sure why."

"Do you think he's up to something?" Heather looks concerned. The aircraft lifts straight up into the air and then accelerates forwards.

"It just seems odd to me. He could drop us both at the Asten building and leave me with the other humans whilst he tracks down Reeteh. You're a scientist, so I'm not sure why he thinks you should be helping with the investigation."

"Maybe he doesn't trust anyone else. Afterall, he is hunting a member of the council."

"That's true," I agree. "But, would you take on two untrained people to help you finish building a quantum device?" I look across Heather at the view through the window of Tammat, as we fly over the city.

"Not to belittle what he does, but a quantum device cannot be assembled by novices," Heather answers. "All he has asked us to do is read the file and head back to Mistep-Hoak to help him find Tina." Heather says, diplomatically.

We are soon above the clouds and I wonder how fast we are flying.

"Hungry?" Heather asks, pulling a biscuit out of her bag.

"No, thanks," I reply. The air steward approaches along the

centre aisle. She is a well-built woman, with an attractive smile. Her uniform is smart and has the obligatory flap across the back of her drainpipe trousers. Boots, which look like motorcyclists' boots, cover the bottom of her trousers, making her look like a sci-fi heroine. I wonder whether she is trained in combat.

I lean back and close my eyes again. Thoughts of Heather in the baltron phase building fill my head and I have to sneak a quick glance at her to convince myself she is really back, alive and well.

Two hours later, we touch down at Verorlanden's aerodrome, which is at the northern end of what I know as Salisbury Plain. Heather calls Frank and he tells her he is busy and unable to meet with us immediately, so we head to a hotel in the city. We check into the lavish hotel under the names Enne Clu-aydo and Chenny Votkz.

"So, am I Enne or Chenny?" I ask Heather as we head for our room.

"You're Chenny. Enne is a female name," Heather replies.

"And luggage?"

"One of Frank's colleagues is having some of my belongings delivered here, along with some clothing for you."

"So how are we paying for this room? It's a luxury hotel."

"This is a common standard for Peripheran hotels and not as expensive as you might think. I am paying for it," Heather explains.

"Do you miss your home," I ask as we reach the room. Heather opens the door with a press of her hand against the pad.

"Yes, I do, especially since my memories returned. When this is over, I will take you there and introduce you to the people of my village." Heather smiles and I assume she is recalling fun times.

We enter the room and Heather closes the door.

"Won't the council be able to trace your handprint on that door sensor?" I ask. We head into a living area, which has a sofa and coffee table, complete with purple poisonous-to-humans fruit in a bowl. Heather picks up the bowl and turns to me.

"The scan they did of my hand is kept only for their door security. Hotels do not pass hand prints to outside agencies," she explains.

"What if the council has told all the hotels to give them all handprints so they can find us?" I query.

"The council wouldn't need to do that. Emilio might, but he would need the backing of the council to do so and they would want to know why he needs it." Heather takes a bite of one of the purple fruit and then takes the bowl into the kitchen area. I follow her into the small room, which has a fold-down worktop and cooker. One entire wall is cupboards.

"If I kissed you on the lips now, would I die?" I ask. Heather turns and looks at me.

"Yes, but only because I would throttle you." She smiles and then takes another bite of the fruit.

"Seriously. How dangerous is that fruit to me?"

"If you kissed me you would be unconscious in seconds. You probably wouldn't die but you would need immediate medical attention to stop you slipping into a coma. If you ate a small piece of the fruit you would be dead within ten minutes."

"Why does it exist?" I ask. As soon as I have raised the question I realise it is a stupid one.

"Simple evolution. It is poisonous to you because of the way it affects the brain. For a Peripheran, that effect stimulates the armaranos lobe. For you, it would overload your brain and put you in a terminal coma."

"Could I have an armaranos lobe transplanted into my back?" I ask.

"I don't think it has been tried. Even with our technology, I

213

think the chances of it working would be remote. And since there are now only thirty-four humans left, I don't think anyone will take that chance. You're an endangered species."

"You need to look after me then, treat me well." I smile at Heather and she smiles back. She has a lovely, friendly smile. I don't think I have ever met someone who smiles as much as her. She takes a bite of the fendura fruit and then waves the half-eaten poison in the air in front of me – just for fun.

"Have I not been doing so?" Heather finishes the last of the fruit and then leaves the kitchen, being careful not to touch me as she passes.

"Yes, you've been doing a splendid job." I say it so it sounds like sarcasm, despite it actually being true. Heather has been the most amazing companion and I trust my life to her. I sit on the sofa as Heather washes her face in the bathroom. She comes to the doorway, her face still wet.

"I don't have any berrinia, so I'll try not to breathe on you," she says. "Don't eat from my cutlery or share any food I have eaten," she adds.

"Diai," I agree. I kick my shoes off and lie out on the sofa. I look at my watch and see that it is almost ten o'clock in the evening. I do a quick time check in my head. It was two in the afternoon when we left Tammat. We got to Mistep-Hoak at about four o'clock, but Mistep-Hoak, like Britain, is five hours ahead of Tammat, so we landed at nine in the evening. I don't feel tired but I am aware that staying up late will make me tired for tomorrow.

"Do you think we should move one of the beds into the same room as the other so we are together?" I suggest. "For safety."

Heather smiles at me. "Really?" she questions. She walks into one of the bedrooms, leaving the door open. "I have a better idea," she shouts.

"What's that?" I shout back. Heather appears at the door.

"They are double beds. We could just share one," she announces. Before I can comment she adds, "as long as you keep to your side and don't get any ideas."

"Diai," I agree.

We both prepare to sleep and then meet in bed. Peripheran hotels supply disposable pyjamas, which seem to be made from cotton, but according to Heather are biodegradable and can be thrown away. We are both wearing identical dark blue pyjamas. I climb into the bed and lie on my back next to Heather.

"What is it like to want to die?" Heather asks, unexpectedly. My instinct is to tell her what I tell Lucy and my doctor. The kind of lies which would make them feel at ease. However, Heather is different. I don't feel as though being judged by her is a bad thing, maybe because I want her to know the real me, the Nathan Glover who has issues. Deep down, I feel as though the more she knows about me, the more she will help. Lucy may be my sister but she still only gets to see the Nathan Glover I want her to see. Sometimes it is hard to hide the real, depressed Nathan, which is why she knows me better than anyone else. I feel comfortable letting Heather see the whole package - Nathan Glover the third in his entirety.

"People have a natural tendency towards self-preservation," I start. "However, when I am at my worst, when I am really depressed, the idea of ending my life seems like a sensible option."

"Can you not just make some changes in your life to stop yourself feeling so sad?" Heather suggests. I keep staring at the ceiling because I feel self-conscious about looking at her whilst discussing this subject.

"It's not about being sad. It's a low feeling, which can come about for no apparent reason. Something as simple as seeing a certain type of car, or smelling a certain smell can bring it on, briefly. However, the low mood is always there, under the surface of my mind, waiting to bring me down. Does that make any sense?" I turn and look at Heather. She looks a little confused.

"I understand what you are saying but I don't really have anything to reference it within my own life, so I don't really get it. I have never felt low without knowing what is causing the low feeling. Then I just do something to take my mind off the cause, or make some changes to remove it from my life. Then I feel better."

"After my wife and son died, I felt dead myself. I wanted nothing out of life. I didn't even want to die. I just wanted nothing. I could have curled up into a ball and just stayed there until I died of starvation. Lucy kept me going and eventually I was able to return to some sort of normality. However, every so often I get these low feelings which take me back to that state of being, well, partially. I have come to terms with the loss of my wife and son but it doesn't stop the feelings resurfacing now and then."

"Smell therapy might help you. I have heard that certain smells can be used in a positive way to help lift your mood."

"Yes, I have heard about that."

"So how do you feel right now?" Heather asks.

"Right now, this very minute, I feel fine. I am happy and the situation we are in is exciting. It's something I have never experienced before, so my mind is enjoying being wrapped up in it."

"So, maybe you should have been a secret agent," Heather suggests.

"I have wondered whether people prone to depression are like it because their minds need that excitement. If you think about it, humanity always had to hunt and gather and fight off predators. The modern world doesn't stimulate the mind in that way."

"I see what you mean. So depressed people just need to be

dropped into a warzone and left to fight their way out?" Heather suggests.

"Well, I wouldn't go that far."

"So how would you explain Peripherans? We haven't hunted and gathered or fought off predators for a lot longer than humans and we have fewer wars, more peace and the kind of dull existence which would send you completely insane. And yet, we have few cases of depression."

"There must be something you do to your children which we don't, which makes it easier for them to exist in your world." I look at Heather.

"We do, we raise them in a community without parents." Heather presses her finger on my nose and her eyes open wide as she smiles to emphasize her point.

"Don't you ever wonder what happened to your children?" I ask.

"No. Why would I? I created them and they are now growing up in a community where they will learn everything they need, with loving companions."

"But, I would want to be one of those loving companions to children I created."

"But, it's not about what you want. It's about what *they* need."

"So you think it's selfish to want to be a parent?" I assume.

"Not necessarily, but your need to know your children is to satisfy yourself and not your children. I grew up in this manner and I don't feel a need to know who created me. I was never lonely and never unloved."

"So what do you think of Theo?"

"I think he was a man who spent too much time on Earth."

"Do you feel a need to get to know who he was now that you know what he was doing?"

"No. He wanted to be my father..."

"He *was* your father," I interrupt.

"He helped create me. That's all. He passed on genetic information - nothing else. I am who I am because of the people who raised me."

"So you think nurture is more significant than nature?" I question.

"Yes, I do."

"Suppose he had a hereditary disease. Without him in your life you wouldn't know you are prone to getting it."

"You underestimate our medical technology. We genetically screen all our babies, so we know which diseases may be passed on from their biological parents."

"Do all Peripherans think they are better than humans?" I ask. I feel a little bad raising a question like that to a Peripheran whom I admire.

"I think that is true, but it's not unfounded. We have learnt from your mistakes."

"It's a bit unfair because you had the ability to hide from us and watch us. So you could learn from us but we could never learn from you."

"One of your pupils is larger than the other," Heather says, changing the subject. I wonder whether she said it to steer me away from an awkward subject or whether she just noticed my differing pupils and wanted to comment.

"Really?" I reply. "You just going to throw that into the conversation?"

Heather pulls the covers over her head and hides underneath. I hear her giggle and I am reminded of the cheerleader I met in the woods. The question now is, do I jump on the lump in the middle of the bed or do I go under the covers and join her?

Chapter Twenty-Two
Killing Time

After several hours of talking and a brief period of playing, Heather and I finally fall asleep. We did everything a new couple would do, except kiss and make love. Heather has let me get very close to her but she still has that human-peripheran line which she will not cross. I wonder whether she agonises internally with her feelings. Does she love me or am I just a good friend? I have never been very good at telling whether a woman fancies me, so I really do not know how to proceed. I'll just have to let her decide where she wants our friendship to go.

I awake to the sound of a buzzer. Heather leaps out of the bed and rushes towards a small screen on the opposite wall. She presses her hand against the wall, under the screen, which is about a foot square. Frank's face appears.

"Huruh," Franks says. Heather gives him a salute, which makes me smile. I didn't realise Peripherans used salutes.

"Any news?" I ask the face on the wall as I sit up in the bed.

"I thought I might join you at Theo's property today."

"Good," I say.

"Have you made any discoveries?" Heather asks.

"I have a few lines of enquiry open. I want to learn more about Theo's secret life, so I thought I would join you at his house," Frank explains.

"That sounds like a good idea," I agree.

"He was a friend of mine," Frank states, "but I had no idea he married a human woman or that he was following Heather. I believe learning more about Theo will lead us to Reeteh."

"So are you going to pick us up or do you want us to meet you there?" I ask.

"I have some things to sort out first, so meet me there this evening. About six."

"See you then," Heather states. She presses her hand on the screen and Frank disappears. Heather turns to me.

"I want you to make a promise to me," she demands.

"Diai."

"Don't try to emphasize or highlight anything at Theo's home which you feel might convince me that a Peripheran having a relationship with a human is right." She waits for my response.

"I will make that promise, but I want you to make one as well," I state. Heather nods her head. "If you see anything that makes *you* doubt those rules you have been programmed with, you must look at it objectively. Don't dismiss what Theo did as wrong if, in your heart, you envy him." Heather frowns.

"Envy him?"

"You might," I suggest.

"I promise to be objective," Heather says.

We get dressed, have some breakfast and then head down to the hotel's lobby. Heather is wearing a long black skirt with Victorian-style boots and a black military marching-band kind of jacket. She looks elegant and sophisticated. I do like Peripheran clothes. Even the men dress well - they remind me of Victorian gentlemen in their waistcoats and long jackets. I am getting used to the trousers having a flap on the back and I can see how long jackets are desired, because they too cover the backside.

In the lift, on the way down, we discuss transport and I suggest we go to Earth and pick up my Delorean from Lucy's home. Then we can drive to Theo's secret human house. Heather agrees.

We leave the hotel and catch a taxi - I assume it is a taxi, although we are not charged for the journey - to the field where we first materialised after the orbs hit. We thank the driver and I follow Heather across the field. She stops halfway and turns to me.

"Ready?" Heather asks.

"Yes."

Heather steps behind me, wraps her arms around my waist and transports us to Earth. We find ourselves standing in the middle of the street, a few hundred feet from Lucy's home. It is raining and there are bodies lying in the road. The last time we were here was during the party. Some of these bodies might be guests. I look ahead at Lucy's home and it occurs to me Jeremy is in there, dead.

"I need to see Jeremy," I say to Heather.

"Why?"

"Lucy needs to know he is dead but she can't come here and see this. I can."

"You sure?" Heather checks. I turn and look at her.

"Absolutely."

"Diai," she replies. Passing my Delorean, we head up to Lucy's front door and try the handle. It is locked, so I pick up a ceramic plant pot, in which a bonsai tree is growing, and throw it through the living room window.

"Sorry, Luce," I say to myself. I climb in through the window. Scattered around the living room floor are bodies of some of the guests. I realise how lucky I am to have survived the genocide and have the opportunity to return here. I feel Heather's hand on my shoulder as she climbs through the window. I help her down.

"I was going to open the door for you," I say.

"I thought you might get distracted," Heather replies, looking at the bodies. "You still alright?"

"I'm fine. You saved me. You took me to Periphera."

"May I remind you that you saved me from this by taking me away from North Silestia House," Heather replies. She pushes me towards the door and we wander through to the kitchen.

"Can you remember where Jeremy was when it happened?" Heather asks.

"I don't know. We were in the garden with Lucy and Frank. Frank had that woman with him. I don't remember seeing Jeremy."

We search the kitchen, dining room, garden and utility rooms but Jeremy is nowhere to be found. So we head up stairs.

"He might be on the toilet," I say as we reach the landing.

"You want to try that first?" Heather asks.

"Might as well."

We head to the master bathroom and toilet but Jeremy is not there, so we check each bedroom. In the third, and largest, spare room we find Jeremy lying on the bed, dead. His trousers are on the floor and he is still half dressed.

"Was he getting changed?" Heather speculates. Her speculation is answered when we discover the body of a woman on the floor at the other side of the bed. She is also half dressed.

"He was cheating on Lucy at her own party," I say as I look at the dead woman.

"It certainly looks that way," Heather agrees. "Are you going to tell Lucy?"

"I don't know." I turn and look at Heather. "What would you do?"

"I would make my own decision and not ask a visiting alien," she says, with a smile.

"Diplomatic. On the one hand, Lucy is devastated at losing him, but on the other, knowing what he was doing might allow her to move on and start a new life," I contemplate.

"That makes sense. It's a decision you must think through carefully. If you tell Lucy, you must be certain it is the right thing to do."

I look at Jeremy and the urge to punch his dead face wells inside me.

"Would you step outside for a moment," I instruct Heather. She looks at me with a curious frown and then edges towards the door.

"Diai," she says as she leaves the room.

I head around to the side of the bed where Jeremy is lying and I touch his face. His skin is cold. Then I punch his cheek as hard as I can. My knuckles hurt but his head hardly moves. I punch him again and a feeling of satisfaction replaces the urge to beat the dead man.

"Feel better now?" Heather asks. I turn and see her standing in the doorway.

"I didn't want you to see that," I say, trying to look apologetic.

"One thing you need to understand about Peripherans," Heather says as she steps towards me. "We are very understanding. You want to punch a dead man? I understand. We don't hold back and we don't judge people harshly for expressing themselves - as long as there is a good reason. Hit him again if it makes you feel better."

"I think I'm satisfied now," I reply. Heather takes my hand and escorts me out of the bedroom. We head downstairs and leave the house through the front door. I rummage through my pockets for my keys and unlock my Delorean.

As I drive us to my home, Heather and I discuss my house and belongings. Whatever happens to Earth, it is *my* home and I intend to keep it, even if it becomes a second home.

Heather helps me tidy and we spend an hour clearing out the food from my fridge and freezer. Then we head into my neighbours' homes and do the same. We release some rabbits from a hutch in one garden and feed some cats, who are hanging around an empty bowl. The bodies of my neighbours are decaying rapidly, so we drag them all into the garden of my next door neighbour, who was in the process of building a large pond. We push each body into the hole dug for the pond and cover them over with some of the mud. My neighbour's dog returns and sits with us as we bury its master.

"You want a dog?" I ask Heather as we pat down the last of the mud. She looks at the dog and then me.

"Do you?" she asks in return.

"No."

"As tough as it might seem," Heather says, "it's survival of the fittest for all the domesticated pets on Earth now. The dog will have to learn to adapt and find its own food."

"I wonder what the Peripheran authorities will do to clear up my home planet," I say.

"My assumption is that they will concentrate on the homes of the survivors. They will clear the bodies away and bury their relatives. The rest of the world will decay naturally and cities will be taken over by nature."

"I wouldn't mind if Peripherans decided to move to Earth and recolonize the planet. At least it would be alive again."

"I understand. I wonder whether the other humans would agree with that," Heather considers.

"Well, if you think about it, somewhere like London was filled with strangers. So what does it matter if Peripheran strangers moved in and made it home?"

"That's a healthy way of looking at it," Heather agrees.

"I feel a bit guilty admitting this but I really don't feel all that bad that the human race has been wiped out. Meeting an alien race was just what I needed to bring me from the brink of self-destruction and I feel alive. Your race is new to me and I actually feel excited. That is so self-centred, I know."

"I do understand," Heather explains. "I don't know how I

would feel. I love being a Peripheran and I would be devastated if the rest of my race was killed. But I can see why you feel the way you do and I don't think you are self-centred. Your survival is now key to the survival of the human race, so you can afford to be a little self-centred." Heather smiles. "Of course, for your race to survive, you need to impregnate one of the other survivors - and keep doing so until you can no longer bear children."

"Yeah, I don't think that's going to happen."

"Really?"

"I can't continue with this conversation without breaking the promise I made to you this morning," I say. I drop the spade on the floor and wipe my hands on my trousers. I look at Heather and she is staring at me, deep in thought. "I would very much like to know what you are thinking," I say to her. Heather stares at me for a few more seconds and then drops her spade on the ground.

"I like you a lot," she states. "I like you more than any Peripheran man," she adds. I feel my heart race as I anticipate what she might say next. "If you were Peripheran, I would be your girlfriend. I have no doubt there," she admits. "I have strong feelings for you."

"But I'm not Peripheran."

"No, you're not, and that is a huge barrier."

"Well, I made a promise to you not to try and convince you that human-Peripheran relationships are okay, so I have nothing more to say on the matter. I am just going to wait patiently until you make a decision yourself."

"What if I am never ready to accept your love?" Heather asks.

"Then I will never be happy."

"What if one of the other humans is just your type?" Heather suggests.

"Unlikely. I've met a lot of human women and, apart from

my wife, I didn't meet one I cared for as much as I care about you. What are the chances that, of the last few surviving women, one of them just happens to be my perfect match?"

"It's possible. Maybe you should meet them all before..." Heather stops mid-sentence.

"Before what?"

"You should meet them all," she replies.

"Diai." I don't push her for an answer. "You could do with a change of clothes," I say, looking at the mud on Heather's skirt.

"We just buried a woman who was my size. Would you object to me taking some of her clothes?" Heather asks.

"I wouldn't and I'm sure she's not going to. That was Mandy. She lived in the house the other side of this one."

"I'll go and see what I can find."

"I'll see what tinned food I can cook up," I reply.

We separate and I head back into my home. While I wait for Heather, I cook some rice and mix in some curry sauce from a jar. There is no meat or veg to add, so I throw in some tinned mixed beans and sweet corn. I am glad I kept the camping gas cooker. It is proving its worth.

Heather returns from her clothes hunt, dressed in skin-tight dark green jeans and her own military band style jacket. She has a t-shirt tucked in the back of her jeans, so it hangs down over her backside. I smile when I see it.

"Even under these circumstances, you still have to hide your arse," I say to her as she does a twirl for me.

"My arse is not for public viewing," Heather replies. She ties her hair back into a pony tail, using a hairband.

"If I asked you to lose the t-shirt, would you?" I ask. Heather touches the t-shirt hanging over her backside.

"If I asked you to walk around in your underpants, would you?" she replies.

"Well, since we are the only people on Earth, yes. I would."

226

"I feel comfortable having the t-shirt in place," Heather says.

"Diai." I accept. It is actually quite sexy.

We eat the food I cooked and then climb into the Delorean. We head to Devon and the town of Tavistock, where Frank should be waiting.

It takes a couple of hours to reach Tavistock, which is as quiet and dead as my home town. We drive through the town and out onto a country lane, towards the house Theo bought for his human wife, Tina.

"Don't drive right up to the house," Heather instructs me. I pull the Delorean over by the side of the lane and turn the engine off.

"Do you have a plan?" I ask.

"Not as such. We don't know what we'll find in there, so it's more of an aim. Just see what we find and deal with it as it comes. Diai?"

"Diai," I agree.

We climb out of the car and tuck our Peripheran pistols into our clothing. I put mine in the back of my trousers. Heather tucks hers inside her Jacket. We walk through the trees which surround the house. It is getting dark and we can only just see where we are going. We should have brought a torch with us.

"We're back in woods again," I say to Heather as we walk side-by-side. She turns and smiles at me.

"You want to climb a tree?" she beams.

"I'd love to."

As we reach the edge of the garden I hear the sound of footsteps. Heather hears them too and we both stop in our tracks and look at each other. I crouch down and point at the floor to indicate to Heather that she do the same. We both lie on the floor and wait. Ahead of us a light comes on at the house, illuminating the wooden country dwelling. A man comes out of the house and stands on the rear porch, which has a bench on it. I don't recognise him.

Behind me I hear a footstep amongst the trees, so I slowly turn onto my back to look.

"Give me one good reason why I shouldn't kill you both," the silhouette of a man says. He has a gun pointing at me. Standing next to him, his colleague has a gun pointing at Heather.

Chapter Twenty-Three
Alliance

The two men take our pistols and then escort Heather and me into the house. We make our way to the living room, where a log fire is roaring in the centre of the room, which is divided in half by a bookshelf and a fish tank, so that the fire heats both sides.

Sitting in a leather armchair is Reeteh Steispeck.

"Hello again," Reeteh says, in his slow James-Mason-like voice. "I must say, I am surprised to see you."

"Yeah, we weren't expecting to see you either," I reply.

"Have a seat." He gestures for us to sit on the leather sofa opposite him. He looks at his two goons and back at us. Heather sits on the sofa, so I sit next to her. I look at the two goons, who stay by the door, silently watching us.

"I would be a fool not to have them protecting me," Reeteh says, when he sees me looking at his men.

"I suppose so," I agree. "Do you see us as a threat?"

"You going to play psychological games with me Nathan?" Reeteh asks.

"Psychological games?" I question.

"You convince me you are not a threat and I relieve my men. Then you apprehend me and take me back to Periphera. I like to think ahead. I can play psychological games too, if you like. Where shall I start? When did you last see your sister, Lucy?"

I try not to react when I hear him say Lucy's name. I don't want him to think he has rattled me. I say nothing.

"Hmm, that's interesting," Reeteh says, rubbing his chin. "Are you not going to tell me not to lay a finger on her or threaten to kill me if anything happens to her?"

"This isn't a movie and I am not the hero," I reply. "My mind doesn't work like other humans, so you might not get the rise you are looking for from me."

"Actually, I have been doing some research and I can see you are an interesting individual. I like the fact you are not like other humans. Tell me, why did you not take in your neighbour's dog?" Reeteh leans back in his chair and watches my reaction. He looks at Heather as well.

"Psychological games?" I ask. "You trying to get that rise in another way? So you have been following us. What do you want a paper hat?"

"A paper hat? What does that mean?"

"It means I think you are trying to be clever. To show how little I think of your cleverness, I would award you a simple paper hat. No gold medal."

"A paper hat. Interesting." Reeteh looks at Heather. "You are very quiet. Do you have nothing to say?" he asks her.

"I am content to just listen," Heather replies.

"Well, I have something for you to listen to," Reeteh says, leaning forwards. "We are on the same side."

"The same side of what?" I ask.

"We seek the same man," Reeteh adds. "You came here looking for Theo's wife, Tina. She is dead. She died with humanity. I came here looking for clues."

"Clues to what?" I ask. Heather is a great thinker, so I am hoping that by me doing all the talking she will have a chance to think of something to get us out of this situation.

"Clues to the man who wants to pin genocide on me."

"You built a machine which killed humanity and you set it off. So *you* are guilty of genocide," I state.

"I built a machine for an anonymous benefactor and he

activated it and killed humanity. If I can determine who that man was I can clear my name," Reeteh explains.

"Who do you think he is?" I ask.

"I thought it was Theo Tandammbian, but my investigation has led me towards someone in Asten."

"That doesn't put us on the same side," I say. "Why did you build the thing for someone who wanted to remain anonymous?"

"They paid me very well."

"Was it worth it?" Heather asks, breaking her silence. Reeteh stares at her for a few seconds.

"No, it was not. I have regrets."

"So what happens now?" I ask.

"Well, I believe the enemy of my enemy is my friend. We are hunting the same man and I believe we could benefit by working together," Reeteh suggests.

"You want us to work with you?" I ask. "I watched you kill Theo, an innocent man."

"That was a mistake. I thought he was the anonymous benefactor and with everything still fresh in my mind I overreacted. I don't do that very often, but I was under duress. Being accused of genocide makes a man edgy." Reeteh looks down at the floor and I assume he is recalling the event.

"Do you know what Theo's connection with this situation really was?" I ask him. Reeteh looks at me and then Heather.

"Yes, I do. Theo was Heather's father and he lived his life like a human - took a human wife: quite a strange thing for a member of the veronmovemen to do."

"Do you think humans and Peripherans should have those kinds of relations?" I ask. The more people I can get to condone it the more it might influence Heather.

"I see nothing wrong, as long as the physical differences are taken into account," Reeteh answers.

"Interesting," I say. Heather slaps my leg discreetly.

"So what happens now?" I ask.

"Well," Reeteh starts. He is interrupted by a knock at the door. We all turn and look as the door opens slowly to reveal another of Reeteh's men.

"We found another," the man says to Reeteh.

"Then bring them in," Reeteh commands. The man steps into the room to reveal two more men, who are escorting Frank. They push Frank into the room.

"Welcome," Reeteh says to Frank.

"I hope I am not interrupting anything," Frank says with a smile. He looks at me and Heather.

"I was hoping you were going to storm this place and break us free," I say to him.

"Yes, that would seem to have been a better plan."

"Please, have a seat," Reeteh says to Frank, gesturing at the space on the sofa next me." Frank sits down. I look at the men by the door and do a mental count. I have seen five men protecting Reeteh. I wonder whether there are more.

"It is so nice of you to join us," Reeteh says to Frank with a smile.

"Reeteh thinks we are on the same side," I say to Frank.

"Really?" Frank questions. He looks at Reeteh. "How do you see that?"

"I am looking for the person in Asten who hired me to build the baltron phase and who subsequently activated it killing humanity and then set me up to take the blame. I believe you too are looking for that person," Reeteh explains.

"Who do you think it is?" Frank asks. He is not giving anything away.

"Well, if I had to guess, I would say Emilio Havente. His name has arisen in a number of places but nothing I can definitively attribute to the baltron phase."

"What kinds of places?" Frank asks.

"Parts for the baltron phase came from a great number of

sources. It is coincidental that Emilio visited many of those sources during the time those parts were being procured. However, I have nothing which proves he was involved."

"How many coincidences are we talking about?" Frank questions. Reeteh seems happy to share his information, which is what I would expect from someone being honest.

"Forty-two," Reeteh replies.

"I cannot apprehend Emilio based on coincidences," Frank states, "even forty-two. Although statistically remote, they may well be just coincidences. We need some actual evidence."

"What we need is a trap," Reeteh suggests. He looks at me, which makes my heart race for a moment. Why is he looking at me?

"Go on," Frank says.

"Emilio tried to kill humanity. Thirty-four humans survived. If we were to use one of those humans as bait, we could lure him into a trap."

So that's why he looked at me. I feel Heather's hand on my knee. I look at her and she shakes her head.

"What kind of trap?" Heather asks Reeteh.

"Theo successfully kidnapped you and held you in North Silestia House, under medication," Reeteh states. "We should do the same to Emilio."

"You can't just kidnap a member of the council," Frank objects. "We would never get that close to him."

"No, but Nathan could, if he pretended to have information about my whereabouts."

"I think you underestimate Emilio's intelligence," Frank disagrees. "He will see through the plan instantly and we'll all be killed."

"You are overlooking one aspect which we have in our favour," Reeteh states. He looks at Heather and I wonder what she has that is so important to Emilio. "Since the event, Nathan has spent all his time with Heather. As far as Emilio is concerned, they are best friends and inseparable. However, if Heather was to publicly assault Nathan and force him into Asten as a refugee, Nathan could convince the council that Heather is working for me. It's not unreasonable. She did work for me, once." Heather looks away from Reeteh and I assume she is regretting their association.

"Then what?" Frank questions.

"Then Nathan invites Emilio to visit North Silestia, where he believes Heather is once again hiding. My men will be waiting for him. We subdue Emilio and hold him until we are able to extract the facts of his involvement."

"And if he had no involvement?" Frank queries.

"We let him go."

Frank stands up and paces the room.

"It's too flimsy to work," he states.

"Then come up with a better plan," Reeteh suggests.

"I need to keep investigating, chasing the evidence. He must have made a mistake," Frank says. He looks irritated.

"Frank, you will be chasing evidence for the rest of your life," Reeteh says. "A man like Emilio doesn't make mistakes. We have to force his hand."

"What would Heather need to do?" I ask.

"Something simple," Reeteh answers. "She could shoot you in public. Not fatally. A shoulder wound perhaps. Then you can go to Asten and ask for help."

"How do we make sure Heather doesn't get caught?"

"She can fend to Earth and my men will pick her up and take her to safety," Reeteh suggests.

"No fucking way," I state. "I don't trust your men with Heather."

"I don't like the plan either," Frank says. He turns and looks at me and Heather.

"What do you suggest, Frank?" I ask.

"I could arrest Reeteh," he replies. He turns to Reeteh "And take you to Asten. Use you as bait," The idea doesn't seem to bother Reeteh.

"That might work," Reeteh agrees. "However I am more use to you as a free man."

"Suppose I visit Emilio and tell him I know Heather is working for Reeteh. Emilio would have to follow up on that," I suggest.

"He might just pass you on to me," Frank debates. "Remember, I am the official investigator. Emilio would not get involved that closely. Someone else would follow up on that lead on his behalf. Besides, the council knows Heather is innocent."

"What if I offer to take him straight to Reeteh? Not to North Silestia House. Here maybe." I look at Reeteh. "Your men could stake out the woods and wait for him to enter the house."

"Yes, they could. This house is built on land which Theo also owns on Periphera. If you fend from this room you will find yourself in another living room owned by Theo. We would need to have my men there as well because Emilio will surely run at the first sign of trouble."

"What if Emilio brings his own men?" Heather asks.

"I'll bring him straight here myself. He won't have time to assemble a team," I reply.

"I still think Heather should publicly assault Nathan, just to add credibility to his claim of not trusting anyone," Reeteh states.

"Frank?" I question. Frank looks at me and then stands up.

"It won't work, but maybe it is worth a try. Heather and Nathan should have an argument near Asten. It would be better if Heather hits Nate with something and then fends to Earth. Nate can then ask to be taken to Asten. If you shoot him, he'll have to go to hospital, which delays things too much. Once in Asten, go to the council but do not approach Emilio directly. Approach the council as a whole. If Emilio is the person we are looking for he will volunteer to help. You must bring him straight here. Do not let him leave your side. It will only take him a minute to call for assistance. If you lose him even for one minute, call it off and go to my safe house." Frank stops to think.

"Sounds pretty straight forward," I say. Exciting.

"I have resources here on Earth," Reeteh states. "I will have a helicopter waiting to pick Heather up. I will deliver her to a place of your choice," Reeteh assures us.

"I want to be on that helicopter," Frank states.

"I have no objection to that," Reeteh agrees. "I will be at my own secret home, keeping in touch remotely. My team will be waiting here for Emilio." Reeteh looks at me. "This house has a basement. If things go wrong, head down to the basement and one of my men will fend you to Periphera, where a craft will take you to Heather and Frank."

"I want to be brought here," Heather states.

"Why?" Reeteh questions.

"I want to be here when Nate arrives with Emilio. If anything happens *I* will fend Nate out of here."

"I understand. You do not trust my men with Nate's safety. Diai. I will arrange for the helicopter to bring you here."

"When do you foresee this abduction happening?" Frank asks Reeteh. Reeteh stands up and approaches a desk in the corner of the room. He picks up a small device and turns to Frank.

"The longer we spend planning the fine details the more likely Asten will hear about us. We need to do this soon."

"How soon?" Frank asks.

"I can have my men ready in thirty-six hours. How does that sound with you?"

Frank turns and looks at me and Heather.

"I have nothing to prepare, so the day after tomorrow is fine for me," I say.

"Heather?" Frank asks.

"Diai," Heather replies. Her tone of voice says differently. She sounds solemn and uncertain. I tap her knee and smile.

"Worst case scenario, you fend me out and we walk away," I say to her. She replies with a fake smile. I suspect she has reservations which she is not comfortable airing here. When we are next alone I will ask her what they are.

Chapter Twenty-Four
Down Time

After discussing the details of the plot to abduct Emilio with Frank and Reeteh a further two or three times, Heather and I leave Theo's Earth home and climb into my Delorean, with no particular destination. Heather takes the driver's seat, without checking whether I want to drive.

"You okay?" I ask Heather as she drives my car along the country lane. It is dark but the moonlight makes it easy to see.

"Not particularly," Heather replies. Her driving is a little aggressive and she is driving quite fast. Unless the Peripherans have already sent their teams to Earth, we are unlikely to meet any other traffic. I watch her drive and I am impressed by her skill at handling the vehicle.

There aren't many right-hand drive Deloreans. This one was converted in the 1990s by a rich owner who eventually sold it when he wasn't so rich. I believe he kept his Aston Martin, though. He kept the hundred thousand pound Aston and sold the twenty thousand pound Delorean. I never did understand his logic.

"I am not comfortable with the plan to abduct Emilio," Heather says.

"Which part don't you like?" I ask.

"The part where we try to abduct Emilio," Heather replies. She looks at me and smiles one of those smiles which seems more apologetic than amusing.

"If I can get him to follow me to Earth it will work," I assure her.

"If?" Heather questions. "Emilio is a member of the council. He will not leave Asten, unprotected."

"What if I told him I knew he was dirty? He won't alert the council about that," I suggest.

"No, he'll just kill you."

We drive up onto Dartmoor and Heather finds a place to park, overlooking a valley in which a river is running ferociously through boulders and trees. The water glistens in the moonlight.

"What do you suggest?" I ask. Without answering, Heather gets out of the car, leaving the door up, and the headlights on. She walks around the front of the car and stands on the grass, which leads down to the river. I open my door and jump out to join her.

With her back to me, Heather says, "I don't know what to suggest."

"If you feel strongly about calling it off, I would be happy to do so." I stand behind her and gently touch her hips with both hands. She doesn't pull away, so I wrap my arms around her waist. Our bodies throw a silhouette onto the grass in front of us as we stand in front of the Delorean's headlights.

"Now you know how it feels when someone is about to fend you into an alien world," I say, pressing my face against the back of her head. Her hair smells nice. It reminds me of lavender. I think about Peripheran shampoo and it occurs to me that I haven't seen a Peripheran shop. I wonder whether they look like human shops. It also occurs to me that I need to wash my hair.

"Go on then. Fend away," Heather replies. Is that a euphemism?

"I think I'll leave the angel impression to someone who knows how to do it properly," I reply.

"You about to break your promise?" Heather asks.

"Do you want me to?" I reply. Heather turns around and

looks at me. My arms are still wrapped around her and we are nose-to-nose. To my surprise, Heather kisses me on the lips and then pulls her face away before I can react.

"You teasing me?" I ask, holding on to her tightly.

"I am facing my fear," Heather replies.

"Is it really that ingrained in you to not mix with humans romantically?" I ask. Without answering, Heather leans forward and kisses me again. I realise she is doing it to see how it feels for her and not because she loves me. This time, I react and we kiss for a few seconds. I feel my hairs stand on end and a shiver reverberates through my entire body. I try to keep the kiss going as long as possible and Heather makes no attempt to stop. I keep my eyes open and watch her. She closes her eyes and then opens them again. Then she slowly stops kissing and pulls her face away. For a few seconds, she just stares at me. I cannot think of anything sensible to say and I don't want to say something wrong, so I keep quiet and wait.

"Hello!" Heather says in that same childlike voice she used on the day I met her. Her eyes are wide and she has a massive grin on her face. For a moment I wonder whether she has lost her mind. Then she leans forward and rests her head on my shoulder.

"You okay? Diai?" I ask.

"I think I love you too," she says leaning the side of her head against mine. I hold her tightly and feel a tear welling in my eye. No, scratch that. There is no tear. I am a big strong man and crying with emotion is not what I do. I raise my free arm and wipe my eye, pretending I have dirt in it.

"I love you so much," I reply.

"You are a brave man," Heather says. I'm not sure what evidence she has to support her assumption that I am brave. I make sure there is no tear residue in my eye and place my hand on her back.

"Brave? How did I manage to give that impression?"

"You have weaknesses which took you to the point of wanting to die and yet you channel those negative emotions into bravery. I have known men who would not do what you have done in the last week."

"I'm still not sure what I have done that is brave," I state.

"You watched your own race die, and then you embraced an alien world and trusted your life to strangers - strangers who aren't even the same race as you. You protected me, you shot a man without hesitation and you faced the man we assumed to be the genocidal maniac, without emotion."

"You're mistaking selfishness for bravery," I reply. I immediately wish I had not said that.

"Selfishness? No. Facing death removed your fear. I don't believe anything scares you." Heather pulls back and looks at me. The headlights illuminate her face. I smile. The urge to kiss her is strong, but I decide to let her be the controller of kisses.

"Losing you is all I am scared of right now," I say. I quickly think about the things which scare me and I realise there really isn't anything other than losing Heather. If she had not been giving me signs that she liked me I would have probably gone back to Plan A.

"I have come to terms with the concept of Peripheran-human relationships," Heather states.

"Really? That's a positive, right?"

"Yes."

"What convinced you?"

"Everyone around us sees us as a unit. Even Reeteh Steispeck saw us as inseparable. I was considering whether I can have a relationship with you and all the time I already was. We make a great team."

"Yes, we do. Well, you're obviously superior to me."

"You have your strengths," Heather says, sounding a little patronising.

"Thanks. Aren't you meant to say, no, I am not superior at all, we are equal?"

"You want me to lie to you?" Heather grins and then pushes me away. She runs across the grass towards the river. There goes the gazelle. I contemplate chasing after her, but I know I'll never catch up. On the other hand, I should make the effort or she will think I am not interested anymore. So I chase her across the grass. Ahead of me, Heather stops by the river and turns to wait. As I run towards her I see pink electricity arc from her back and rise into glowing angel wings. She lights up the field. Then there is a bright flash and she is gone. I stop running.

After a few seconds, another flash of light takes my attention and I turn to find Heather standing behind me. She leaps forward and wraps her arms around me, kissing me. Today has just become the best day of the year.

"Lie with me," Heather says.

"Is that a euphemism for sex?" I ask. I never was any good at understanding subtle hints.

"Er, no," Heather replies. She points at the grass. "It was a request for you to lie on the grass," she pauses briefly, "next to me."

"Diai."

I quickly drop to the ground and lie down. The grass is dry. Heather lies down beside me and turns onto her side, so we are facing each other. The Delorean's headlights shine across us.

"There are things about Peripherans you need to know if we are to be lovers," Heather says, with a clinical tone.

"You don't eat your mates do you?" I joke. Heather laughs at my comment.

"No. I was going to say that we can be quite literal. If I say I'd like you to put your car in my garage, I mean I want you to put your car in my garage. Nothing sexual."

"Diai," I acknowledge. "That's good to know," I say.

"Peripherans don't tend to hint or suggest things discreetly. If I want you to make love with me I will suggest we make love. I understand humans liked to be suggestive with their requests."

"Yes, some did. Actually, they may all have been like that. I was never really any good at telling what was being suggested."

"Peripheran women don't use touch as a way of telling a man they like them. So if a woman links her arm with yours and seems to be very friendly, she is just being very friendly. If she is interested in you sexually, she will tell you straight."

"I suppose that avoids confusion. So you haven't been flirting with me for the last week? You've just been friendly."

"Flirting?" Heather looks genuinely confused.

"You've been touching me a lot and being very, well, close."

"I liked you. I wasn't flirting."

"So, just to get things straight, today, the kissing; that's romantic. Not just friends anymore?" I have to check."

"No, not just friends anymore," Heather clarifies. "I am falling in love with you and I want to explore those feelings." Heather slithers across to me and pushes me onto my back, then climbs onto me and lays her head on my chest. "I feel happy when I am with you," she says.

"I feel really happy when I am with you," I reply.

"Your heart is beating very fast," she notices.

"Well, I have just found out the woman I adore feels the same way about me. And, we have just had our first kiss. You are now lying on me, so yes, my heart is racing. Are you as excited as I am?" I ask. Heather lifts her head off my chest and looks at me.

"My heart is beating fast, too." She smiles and drops her head back onto my chest. I place my arms around her and I become aware I have my hand on her back, over the lobe thingy.

"Would it be weird if I asked to look at your back again?" I ask.

"Why?" Heather asks.

"It fascinates me."

Heather rolls off me, onto the grass and lies on her front. She undoes her jacket and slips it off her shoulders to reveal her upper back.

"Keep your face away," she says. A second later, the lobe turns white and a crackle of pink electricity arcs across her skin. The electricity rises in two lines about six inches from her back and then disappears.

"That's amazing," I say without exaggeration.

"Something important you must understand," Heather states, turning to look at me. "Never stand behind a Peripheran. If I armaranos fend with you behind me it will kill you."

"Will I get cut in half by the angel wings?" I wonder.

"No. Physically, you'll be fine but the quantum effect of fending will mess with your brain's electrical activity."

"Like the baltron phase?"

"Yes. So never stand behind a Peripheran."

"I'll keep that in mind." I climb onto Heather's back and place my face on her back, so my cheek is touching the skin over her armaranos lobe. I feel Heather's face drop onto the grass. Is she despondent with me?

"Do you know how hard it is to stop yourself from doing something you know you must not do but can do really easily with a simple thought?" Heather asks.

"What are you implying?" I ask.

"My armaranos fend is very easy to switch on and you lying on my back means I *have* to keep it off. That means distracting my mind."

"Like when you stand by a cliff and you think about jumping even though you know you don't want to?" I roll off her back and Heather quickly pulls her jacket back on.

"I have never stood by a cliff and wanted to jump," Heather states.

"Must be a human trait," I assume. Heather nods her head and I see by her expression she is mocking me, but in a non-offensive way. She looks like she is on the verge of smiling.

"Okay, so I am just weird," I say.

"Really? You seem so normal!" Heather says with pure sarcasm. She adjusts her clothing and lies on her back, looking up at the dark sky. The moon is almost overhead.

"Where is your Peripheran home?" I ask. Heather pauses to think before answering.

"I don't officially have one," she answers. "I had been living in a shared apartment with the other scientists when I worked for Reeteh. When I left him I was going to go straight to protected accommodation. My last proper home was in Mallam; what you call Oxford. That's where I grew up."

"So you have friends there?" I query.

"Yes."

"Is that where you would like to move back to when this is all over?"

"I haven't given it any thought. I suppose it depends on what happens to you."

"Me? Why? Are you not expecting me to survive?" I may have misunderstood her comment.

"No, of course I am. I meant, where Asten decides to locate you."

"What if I want to move to Mallam?"

"I would be happy with that. But we should discuss it with Asten," Heather insists.

"Do you think Emilio is the only corrupt member of the council?" I ask. Heather sits up and crosses her legs. I don't even try to copy her. I place my hand on her knee and she covers it with her hand.

"I hope so. Frank will find out."

"So, who does he work for, exactly? Not Asten?"

"No, he works for the government."

"Is he above Asten or below?"

"What do you mean?"

"Could he overrule something they do or is he just a state employee?"

"As an investigator, he can arrest Emilio. Asten is an independent organisation, which reports to the government. The veronmovmen. If the veronmovmen believes Asten is aware of Emilio's corrupt business, they will close Asten and investigate the entire council."

"That wouldn't be a bad thing."

"I think there are players in this game we have not seen," Heather says, somewhat cryptically.

"You think government ministers are keeping a close eye on what is going on?" I check.

"Definitely. I trust Frank, but I believe he has information he would not share with us and for good reason. He is trying to pull his investigation together and he is using us to achieve one small victory. I would be surprised if he did not have other people doing jobs for him as well."

"He's keeping his cards close to his chest." To think I might be the last human to ever use that metaphor.

"Yes. But he's doing it for a good reason," Heather agrees.

"So this sting to capture Emilio. Do you think Frank will let it go ahead?"

"I think Frank will put a few secret components of his own into the sting," Heather says, looking down at me.

"You have a lot of faith in him."

"I like people who are good at what they do."

"Not too much, I hope." Heather turns and drops onto my chest, her face nose-to-nose with mine and her hair creating a tent over my face. I think this is my favourite view.

"You jealous?" she says, smiling.

"Of course I am. I don't want you to like any other man, ever!" I laugh.

"Remember what I said about Peripheran relationships. If I fall out of love with you, you'll be the first to know," Heather reminds me.

"I better keep you happy," I say playfully.

"Yes, but I'll keep you happy, too."

I wrap my arms around Heather and we kiss. I roll her onto her back and we continue kissing. When we stop, I roll off onto my back.

"I need to make a suggestion," Heather says with a tentative sounding voice. I immediately worry that I have done something wrong.

"Yes?" I reply. I turn onto my side to look at her. Heather turns her head towards me.

"I would like you to meet the other human women and be certain you wouldn't prefer them over me," Heather states.

"Really?"

"Yes," Heather acknowledges. She looks serious.

"Do I detect some insecurity?"

"We all have insecurities of some form. I really like you and I would be devastated if you met a human woman who you liked more."

"So, you want me to meet them now before we get more serious?"

"Yes. Does that sound selfish?"

"Not at all. I will meet the human women and I'll give you a critique of each one, so you know whether any of them is a threat." I smile at Heather but she does not smile back. "You have qualities I have never seen in a human woman," I quickly add. "So they would have to be of a ridiculously high standard to beat you for my affection. Aside from that, I don't think human women find me attractive - apart from my late wife. I was pretty awful at attracting them. I am more worried about losing you. I fell in love with you quickly and I don't see how any human woman could change that."

"Thank you," Heather says. I receive the smile I was after and we embrace. I like holding her. She is really special to me and I never want to let go.

Chapter Twenty-Five
Roles

Back at my home, I move the Audi off my driveway and park my beloved Delorean in its place.

Heather and I spend the night sleeping on the sofa in my living room, entwined in a human-Peripheran embrace. My leg goes numb but I put up with the discomfort because Heather is asleep and I don't want to disturb her.

The following morning, we are awoken by Frank, who arrives to discuss the plan to abduct Emilio. I offer him breakfast but he is not keen on tinned beans. He seems preoccupied and I wonder what else he has on his mind. I make some tea on my trusty camping gas cooker and the three of us sit around my kitchen table.

"Just to confirm," I say. "We are going ahead with the plan."

"Yes," Frank agrees. "You and Heather will head to Asten and have a public argument."

"Do you trust Reeteh?" Heather asks Frank, interrupting his briefing.

"No," Frank replies.

"Then why are we doing this? It was his plan," Heather argues.

"It's my plan now," Frank states. "Before we do anything, we are going to meet with Reeteh and make a few minor adjustments. Whatever Reeteh's motivation, I want to make sure the three of us come out of this alive. Especially you." Frank looks at me.

"I don't need special treatment," I say. "I may not be able to fend myself but I can fend for myself." I feel myself frowning at my own comment. Heather is smiling discreetly. She doesn't want Frank to see her.

"There are thirty-four humans left," Frank states. "And you are one of them. Like it or not, you need special treatment."

"I'm still not comfortable with the plan," Heather says.

"It's all we have right now. The alternative is to wait until Emilio makes a mistake. That could take years and may never happen." Frank stabs his index finger on the table several times as he makes his point.

"What should I say to Emilio?" I ask. "Should I tell him you have evidence implicating him?"

"Not at all," Frank replies. He'll just kill you - if he really is corrupt. Remember, this is the man who orchestrated the genocide of the human race. You are a loose end and he would relish the chance to kill another human. No, you must not force anything on him. You need to let him discover what you know."

"Discover?" I query.

"Don't tell him about Theo's home. Let him ask you questions and discover that information. If you say all the things you want him to hear without him asking he'll know something is going on. Don't even offer to take him to Theo's home. Try and manipulate the conversation so that he asks you to take him there." Frank stares at me for a moment. "It's a tough assignment. Do you think you can do it?"

"Yes."

"I'm going to take you to Reeteh. We have agreed to put your skills to the test."

"Skills?" I question.

"Reeteh has a friend who is going to role-play some scenarios with you. If you handle it well, we'll proceed with the plan. If not, we'll call it off. You have to understand,

Emilio works for Asten. His job involves reading people. A lot of his work is covert and the people he is involved with are incredibly devious. You are stepping into his world."

"I literally already have," I comment. "Can I wear a wire? Do you have a Peripheran equivalent? Something like that mind projecting device you had." I look at Heather.

"No," Frank answers. "If you walk into Asten with any kind of device they will detect it. You have to do this by yourself. We can't even give you protective clothing."

"Okay," I say. I look at Heather. She looks worried.

"No one will think less of you if you decide not to do this," she says.

"I know. I *need* to do this. I may not have liked humans when I lived amongst them but I'll be damned if I am going to let a prick like Emilio get away with killing them all."

"What about Reeteh?" Heather asks.

"He'll flee the moment we succeed," Frank states. "We'll let him flee and then I'll bring him in later. He may be working with us now, but he's not getting off free for what he has done."

We finish our drinks and then clear up. With my Delorean parked safely back on my driveway I feel more relaxed about leaving. Frank transports himself to Periphera. Heather steps behind me and wraps her arms around my waist. The last time she did this, we were friends. This time, we do it as lovers. There is a bright flash of light as I leave Earth and arrive on Periphera.

Parked nearby is Frank's car. We climb inside and he drives us to a town which, on Earth, would be near Bristol. On Periphera, it is called Kiranarik. The journey takes about an hour and a half and I am fascinated to see the Peripheran towns and vehicles we pass along the way. There is no motorway. The roads are like our main roads, with a single carriageway on each side, except the centre of the road is not a dotted line, it is a physical barrier. There aren't many cars on the roads, which makes me wonder what the population of Periphera is. I see several aircraft fly overhead and I wonder what the lives of the Peripherans on those planes are like.

We reach Kiranarik in the early afternoon and Frank drives us to a large building in the centre of town. The town is like a small version of Verorlanden, with most of the buildings constructed in white with ornate twisted, tree-like decorations on their walls. Reeteh's building has nine large windows facing onto the street. A few cars pass us by as we approach the front door, but the town is relatively quiet.

One of Reeteh's employees lets us into the building and escorts us to a room at the rear, where Reeteh is waiting. The room is stylishly decorated and gives the impression of wealth. There is a wall of books and a number of leather armchairs scattered around the room. Against one wall is a large sofa, which has curved wooden legs and an upholstered cover. The legs have the shape of a cat's paw at the bottom. Reeteh is sitting on the sofa with a glass in his hand.

"Brandy?" Reeteh asks as we enter the room.

"No thanks, Frank and Heather both reply."

"What else do you have?" I ask.

"Anything you wish," Reeteh answers. He stands up and walks over to a cabinet, which is against the adjacent wall. He pulls out a bottle of whiskey and waves it in the air at me.

"Whiskey?" he asks.

"Diai." I reply.

"Are you still eager to approach Emilio?" Reeteh asks as he pours my drink.

"Eager is not the word I would choose, but I feel the need to do this."

"Did Frank explain to you why he brought you here?"

"Yes. Role playing," I recall.

"There are advantages and disadvantages in sending you to

Emilio," Reeteh says, "Today we will determine which outweighs the other." He hands me the drink.

"I understand." I feel Heather's hand on my back.

We sit down and start to discuss the plan in more detail. After twenty minutes the door opens and a man enters the room. Reeteh stands up and enthusiastically greets him. He turns to me.

"This is Dyorc," Reeteh says. "He will be helping you prepare for your meeting."

"Dork?" I query.

"Dyorc," Heather whispers. "It's quite a common name."

"Hello Dyorc," I say, standing up. We shake hands.

"Hello Nathan," Dyorc replies. He smiles a friendly smile and then turns to Reeteh. "Shall we get started immediately?" he asks. Frank stands up and steps to my side.

"I see no reason not to," Reeteh replies. He looks at Frank. "Frank?"

"Of course," Frank replies.

"So, Nathan," Dyorc says. His voice is soft but clear. "I will pretend to be your subject and you must convince me to divulge something specific."

"Like what?"

"That, I must not know. If I guess what you are trying to find out from me you fail."

"So, I have to get you to say something but you mustn't know what it is I am trying to get you to say?"

"Yes," Dyorc confirms. "I will leave the room whilst you discuss amongst yourselves what you want to know. When I come back in, you must try to get me to divulge the information." Dyorc leaves the room.

"How am I supposed to know what to get from him?" I ask. Reeteh picks up a piece of paper and hands it to me.

"This is a list of relevant information about Dyorc's life."

"I would suggest you try to get him to tell you what he had for breakfast," Frank interjects.

"That is a superb idea," Reeteh agrees. He heads over to the door and let's Dyorc back into the room.

Dyorc stands silently and stares at me.

"So, Dyorc," I start, "when I was six I watched a cat get run over by a tractor. At no point did it occur to me that a cat sitting still for long enough to be run over by a tractor was unusual. I suppose it's because I hadn't lived in the countryside for long and the sight of a tractor was new to me."

"That's interesting," Dyorc responds. "So, in hindsight, why do you think the cat sat still and allowed the tractor to run it over?"

"I have no idea. If I had been born a country lad I might have understood. Do you know what I mean?"

"I'm not sure I do?" Dyorc replies.

"I was born in a large town; how about you?"

"Yes, I was too."

I turn to Reeteh. "I am hungry. Could we do this with some snacks?" I ask. Reeteh nods his head and stands up. "Anyone else hungry?" I ask, looking at Heather, then Frank, then Dyorc. Heather and Frank nod their heads. Dyorc shakes his head. "Shall we keep going while we wait for the snacks?" I ask.

"If you please," Dyorc replies. Reeteh leaves the room briefly and then returns.

"I skipped breakfast this morning," I explain.

"Were you in a hurry?" Dyorc asks.

"I overslept. I could murder a full English breakfast? I state.

"I'm not entirely certain what that is," Dyorc replies.

"Sausage, bacon, egg. Don't you eat those?"

"I myself prefer toasted bread with peanut spread."

"And you're not hungry now? You must have eaten a lot of toast this morning!" I smile at Dyorc and wait for his reply.

"Just a couple of slices. I am not a big eater."

"Diai. So, the first time I went to the country," I say, quickly changing the subject, "I see a cat get hit by a tractor."

"Why didn't it run away?" Dyorc asks.

"It did. Well, it limped. So, have you always lived in a town?"

"Yes," Dyorc replies.

"Dyorc," Reeteh interjects, "could you leave the room for a moment, please." Dyorc nods his head and then leaves the room.

"So, you found out what he had for breakfast. Do you think he knew that was what you were after?" Reeteh asks.

"I don't know. Shall we ask him?" I reply.

Reeteh pokes his head around the door and asks Dyorc to come back into the room.

"Do you know what Nathan was trying to find out?" Reeteh asks.

"Well, his story about the cat was untrue. He seemed fixated on whether I grew up in a town or the countryside," Dyorc replies.

"I think Nate will do well," Frank states.

"Yes," Reeteh agrees. "Let's do another."

"Should I assume I was wrong?" Dyorc asks.

"Not even close," Heather replies, smiling.

We spend the rest of the afternoon role playing more scenarios and I somehow manage to convince Reeteh and Frank that I can fool Emilio. Frank leaves us early to make more of his own preparations. Heather and I finally leave Reeteh's house during early evening, having declined an invitation to stay for dinner. A car is supplied to take us back to Verorlanden, which Heather drives, giving me step by step driving instructions as we travel. She is keen to help me integrate with the Peripheran society.

My instinct is telling me that planning to kidnap a member of the council in Asten is a very bad idea and I wonder why Frank is even entertaining the idea.

Chapter Twenty-Six
Emilio

"What the hell is wrong with you?" I shout at Heather as we walk around the corner of the street onto the road where the Asten building is situated. It is mid-morning and there are plenty of people to witness our argument. The tall buildings loom overhead, their white structures reflecting the sunlight into the street. The roads are busy but not as busy as the streets of London or New York at this time of day.

Heather pushes me and I turn to face her.

"You have to understand," Heather replies. She tries to grab my clothing, but I step back, unexpectedly leaving the pavement. A car swerves to miss me as I turn away from Heather. A second car skids to a stop at my feet and the door opens as the angry driver gets out. I jump back onto the path and push Heather away as she tries to take my arm.

"Leave me alone I shout at her," not meaning a word of it. I never want her to leave me alone. I walk away, briskly, heading for the Asten building.

The grounds of the Asten building are surrounded by a large stone wall, with no gateway. I look back and see Heather run away, disappearing around the corner of the street. Several onlookers watch her. I approach the wall, where there is a communication screen.

Frank had explained that access to Asten could only be achieved by talking to the security team via the screen. I press a button on the wall and the screen lights up. The face of a woman appears.

"Huruh," the woman says, with a smile.

"Do you speak English?" I ask.

"Yes, I do," the woman replies. I see her look away at something and then back at me. "Are you Nathan Glover?" she asks.

"Yes, I am. How do you know?"

"We have your details. I am looking at your file right now. Why are you standing in the street alone? You are supposed to be under protection."

"Something went wrong with the protection," I answer. "I need to come inside and speak to the council." I wait for her response.

"I am sending a transporter down to bring you in. Please stay by the screen until it reaches you," the woman instructs me. I nod my head and turn to look up and down the street. I wonder whether I am actually safer out here than in Asten. After all, the person who killed humanity is inside the building and the criminal on the outside is now my collaborator.

A flying-car-type-of-craft descends from the roof of the building above me. A green car pulls up beside me and two men jump out. They are wearing grey uniforms and have guns attached to their belts.

"Please stay where you are," one of them says to me, holding a hand up. "We need to clear the road to allow your transport to land."

"Are you the police?" I ask. The two men look at each other and then at me.

"The Peripheran equivalent of police," the man replies. They redirect the oncoming traffic to make a space on the road. They also tell pedestrians to keep back as the transport drops into the space they created. With a quick bow of their heads, the policemen jump back into their car and wait. The door on the transport opens, so I climb inside.

The aircraft is empty. I cannot see the pilot because there is a blacked-out screen between them and me. I sit on one of the four seats and the door closes. I am lifted up to the top of the Asten building, where Edruth is waiting. She smiles as she approaches the craft. The doors open, so I climb out.

"What happened?" she asks.

"Heather is working for Reeteh Steispeck," I state. Edruth escorts me into the building.

"How do you know?"

"I met Reeteh."

"You met him?" Edruth looks concerned. She stops and holds my arm.

"Where?"

"I think I would feel safer if I addressed the whole council with my information," I say to her.

"Diai," Edruth replies.

We head to the lifts and Edruth escorts me down to the level where the council has their huge cathedral-sized chamber. We step into the huge dark room and head for the small doorway which leads to the room with the conference table. To my surprise, all the council are sitting in the room, waiting. Do they stay in here all the time?

"Hello," I say, as I enter the room. Edruth Finds her seat and stands by it.

"So you met Reeteh," one of the council states. How does he know that? Edruth must be wired, unless this building is rigged with cameras and microphones everywhere.

"Yes."

"And Heather Tasston is working for him," a woman at the end of the table checks.

"Yes. She helped him build the baltron phase."

"We are aware of that," a man at my end of the table states. He gestures for me to sit down on one of the spare seats, so I comply. "I must admit, I am surprised she is working for him again," the man adds. "It contradicts what we already know."

"He wanted me to help him," I explain. "I turned him down, so Heather tried to convince me."

"You did the right thing, coming here Edruth states. I look along the rows of faces and spot Emilio, sitting half way down the table. I make sure I don't look at him longer than appropriate otherwise he might guess my intention.

"I don't feel safe," I lie.

"You are perfectly safe in Asten," the older man next to me states.

"I know where they are hiding," I state.

"On Periphera?" Emilio asks.

"No. They have a house on Earth," I reply.

"Not North Silestia House?" the woman at the end of the table asks. "We have North Silestia House."

"No. Not North Silestia. The house belonged to Theo Tandammbian," I say.

"On Earth?" Emilio questions. "Theo Tandammbian was a government advisor. He was based in Verorlanden."

"Maybe it was his holiday home," I reply. "The house definitely belonged to Theo."

"Do we have a list of Theo's residences?" Edruth asks the older man next to me.

"One moment," he replies. He looks down at a device on the table and then presses his finger on the table itself. The table lights up with a screen, showing a list of commands. The man touches a few of the commands in turn and then some addresses appear on the screen. "Theo had a residence in London," the man reads from the screen.

"This wasn't in London," I state. "This was the opposite direction."

"Are you sure?" the old man asks.

"Absolutely. I could fly you to it within an hour," I reply.

"None of these other residences is located on Earth," the man states.

"Why would Theo have a non-disclosed residence on Earth?" Edruth asks.

"A safe house?" I suggest.

"And you are certain, Reeteh is in that house?" Emilio asks.

"Yes, I am."

The council members look at each other and then discuss what to do amongst themselves quietly. I wait to see what they suggest.

"We need to arrange a tactical team," the old man says.

"That sounds like a good idea," I agree.

"A room is being prepared for you," Edruth tells me. "Somewhere for you to relax."

"Is Lucy still in Verorlanden?" I ask.

"All the humans have been transferred to a hotel," the older man states. "We can have her transported back here if you wish."

"I'll phone her and see what she wants to do," I reply.

"I will escort you to your room," Edruth says, as the entire council rises to their feet. I'm not entirely certain what these people actually do. They aren't the government and Heather said that Asten was a secret service. However, despite having lots of CCTV, I don't see how this group has any intelligence; especially since one of their own is more than likely the man who killed humanity. The worrying thought is that they might all be involved. How do you fight the entire council?

Edruth escorts me to a small apartment a few levels above. It has windows which look out across the city. The sun is shining and it is a beautiful day. For the first time in years I feel as though I can actually appreciate it. The Peripherans are different from humans in their attitudes and I hope they fulfil my expectations of being the friendly helpful race I would like them to be. Certainly, so far they have been very friendly. I like the fact that they say hello to strangers in the street. It somehow makes me feel secure as though everyone is looking out for me. I

260

think that is the difference between Peripherans and humans – well humans in the few countries I have visited – there are places in the human world where you feel unsafe, simply because of the people in those places. So far, I don't feel that way in the Peripheran world. Maybe I should find out whether there are any places on Periphera which are not safe. I am aware that my fondness with Periphera is a rose coloured spectacle created from the dislike I had for humanity. Given time, and experience, I may well end up disliking Peripherans as well.

I offer Edruth some tea but she declines. I want to ask her about Emilio and gain another ally but I resist. I believe Edruth is straight but I cannot let her know what Frank has planned. She leaves me alone in the small apartment. I press my hand on the communication screen and the image of a man appears.

"Huruh," the man says. He smiles.

"Huruh," I reply. I remember when I first said 'Bonjour' to a French woman. I felt excited to have spoken to her in her own language. I was a teenager though. Saying 'Huruh' to a Peripheran gives the same buzz but that may be because they are technically an alien race.

"Surecks quahnrhuic jwet sibbis," the man continues. That's what it sounded like he said. I have no idea what it means.

"Wow, hold on. I don't speak Peripheran," I interrupt him.

"I'm sorry. How can I help?" the man asks.

"I am Nathan Glover and I would like to speak to my sister, Lucy Patterson," I tell the face.

"I would be happy to connect you to her. Please wait." The screen goes blank for a moment and then there is a kind of screensaver which shows a view of Earth – Periphera - from space. I wonder whether the Peripherans have set foot on the moon. Do they even call it the moon? My thoughts are interrupted by Lucy's face. She smiles but I can see she still looks troubled by what has happened.

"Hi sis," I say. "How you doing?"

"Nate. I'm coming to terms. Peripherans are friendly people but I wonder whether they are being extra friendly to us because of what happened. How are things with you and Heather?" Damn, a question I cannot answer truthfully. I have to tell her things turned sour just in case this call is being monitored, but doing so will make Lucy worry about me and I don't want that.

"We're spending some time apart," I say with as much diplomacy as I can manage. I decide to change the subject. "I picked my car up from your home," I say. As I say the words I realise it was the wrong way to take the conversation.

"You've been back to Earth?" Lucy questions.

"Yes."

"You went into my home? Did anyone else survive?" she questions. She looks eager and I assume she is hoping I have good news about Jeremy.

"I went inside," I start. I stop to think about my choice of words. "There were no more survivors." I add.

"Did you see Jeremy?"

"Yes."

"I'm sorry, sis," I say. Lucy's eyes well with tears. Should I tell her he was cheating on her? Would turning her emotions from sorrow to hate make her life better from now on?

"What?" she says unexpectedly.

"Sorry?"

"What else? Come on little bro. We grew up together. I can tell when you are holding something back. What did you see?"

"Do you think Jeremy was a loyal husband?" I ask.

"The bastard!" Lucy shouts. "It was Carry, wasn't it."

"I don't know who Carry is. Jeremy was in your spare room when he died. He wasn't alone."

"What did she look like? Short, with long blonde hair. It was all bleach and hair extensions. Did she have a tattoo on her shoulder?"

262

"I didn't look that closely. If it's any consolation they never got around to doing what they intended."

"During my party! The bastard! I want him out of my house."

"Sis, take some time to calm down and think about the future," I say to her. I don't think she is listening.

My attention is taken by the sound of the bell at the apartment entrance.

"I have to go. There is someone at the door," I say to Lucy.

"Ok, take care little bro. When are we going to meet up?"

"Soon, I hope. Bye sis." I press my hand on the screen and Lucy's face disappears. I head to the door and open it slowly with the wooden handle. The door locks in the same manner as other Peripheran doors, with a hand scanner but it has an ornate wooden handle for pulling it open.

"Hello Nathan," Emilio says, as he steps into the apartment.

"Hello," I reply. Should I pretend to have forgotten his name? I can't remember how much I interacted with him previously. "I am sorry, I forgot your name," I add as I close the door. We head into the living area. Emilio turns and looks at me. He smiles.

"I have read your file, Nathan," he says. "You remember my name."

"I do?"

"Of course. I know everything there is to know about you. I have seen your school records, your evaluation reports from the psychiatrists you have seen, your medical notes, your work records and all the information the government and local authorities were holding about you. I even know how much money you had in the bank. It's amazing how much of a human's life was stored in documents," he states.

"Okay. So that means I know you name. How?"

"I know what you used to achieve, before your wife and son died. You were quite a thinker. You did the entry test for MI5.

You wanted to be a code breaker. What happened? Why didn't they accept you?"

"My wife and son died whilst I was in London attending an interview. They did offer me a training position but I turned it down."

"And by doing so you ensured that MI5 would follow your every move. What are the chances that Theo Tandammbian just happened to hide his daughter in an abandoned stately home a mile away from a burnt out wannabe code breaker? Of all the people in your home town that she should accidentally bump into, she chose the one under surveillance."

"I was under surveillance?"

"Yes. Surveillance that we at Asten were also watching, discreetly."

"It was chance that I found her," I state. "I haven't been good at anything for seven years."

"No, you've been awful. Your life spiralled to the point that you wanted to die. Events happened that were destined to pull you in. And here you are. Why do you think Frank entrusted you with parts of his investigation? He has read your file. He knows you are spy material. He's probably going to enrol you on a training programme when this is over."

"As soon as what is over?"

"The charade. I've just been reading the testimonies of the people who saw you arguing with Heather. Convenient. Have a little public argument, and then turn to Asten for protection."

"What are you implying?" I ask. I have a feeling he's going to kill me in this room. I scan his clothing for signs of a hidden gun.

"I am implying that you came here with an agenda. As I said, you know exactly what my name is."

"Emilio Havente. Did you know your name is an anagram of 'I am the evil one'?"

"No, I did not."

264

"You killed humanity."

"I am not going to monologue, Nathan. I have no need to tell you my reasons or try to convince you I am a good man. It's none of your business."

"You killed my race. Of course it's my business."

"I saved my race," Emilio snaps.

"How? Humans weren't a threat to you."

"They were going to bring humans here. Veronmovmen decided it was time to let our races interact openly. Humans on Periphera: it couldn't happen."

"So you killed the humans?" I question. I am getting him to monologue. It does work. Evil people like to explain themselves.

"The Peripheran way of life is harmonious. Bringing humans here taints us."

"Humans *are* here; thanks to you."

"What harm can thirty-four humans do?" Emilio smiles.

"Shouldn't you be more worried about what harm one human can do?" I ask.

"Is that a threat?" Emilio replies.

"Not at all," I reply. I sit on the sofa and, to my surprise, Emilio sits next to me.

"You are to tell me where Theo's Earth residence is."

"I can't. I know how to get to it but I don't know the address."

"Could you show me on a map?"

"I could, but I don't feel inclined to be that co-operative." I look at him for a reaction. Emilio stares at me and I assume he is thinking about what to say.

"You love your sister," he states.

"And?"

"If you were any other person I would threaten to kill her if you don't co-operate. However, you are Nathan Glover the third and I know you won't respond to that kind of threat."

"So why mention it?"

"Just thought you should know it is an option."

"So is suicide. I recommend you try it."

"You're the kind of person who reacts to positive reinforcement, so let me offer something to you. Tell me where Theo's residence is and I will retire from my post as a member of the council of Asten Mistep-Hoak."

"Really?" I question. "You'd quit your job?"

"I am due retirement soon."

It's my turn to take some time to think. I believe his retirement is inevitable and he is planning on disappearing regardless of what happens. He knows Theo was on to him and he wants to know how much Theo knew. That's my hunch. Why else would he be so interested in Theo's Earth home? He wants to make sure that when he disappears no one comes looking for him.

"I need some time to think," I say. Technically, I am free to walk out of Asten. I am curious as to what he would do to stop me.

"Are you trying to stall?"

"Stall what? You're the one who is eager to go to Theo's home. I am happy just to sit back and put my feet up." I stand up and head for the door.

"If you don't mind, I am going to go for a walk around this fine city," I state. Emilio tries hard to suppress his annoyance but it shows through in his distorted face. I open the door and leave the apartment. Emilio follows me closely.

"You think you are clever, Nathan," he whispers to me as we walk along the corridor.

"No, I think I am hungry. Can you recommend somewhere to get some lunch?" I ask. This feels good. We are in Asten and he cannot touch me. We are surrounded by the people who protect his world and he has defied them. He cannot do anything until I leave. Ahead, I see Edruth, talking to another member of the council. It is the old man.

"Hello," I say as we approach them.

"Hello Nathan," Edruth replies. She looks at Emilio. "Emilio."

"Edruth," Emilio replies. "Bardel," he says to the old man. I wondered what his name was.

"Emilio," the old man – Bardel – replies.

"Would it be possible for me to borrow a car?" I ask. I would like to go for a drive."

"I'm sorry Nathan, but Peripheran cars are not like the combustion engines you are used to. We cannot let you drive until you have been properly trained," Bardel replies.

"Perhaps I can drive you somewhere," Emilio volunteers. "You would then have Asten's protection."

"I would be happy with that Bardel," agrees. I feel Emilio's hand on my back and I want to tell him to take it away but I resist.

We leave Edruth and Bardel and Emilio escorts me to the top floor, where we head for a hangar. Inside are three of the small transport aircraft. I wouldn't call them planes because they have no wings. They are like flying cars without wheels. We climb into one of the aircraft – a nice royal blue colour – and Emilio manoeuvres it out of the hangar onto the landing area of the building. He flies us across Verorlanden, heading for the countryside.

"Where would you like to go?" Emilio asks.

"Head north for a couple of miles," I reply. I haven't actually told Emilio that I want to go to Theo's secret home but he must assume it to be so. I have a nagging feeling in the back of my mind and I think it comes from the thought that Emilio seems happy to venture out unarmed. I consider whether he has a security team following us.

We hover over a field I recognise and I instruct Emilio to land in the valley to the east of the field. Once we touch down, Emilio cuts the engines.

"Now where?" he asks.

"I would like to go to Earth," I state.

"I bet you would," Emilio replies. "How far is Theo's residence from here?"

"I would need to be on Earth to tell you. The landscape is different."

"Was this your plan?" Emilio asks. "Take me to Theo's home, where an ambush awaits? Look out your window."

I look out my window and see at least a dozen other aircraft landing in the valley around us. Emilio opens his door and climbs out. I follow him and watch as another dozen aircraft drop from the sky. Emilio smiles.

"Whoever you have waiting for me on Earth, they're going to have a big surprise," he says. "Are you still coming?"

"Absolutely," I reply. Emilio steps behind me and wraps his arms around my waist.

"Take a deep breath," he says, "it may be the last Peripheran air you breathe."

Chapter Twenty-Seven
Ambush

We arrive on Earth on the front driveway of North Silestia House. As my eyes start to focus I see a soldier running towards us. He is holding a small screen, like a tablet PC but probably a lot more sophisticated. He reaches Emilio and speaks a few words in Peripheran. The only word I recognise is North Silestia. Emilio turns to me.

"North Silestia?" he questions. "You brought us to North Silestia." We both turn around to see the large house, silent and empty.

"This is Theo's Earth home," I state. Frank had informed me that there would probably be evidence in Theo's other residence which would prove Emilio's participation in the genocide. Under no circumstances was I to return to the house in Devon. North Silestia, on the other hand, is a good place for an ambush.

Around us the rest of Emilio's armed force arrives by electric angel wing – armaranos fend. Every one of them armed with Peripheran weapons.

"This is not Theo's Earth residence," Emilio states. "This building belongs to a human family who fell on hard times and left it abandoned. Theo merely used it to hide Heather." Emilio turns to the soldier.

"Search the house. Kill anyone you find," he commands. The soldier nods his head and then joins his men to pass on the order. Emilio turns to me and takes hold of my arm. "What are they going to find in there?"

"Absolutely nothing," I answer.

"So why bring me here?"

"I didn't. I came here for some peace. You volunteered to drive me here - well, fly me here. I never asked you to bring an army."

"You know full well why I accompanied you. Where is Theo's Earth residence?"

"What makes you think there really is one?" I ask. If he gets angry I might die here. Should that make me excited?

"I know there is, I have just never been able to locate it. You didn't just guess the existence of a residence I have been searching for. You've been there. Tell me where it is."

"Do Peripherans have the ability to read minds?" I ask, pulling my arm away from Emilio.

"What do you think? Would I be asking you where Theo's residence is if I could do that?"

"Then you're out of luck."

"Actually, I think maybe I have been coming at this problem from the wrong angle. Why are you here? If you think I am guilty of crimes then you must assume I would kill you to protect myself. And yet, here you stand, unprotected, at my mercy. Why?"

"I suppose I am just incredibly stupid. Oh, and I am not at your mercy. I chose to be here." Emilio stares at me and I wonder what he is thinking.

The soldier with the tablet PC returns, holding it in the air.

"We just monitored a human helicopter leaving the vicinity," the soldier says, pointing along the valley.

"Your ambush?" Emilio asks me.

"I suppose they weren't expecting you to bring an army," I reply. The helicopter was part of the ambush. Frank must have decided to call it off once he saw the weaponry Emilio brought with him.

"Never leave home without your own private army," Emilio

says, his face showing the smuggest smile I have ever seen. It would be nice to wipe that smile out. "So, how are you going to get away?" Emilio asks.

"I'm not," I reply. "The council know I am with you, so you need to get me back to Asten safely, otherwise questions will be raised."

"You have obviously thought this through," Emilio says. He doesn't sound bothered and that bothers me. "So, if I shot you now and told Asten that a helicopter attacked us, would they believe me? A helicopter just left this area. Asten can track that."

"If you shoot me, you'll never know where Theo's secret home is," I suggest.

"Only if I kill you." Emilio looks at the soldier and then holds his hand out. The soldier takes a pistol from his side holster and hands it to Emilio. I feel my skin pulsate as a shiver runs up my spine. I am not afraid of dying but I don't want someone like Emilio to have the satisfaction of killing me. As Emilio aims the gun at me, I whack his hand, knocking the gun to the floor. Then I steal the opportunity to run, heading for the slope up to the woods. I reach the first trees and then fall to the ground. My left arm stops working and I feel my shoulder burning. The bastard shot me.

The last image I see before I pass out is my bloody hand pressed against the trunk of the nearby tree.

Chapter Twenty-Eight
Hospital

I awake to find myself in hospital. My left shoulder aches but I can move my hand. My arm is restrained in a sling. I look around the room: the hospital seems very human. Just like my local hospital. I am in a private room, with a wall between me and the nurses' station. The wall has a glass screen with curtains, which are open. There are two nurses sitting at the station; one is looking through files, the other is doing something on a computer. Opposite my bed is a large window, with closed curtains. I can see daylight through the fabric. As I attempt to climb out of bed one of the nurses enters the room.

"Don't try to get up," she says, pushing me back onto my pillow. The other nurse is immediately by her side.

"How do you feel?" she asks. Her name badge says she is Angela.

"Thirsty," I reply. "Where am I?"

"You're in District Hospital, Salisbury," Nurse Angela answers.

"You've been in a coma," the second nurse states. I glance at her badge and see she is called Jodie. She presses a glass of water to my lips, so I drink. The water tastes refreshing. As I drink, the first nurse opens the curtains, filling the room with light. I close my eyes and then open them slowly to adjust to the light.

"How long have I been in a coma?" I ask.

"About a week," Angela replies. You were shot in the shoulder, so don't try to move too much.

"How did I end up here?"

"Your sister brought you in," Angela informs me. Nurse Jodie puts the plastic beaker down and leaves us.

"My sister?" I question. How did I get from being with Emilio to being with Lucy? "Are you sure?"

"Yes."

Nurse Jodie comes back into the room.

"Doctor Brewer is on his way," Jodie states.

"The doctor will answer all your questions," Angela says as she adjusts my covers. "Are you okay with the curtains open?"

"Yes."

The two nurses leave me and return to their station. I can think of no circumstance in which being shot by Emilio has led me to be brought into Salisbury District Hospital by Lucy.

An hour later, a doctor, who introduces himself as Doctor Brewer, visits me.

"The nurses said I was in a coma," I say to the doctor as he sits against my bed.

"Yes, you were. Your sister has been here every day."

"Did she bring me in?"

"You came in by air ambulance. Your sister found you in a forest having been shot."

"In a forest?"

"Yes. Now you are awake the police will want to talk to you. I believe you were shot accidentally by a gamekeeper."

"Really?"

"Do you remember anything?" the doctor asks.

"What I remember doesn't involve a gamekeeper," I state.

"Memories can be distorted after being in a coma." The doctor picks up my chart and reads from it. "You are on our list of vulnerable patients. You were found with a noose. Have you previously been suicidal?"

Before answering his question I think about the events which brought me here. Is he suggesting I went to the woods and instead of meeting Heather I was actually shot by a gamekeeper?

"I have been," I reply. "Can you contact my sister and ask her to come here?"

"She has visited you every day, so I expect she'll be back tomorrow."

"Tomorrow? What time is it?" I ask. Doctor Brewer looks at his watch.

"Just after four." He puts the charts back in their holder and heads to the door. "You relax and let your shoulder heal." Then he leaves the room and I see him through the window talking to the nurses.

I refuse to believe my entire experience on Periphera was a figment of my comatose imagination. It was too detailed. I kick my covers off and slide myself onto the side of the bed, letting my feet touch the floor. I stand up slowly and stagger across to the window, leaning on the glass to stop myself falling over. Outside I can see part of the car park. A bus is parked by the side of the road and several cars are looking for parking spaces. A dozen pedestrians are walking to and from the hospital. Everything looks normal. For this to be real, Heather must be a figment of my imagination. I find my legs buckling and I fall to the floor with the thought that Heather, my new love, does not exist.

The two nurses help me back to the bed.

"I can see you are going to be trouble," Angela says as they tuck me in.

"I'm sorry. I had to see."

"Would you like some food?" she asks, as Jodie heads back to the nurses' station.

"Some fruit would be nice," I request. Angela smiles and then leaves the room. I close my eyes and try to recall Heather's face. How did my mind make up such a beautiful image? I cannot accept that I will never see her again. During my time on Periphera - in my coma - I lost her when I thought she had blown herself up. I wanted to die then and now I feel the same again. I realise how self-centred that is. If I can't have her I would rather die. It's not really like that. I wanted to die before but she came into my life – my mind - and gave me a reason to live. Now that reason has gone.

After eating a small bowl of chopped fruit I fall asleep. I awake during the middle of the night. The lights are dim and a different nurse is sitting at the station. I drink some water and then fall asleep again.

I am awoken the following morning by a nurse adjusting my covers. She is accompanied by a man wearing a casual suit, with no tie. The nurse passes me some breakfast: two pieces of cold toast and some cereal.

"Hello Nathan," the man says as the nurse leaves the room. "My name is John Ryan. I am a psychotherapist. Would it be okay for us to talk?"

"What about?" I ask as I bite into the toast.

"I have been in touch with your therapist. Your sister has told me that before the accident you were suicidal. You went to the woods with a noose. Can you tell me what you intended to do?"

"Is it not obvious?"

"I'd like you to tell me about what you were feeling."

"I wanted to die."

"And how do you feel now?"

"Confused."

"Why is that?"

"Because I have a week's worth of memories and apparently they were all a dream I had whilst in a coma."

"Tell me about the dream. How did it start?"

"I met a woman in the woods and..." I stop talking because a thought occurs to me. My time on Periphera was special to me. Despite all the bad things which happened, I really enjoyed

275

myself. Now I am back in the real world - back on Earth - being quizzed by another damn shrink. If I want to die, who is he to stop me? Why try to convince me that life can be fun when I know it cannot? Nothing is going to live up to the week I spent with Heather.

"You met a woman. What was her name?" John asks.

"Meredith," I reply. "She was called Meredith Spaniel." He wants to know what I dreamt; I might as well just make up a story. I feel slightly amused at the thought of feeding him a fictional creation. That is, until I see John's expression change. He looks irritated. Why would that irritate him?

"If I am to help you, you must be honest with me," John says. "I am a trained therapist. I can tell when someone is making stuff up."

"Really? I only told you her name." I finish the piece of toast and have a drink of water.

"Let's move forward. What do you remember before you woke up?"

"Before I woke up?"

"Yes. Where were you?" he asks.

"I was in the forest. Why?"

"Where were you going?"

"Nowhere. It was a dream. What does it matter?"

"I specialise in coma recovery. Part of the recovery involves recalling the images and thoughts you had whilst unconscious. It helps us understand what happens to the brain whilst in a comatose state."

"Do we have to do this now? I don't feel in the mood."

"No, we don't have to do this now. You finish your breakfast and I'll come and see you later."

John stands up and heads for the door. Before he leaves, he turns around and I am reminded of lieutenant Columbo, a fictional TV police detective who used to do the same thing. He would say, 'Just one more thing' and it would be that one thing which was crucial to his investigation but he would throw it in as though it was an afterthought.

"I am here to help you Nathan."

"Okay," I reply. Then John leaves.

I struggle to get out of bed and stagger to the window. Outside, the view is much the same as yesterday. There are people wandering around. Another bus is parked by the bus stop and car drivers are looking for parking spaces.

I try to look further than the car park but the trees obscure my view. I really do not know how I am going to adjust to returning to the life I had before. I return to the bed and take my arm out of the sling. I fiddle with the dressings to see whether I can look at my wound but the bandages are taped to my chest. I decide to go for a walk and head out to the nurses' station. The nurse on duty smiles and says hello as I pass. I look into the next room and see a man lying on the bed, asleep. I pass his doorway and head further along the corridor. I am intercepted by another nurse who asks whether I need any help. I tell her I am getting some exercise and she nods. She advises me not to go too far in case I feel drowsy and need to lie down. She takes my arm and escorts me back to my room.

"Can I see your back?" I ask her.

"Sorry?" the nurse replies. I look at her name badge.

"Jenny. I'd like to look at your back," I repeat. She looks confused but then turns around.

"Just a normal back," she says, turning to face me.

"I mean your actual back," I state. "Your skin."

"Why would you want to see my skin?"

"Just curious." I say.

"Well, you'll just have to imagine what my back looks like." She leaves the room and heads over to the nurses' station to talk to the other nurse. I lie down and stare at the ceiling. I feel frustrated; restless. My mind is mixed up and I don't know what to do.

After some lunch I am surprised to hear my sister's voice in the corridor. I sit up and look through the glass. Lucy is talking to the nurse.

"Lucy!" I shout. Lucy turns and runs into the room.

"Nate!" she screams excitedly. She leans over me and hugs me gently.

"I am really glad to see you," I say to her. She is the only person in the world I trust unreservedly.

"It's good to see you awake," Lucy replies. "You had me worried."

"Is it true what they say? I was shot by a gamekeeper?" I ask. Lucy sits on the edge of the bed and pats my leg.

"You took a noose to North Silestia woods and a gamekeeper shot you," she confirms. My heart sinks. It is true. Heather does not exist. Lucy would not lie to me.

"I want you to come and live with me when you get out," she says. "I am going to personally help you recover."

As she talks I notice that she has ink on her hand. She has a doodle of a smiley face on her palm.

"You been scribbling on your hand?" I say. Lucy pulls her sleeve back a little to reveal writing on her wrist. She quickly pulls her sleeve back down before I can read the writing.

"You know me, I like to doodle," Lucy replies. She looks up at the corner of the room and then at me. She looks worried.

"How's Jeremy?" I ask. Lucy's face drops and she tries to hide her feelings. Jeremy is a sore subject. Since the last week for me has been a dream, my suspicion of Jeremy's infidelity is based on prior knowledge. Maybe Lucy has discovered his secret.

"He's fine," she lies. "So, remember when we were kids and you tried to make up a language?" she says, changing the subject.

"I remember."

"We had some good times," Lucy recalls. "Do you ever use that memory technique you used to do?"

"Not much," I reply. As a teenager I became obsessed with improving my memory and I developed memory palaces and all sorts of ways to store random information. It was fun.

"They said you might be able to leave by the end of the week," Lucy says. As she talks she slowly pulls her sleeve back to reveal the writing on her wrist. I realise her recollection of my memory techniques was a prompt. On her arm is a series of numbers. I quickly make up a story with each number assigned to an animal. I already have nine animals assigned to numbers from my previous dabbling with memory techniques. The numbers on Lucy's wrist are 824 2111 5424 2152. Eight is a shoe. Two is a chicken. Four is a dog. One is a cask of beer. Five is a bee. So my story is that I walk (8) a chicken (2) to the dog (4) where another chicken (2) is waiting with three casks of beer (111). A bee (5) irritates the dog (4) and then lands on the chicken (2). The dog (4) chases the chicken (2) and knocks over a cask (1). The bee (5) then lands on a chicken (2). I double check my story to recall the numbers just as Lucy pulls her sleeve back down.

"Would you like a drink?" I ask her.

"No, I'm fine. You just relax. I'm happy just to sit with you." In the corner of the room is an arm chair. Lucy walks over to it and sits down. She's giving me time to work out what the numbers on her arm mean.

One of my memory palaces involved assigning numbers to the alphabet. However, not in a simple way, like A=1, B=2. I assigned the alphabet to bookshelves in a stately home I had a photo of. So 'A' was on case 1, shelf 1. 'B' was on case 1, shelf 2. There were seven cases, each with four shelves. As a marker, I assigned unused numbers to help confuse people who don't know the code. The number 8 is one of those numbers, so I can disregard it from Lucy's code. So her code is 24 2111

5424 2152. Those can be put into pairs - 24 21 11 54 24 21 52. The first pair is case 2, shelf 4. That's an H. The second pair is case 2, shelf 1. That's an E. I follow this pattern until I have assigned a letter of the alphabet to each pair of numbers. My heart races when I realise what it spells. HEATHER.

"Holy crap," I say aloud.

"Welcome back," Lucy says from the chair. I turn and look at her.

"Are you going to visit me tomorrow?" I ask. Lucy stands and approaches my bed.

"Of course."

"What time?"

"Same time as today," she says. Then Lucy sits back down in the chair and eventually falls asleep. I go over the numbers in my head again to double check the code. I remember that I used to include a signature in my codes. The spacing of the numbers spells letters as well. Lucy's code was 824 2111 5424 2152. That's a group of 3, then 4, 4, 4. 34 is case 3, shelf 4. That's an L. 44 is case 4, shelf 4. That's a P. Lucy's initials. LP. Lucy Patterson. It was our way of indicating that the code works and assigning a signature. If it didn't have the signature it might be someone else using the code. I feel excited as I realise Heather is out there, somewhere. She is probably trying to find me.

During the afternoon, the doctor checks my bandages and allows me to try spending some time without the sling. He then leaves. John Ryan returns but leaves when I continue making up stories.

The only thing I can think about is Heather. If the last week was a dream, Lucy could not have known Heather's name. I realise she must be under pressure to play along with the facade. This entire setup must be a way for Emilio to get me to tell him where Theo's secret house is. Lucy is as much a prisoner in this hospital as I am and we both need to get out.

Chapter Twenty-Nine
Doctor Drake

Lucy is awoken just before my evening meal by a nurse who tells her it is time to leave. We don't say goodbye; we just exchange smiles. I would hate to be Lucy right now. She doesn't know for definite that I understood the code; after all it has been fifteen years since we played with the concept. Also, I suspect Emilio is keeping her in the hospital against her will. If she was able to leave she would go straight to Asten and tell them what is going on.

My biggest problem now is deciding how Lucy and I can escape. I have to get past whatever security guards are guarding me and then find Lucy. No matter how many ways I try to think of a plan, nothing works. I decide to sleep on it.

I am awoken a couple of hours later by a nurse who informs me that a doctor wants to talk to me. I ask her what the time is and she tells me it is just after eight o'clock. It seems later. The nurse switches on the light and brings me a beaker of lemonade. She helps me sit up as I wait for the doctor to call.

"Do you live locally?" I ask her.

"Yes, Salisbury," she replies.

"Do you like it?"

"It's home," she says diplomatically. She must be Peripheran. I wonder how much she knows about why I am here. "How does your shoulder feel?" she asks.

"It aches but seems ok," I tell her.

"If you need your pain killers increased I will ask the doctor," she says, sympathetically.

"Diai," I reply. She smiles and then leaves. I wonder at what point the penny will drop and she will realise she just responded positively to a Peripheran word - a word which sounds like a negative English word. You say 'die' to any English nurse and they will take offence. She just smiled - because her first language is Peripheran and she knows the word means 'ok'.

As I sit, thinking and waiting, the doctor arrives. I see his entourage at the nurses' station. There are two other men in white coats and a woman. The doctor has his back to the window, so I cannot see his face. As he turns to approach my door I see his profile and I immediately recognise him. He steps through the doorway into my room, confirming my suspicions.

"Hello Nathan," Emilio says, with a smile. "I am Doctor Drake. How is your shoulder?"

"Doctor Drake? How many doctors are looking after me?" I ask. I am not sure why Emilio has chosen to visit me but he wants me to believe he is a doctor at the hospital, so I play along.

"Several of us have to check you during our shifts," he replies. He pulls the arm chair over to the bed and sits down beside me.

"You look just like a bloke in my dream," I tell him.

"Really?"

"Yes. His name was Emilio," I state. I watch his face for a reaction. He hides any sign that he recognises his own name.

"Tell me about him. What role did he play in your dream?"

"He was a weak-minded sadist," I mock.

"Really?" Emilio queries. "What kind of dreams do you have?" He smiles to show he is taking the comment as a joke.

"The kind with genocidal maniacs in them. They shoot me in the back because they are too cowardly to fight like a man."

"I am sensing hostility in your voice. Do you have issues

you would like to discuss?" Emilio asks. He is a great actor. It is almost as though he really is Doctor Drake. The thought occurs to me that I might be suffering from some kind of delusion. Could it be that Periphera really was a dream and Doctor Drake is a genuine medical professional? Were the numbers on Lucy's arm real or did I imagine them? All she did was pull her sleeve up. She didn't point at them or look at them at all. It would be easy to give in and assume Doctor Drake to be genuine. However, I am certain I saw the numbers on Lucy's arm. Her whole personality was different as well. She seemed lost, despondent.

"When can I leave the hospital?" I ask.

"A few days," Emilio replies. "We have to make sure your shoulder is healing properly and with your psychological past we must ensure you are mentally able to return home."

"Do *you* think I am mentally well enough to go home?" I ask.

"I don't know. How do you feel yourself? Do you still feel suicidal?"

"No. I don't want to kill myself anymore."

"It is sometimes good for coma patients to recall the dreams they had during their coma," Emilio states. I have never heard that before. I expect he made it up to get me talking.

"Diai," I say.

"Die? I don't understand." Emilio looks genuinely confused. He really is a good actor.

"It's what they said in my dream."

"They told you to die?"

"Well, yes, one of them did, sort of. He wanted to know where Theo's secret home was."

"Who is Theo?"

"A government man."

"Why did they want to know where his home was?"

"Because there was evidence that would condemn him."

"Did you know where his secret home was?"

"Yes, I had been there."

"So where was this Theo's home?" Emilio asks. He must be getting desperate. What I don't yet understand is how he is going to hide the fact that he used all these people to make me believe I am back on Earth and that none of the events of the past week actually happened. Do all these people work for him? Has he told them I am dangerous? Do they think they are working for the good guy? I suppose I could call them his minions. I thought minions only existed in movies but apparently anyone can have them. The realisation hits me that Emilio's minions are relatively innocent pawns in a chess match between Emilio and me. I will need to remove them from the board to get me and Lucy out of here. Could I kill someone whose crime might only be that they work for the wrong man?

"It's in Salisbury," I lie. "It's just past the supermarket. You cross a big junction with traffic lights and then turn left at the next roundabout. You'll find it on the right hand side." I see Emilio thinking about my directions. If he knows this area, he will be picturing that route in his head.

"I don't know where that is," Emilio replies.

"I'm not sure how else to describe it," I add.

Emilio stands up and heads over to the window. He looks out at the view. I wonder what he is thinking. If he thinks I cannot be persuaded to give the information he wants he may well turn to plan B, which I guess would mean hurting Lucy. One thing I think it would be safe to assume is that once Emilio has the information he wants, Lucy and I will die. There are thirty-four humans left and I am certain he would relish the chance to reduce that to thirty-two. Aside from that, we know too much about him. Once we are dead, I expect Frank and Heather will follow. Emilio seems to be the kind of person who doesn't like loose ends.

285

"I have been a bit uncooperative," I say to Emilio, who has his back turned to me.

"Why?" he asks without looking at me.

"It was all a bit of a shock waking up to the realisation that the events of the last week were all in my mind. I fell in love and I feel a great loss."

Emilio turns and looks at me.

"So why the stories?"

"It made me feel in control. I don't like not being in control. I also didn't really see how recalling my dreams would help me recover." I drink some water as Emilio approaches the bed and sits by my feet.

"Being in a coma has a significant effect on the brain. By getting you to recall the things your mind created during the coma we can understand how your brain has been affected." Emilio sounds sincere. If he wasn't talking absolute rubbish I might believe him.

"I'm quite tired. Will you be on duty tomorrow?" I ask.

"Yes."

"Once I have had some sleep I will cooperate fully and tell you all about my dream, from start to finish."

Emilio pats my leg reassuringly and then stands up.

"I look forward to helping you through this," he says as he heads for the door. "Get some sleep."

I am finally alone again. I watch as Emilio chats briefly with the nurse at the station and then leaves. I try to go back to sleep but find it difficult with so much playing on my mind. I have no intention of telling Emilio where Theo's home is, so I will have to attempt to find Lucy and get her out of here. I need a weapon. I suspect the nurses keep weapons at the station. They would need to stop me if I tried to leave. Either that, or there is a team of security outside the ward, waiting for me to break out. I also need to find clothes. They probably burnt mine assuming I will never need them again.

After a couple of hours of lying in bed thinking, I get up and head quietly to the nurses' station. Just one nurse is at the station and she is doing something on the computer. She sees me approach and turns the screen off.

"Hello," she says, smiling.

"I can't sleep," I tell her. "Can I get some sleeping pills?"

"I don't think you are allowed them," she replies. She picks up the telephone and presses a single button. "Can Nathan have sleeping pills?" she asks the person on the other end. She pauses and then thanks them. As she puts the phone down, she looks up at me and smiles. "I'm afraid you are not allowed sleeping pills. However, I can make you some hot milk or cocoa. Would you like some?"

"Yes please. Could I have hot cocoa?"

"Of course. You go back to bed and I'll make you some." She stands up and waits for me to start walking back to my room, so I comply and turn my back on her. As soon as I hear her start to walk away from the station, I turn and jump to her side, taking hold of her arm. I wrap my arms around her.

"What are you doing?" she shouts.

"Where is Lucy being held?" I ask. The woman says nothing.

As we struggle, the ward doors fly open and a man rushes in, holding a gun. I push the nurse towards him and, to my surprise, she armaranos fends herself out of the ward, her electric angel wings illuminating the corridor and temporarily blinding the man, who is facing her back. I seize the opportunity to jump on him and grab his gun. Without thinking I aim it at his head and pull the trigger. A ball of charged air drills a hole through his brain, killing him instantly. I jump to my feet and turn the dial on the gun to allow it to shoot at its maximum distance. The nurse has removed any doubt I had that Periphera is real. I now know Heather is out there and Lucy needs my help. From the corner of my eye I see the familiar flash of light as a Peripheran materialises on Earth. I quickly turn and shoot them in the chest before they can do anything.

I pull the trousers off the dead security man and put them on. Then I run out of the ward, checking for people as I go. I find a room where three nurses are sitting, chatting. I jump in through the door and aim my gun at the nearest nurse.

"Tell me where Lucy is being held or die?" I command. She looks surprised.

"I don't know," she replies. I shoot her in the chest and then aim the gun at the next nurse.

"Your turn," I say.

The nurse is frozen with fear. You have five seconds before I move on," I say.

"She's on floor three, room 18B." the nurse says. The third nurse starts to fend, her back lighting up with pink lightning, so I shoot her in the chest. Then I take hold of the second nurse and drag her out of the room.

"I am seriously pissed off," I say to her.

"I am not going to stop you," she says. "Please don't kill me."

"Take me to Lucy and I'll let you live," I say.

"This way," she says, pointing at a door to the stairs. I may have just killed two innocent women but my mind is buzzing with so much adrenalin I don't give it a second thought. This is a time of kill-or-be-killed and I would gladly kill everyone I see if it means I can save Lucy and get her out of here.

Chapter Thirty
All Hell

The nurse and I head down the stairs until we reach level three. As we leave the stairwell, two men shoot at us from the end of the corridor. They don't seem to be aiming solely at me because the nurse flinches as a shot catches her sleeve. I quickly pull her back into the stairwell and wait. I push her to the floor and crouch down next to the door. In movies, the good guy will run up to the roof or down to a lower floor. In reality, I have no intention of going anywhere. When those two men enter the stairwell I intend to shoot them and continue my search for Lucy. Sitting on the floor puts us in a place outside their natural field of view. It will take them a moment to see us down here – just long enough to...

The door opens and the men peer around the door. I quickly point the gun up at the first man and pull the trigger driving a hole through his throat. The air bullet continues to make a hole in the ceiling, taking some of his brain matter with it. Before the second man can do anything, I shoot him in the chest. I then pull the nurse to her feet and we enter the corridor. I run as quickly as I can along the corridor, pulling the nurse with me. When we reach the end, we turn into another corridor, which has signs telling us we are heading towards the cardiology department.

"Just need to go to the end of this corridor and turn left," the nurse shouts as I pull her along. "Please let me go."

"No, keep up," I reply. I'm not letting go until I find Lucy.

We reach the end of the corridor. I peer slowly around the

corner and see four men standing next to a doorway. The door has the number 18B on it. I step back and turn to the nurse.

"I'm going to let you go, but I need you to do something," I whisper. She nods her head.

"I want you to walk around the corner and go straight past the room. I'm going to use you as a shield so I can see the room, so walk slowly. Once you are past the room you can go wherever you want to. Do you understand?"

"Yes," the nurse replies. I notice her name badge says she is called Yvonne.

"Before you go," I say, still holding her arm. "What do you do for a job?"

"I am a nurse," she replies, which surprises me at first. She is probably not a bad person and may not have known she was working for the man who killed humanity.

"What is your real name?"

"Neri," she replies. I let go of her arm and lower the gun.

Neri steps away from me and then walks slowly around the corner towards the men. I peer around the corner and look over her shoulder as she approaches the room. Neri says something to the guards in Peripheran as she passes and then continues along the corridor. I quickly drop to the floor and lie against the wall, with my gun at the corner. A moment later a man comes into my field of view, so I pull the trigger and shoot him in the face. As he drops to the floor another man appears. He doesn't have time to turn before I shoot him. That's two down. The other two will not be stupid enough to come to me, so I quickly stand up and step backwards to a nearby doorway. As I peer around the door a man turns the corner, shooting at the floor where I had been lying. I seize the opportunity and shoot him in the chest, knocking him backwards.

Behind me, I hear a door open and I realise the room has another entrance. I quickly step into the corridor and skip along to the corner, where I peer around to look at the room where Lucy is being held. The remaining man has gone, which means he is now behind me. I flip myself around the corner, just as the man comes out of the doorway I had hidden in. He shoots at me but hits the corner of the wall. I run over to room 18B and push the door open. Inside I see Lucy sitting on a bed, listening to headphones. She is alone. I wait for the man to come around the corner so I can shoot him but he doesn't come. I cannot go into the room and lose sight of the corridor, so I wave at Lucy. She sees me and pulls the headphones off.

"Nate!" she shouts. Her voice is loud enough for the man to hear and he must assume I am in the room with her, because he steps around the corner. I shoot him in the chest and watch him fall to the floor. I turn to find Lucy by my side.

"Would you like to leave?" I ask her.

"More than anything in the world," she replies. Before we can leave, a shot of air bullet hits the wall by my head and I realise there are more men in the corridor, coming from the opposite direction. I step back into the room to avoid being hit and see more men appear at the corner from which I had come. I close the door and turn the latch to lock it.

"Are there any other doors?" I ask Lucy.

"No. Just a window but it has bars."

"Show me." I head to the back of the room, where Lucy shows me a walk-in cupboard. The cupboard has a window which opens out to an enclosed, grassed area in the middle of the building. It is dark outside but the exterior wall has a light on it. I open the window and then adjust the dial on the gun.

"Stand back," I say to Lucy as I aim at the first bar. I pull the trigger and a bullet of charged air drives a hole through the metal. I pull the bar up, bending it to the top of the window. Then I do the same with the other four bars.

Lucy climbs out first. As I start to climb out I hear the door to her room being forced open. I dive through the window and land in a heap on the gravel outside, making my injured shoulder sting with pain.

"Hide," I say to Lucy, as I jump up and run along the side of the building. We find a small alcove where an oil tank is located, so we hide next to it. I can see the window we climbed through so I adjust the setting on the gun to allow maximum distance and wait for someone to make themselves visible.

As we wait I hear a buzzing sound. I look up and it takes me a few seconds to see a small remote-controlled drone hovering over us. It looks like the type used by the army for reconnaissance and is spider shaped with two sets of blades on the top. As the drone hovers I aim the gun at it and shoot, knocking it out of the air. It lands on the ground near my feet. Since it may still have working cameras, I look around for something to put over it. Lucy anticipates my action and takes her jacket off, throwing it over the drone.

"We're trapped," she says.

"Yep. But we have a gun that doesn't need bullets, so I am going to shoot everyone who tries to come near us."

The sound of an explosion makes us both jump. A cloud of black smoke rises from the building opposite us, into the night sky.

"What was that?" I say. The sound of smaller explosions can be heard inside the building.

"Is that gunfire?" Lucy asks. Another explosion rocks the building we are leaning against. Peripheran guns don't sound like the guns we are used to so it might be.

"We're sitting next to an oil tank," I say. "I think we should find somewhere less explosive." I stand up and edge out of the alcove. More explosions occur in succession, creating more clouds of black smoke over the buildings. I shoot a nearby window and peer inside to see an empty room. I use the gun to break the rest of the glass and then help Lucy climb inside. I follow her into the room, which has a large x-ray machine in the centre.

"Do you know the way out of here?" I ask my sister.

"The entrance is on level three," she replies.

"This *is* level three," I recall. I open the door and peer into the corridor, which is clouded with smoke. I can hear gunfire in the building. It sounds like lots of Peripheran air guns going off, interspersed with explosions and shouting.

"We're going to have to make a run for it and hope for the best," I suggest. Lucy nods. I take hold of her hand and, holding the gun in front of me, we run into the corridor. A quick glance at an overhead sign tells me that the entrance is left at the end of the corridor, so we run as fast as we can in that direction. When we reach the end an explosion destroys the wall, knocking us over. I drop the gun and lose it under some of the rubble. My arm is bleeding and my injured shoulder hurts more than ever. I look at Lucy and see she is unharmed. My body shielded her. She pulls me to my feet.

"Can you walk?" she asks.

"I'm not staying in here," I shout as the noise of another nearby explosion drowns out the sound of my voice. We make our way along the corridor, which is now full of smoke. We head through a set of double doors, straight into a gunfight. There are men on the left shooting at men on the right. I drop to the floor, pulling Lucy down with me. We scramble into a doorway as holes riddle the wall, door and door frame, from the gunfire. Some of the men are shooting at us. I have no idea whether they are all shooting at us or whether one side is here to save us. I cannot shut the door because most of it is missing from the impacts of the air bullets, so I push Lucy along the floor.

"Head for the other door!" I shout as pieces of the wall start to fly across the room from more gunfire impacts. We clamber to the door, diving into another room. We crawl across the floor until we reach another doorway, where we stop briefly and lean against the wall.

"Do you think we crawled towards the good guys or baddies?" I ask Lucy.

"Who the hell is who?" she replies. The smoke is starting to affect my breathing as it wafts into the room from the holes in the adjacent room's wall.

"We need to get out of here," I say as I stand up. I slowly open the door and peer into another smoke-filled corridor. "Which way?"

"Go left," Lucy instructs.

"That takes us back to the gunfight," I tell her.

"That's where the exit is."

"Diai," I reply. I head into the corridor, with Lucy clutching my hand. We walk briskly along, staying close to the wall. Ahead, is another set of double-doors. Through the small windows in the doors I can see soldiers in full combat gear, complete with helmets and gas masks.

"Now what?" I say. "I lost the gun."

Across the corridor a single door leads into another room. I am about to suggest to Lucy that we go into the room when the door opens and a soldier comes out. He sees us and holds his gun up. I start to run but Lucy is in the way. I knock her over and we fall to the floor. I quickly roll onto my back.

"Nathan Glover?" the soldier asks, as he takes his mask off.

"Depends who wants to know," I reply. He hasn't shot me, so he may be a good guy.

"Consider yourselves rescued," he says.

"Really?" I question. "Have you looked around you?"

The soldier holds his hand out and helps me to my feet. I turn and help Lucy up.

"This way," the soldier says, as he runs towards the double-doors. "I have Nathan Glover," he says to no one in particular. He must have a radio. We head through the double-doors and are met by half a dozen more soldiers, who surround us and escort us to the main entrance, shooting at anything that moves. There are more explosions and we have to climb across debris to get through the entrance doors. Once outside we are met by Frank, who is dressed in combat fatigues. The air is cold and there is smoke everywhere.

"Hello Nate," he says with a smile. "How's that for storming the place and breaking you free?"

"Emilio is in the hospital," I say to him. Frank turns away and issues commands to a soldier who looks like he is in charge. He has a mobile command centre strapped to his back and is talking to the soldiers via a communicator. The whole area is illuminated by a set of spotlights on a small mobile tower. Frank turns back to me and Lucy.

"We'll get him." He pats me on my good shoulder and quickly visually assesses my injuries "Are you badly hurt?"

"Just superficial scrapes," I reply. "Where's Heather?"

"She is waiting for you," Frank replies. He leads us through the car park to a helicopter, which is sitting with its engines running.

Peripherans can only bring to Earth objects they can carry, so they have to use human transport to get around. The three of us climb inside and are immediately lifted into the air. I look at the hospital through the window and see several fires and smoke billowing out of the windows.

The helicopter flies us away from the city and continues north until we reach Salisbury Plain, right next to Stonehenge. It is dark and the stones look like tall shadows. The helicopter lands so I get out with Lucy and Frank. The helicopter pilots also get out, abandoning their aircraft. Frank stands behind Lucy and wraps his arms around her. He smiles at me.

"I'm taking the attractive sibling," he says.

As I watch Frank armaranos fend my sister to Periphera, one of the helicopter pilots wraps his arms around me. There is a flash of light and I find myself standing on the outskirts of Verorlanden. Frank and Lucy are waiting. We climb into a Peripheran aircraft and are transported to the top of the Asten building, where Bardel and Edruth are waiting. Behind them, is Heather.

Chapter Thirty-One
Home

Once out of the aircraft, I push my way past Frank and Lucy and run towards Heather. She pushes Bardell and Edruth aside and meets me at the centre of the rooftop. We embrace and kiss each other. She feels warm and smells great – that familiar lavender smell. We stop kissing briefly to look at each other.

"So that's twice I have been led to believe I would never see you again," I say to my love.

"Never again," she replies. "You stay by my side forever."

"I will," I say. Heather rests her head on my shoulder and we cling tightly to each other. I try hard to fight the pain in my shoulder. I don't want Heather to let go of me.

I see Edruth standing in my field of vision, her face looks stern. I realise Heather has just publicly shown she is in a relationship with a human. I am glad. We shouldn't have to love each other secretly.

"You got a problem with this?" I say to Edruth. I am surprised to see her smile.

"Not at all," she replies, stepping closer. Heather turns to face Edruth, keeping both her arms around me. Frank appears at my side, with Lucy. I turn to him and glance at my sister. I don't think she is ready for a relationship but when she is, Frank would be a reliable suitor. I hope she finds happiness in this new world.

"You must go to the infirmary and have your wounds treated," Bardel says, looking at the blood on my clothing.

"I'll take him," Heather says. We head into the building just as rain starts to patter across the rooftop. A clap of thunder in the distance breaks the silence.

We make our way down to Asten's infirmary, where a team of doctors awaits. Heather stays by my side as they tend to my shoulder and bandage the other wounds.

Afterwards, Heather and I head back to the Asten apartment I had previously stayed in. I collapse on the bed, whilst Heather makes us some tea. I fall asleep and awake to find Heather pulling my trousers off. She undresses me, pulls the covers over my naked body and then climbs into the bed. She is wearing some of those disposable pyjamas.

"How do you feel?" she asks, picking her tea up from the side table and sipping some.

"Content," I reply. "Very, very tired, but content. If I fall asleep, don't leave me. I don't want to wake up alone."

"I'm not going anywhere," Heather assures me. "There is tea on your side."

"Thank you," I say, closing my eyes.

"Peripherans like to give news as it comes," Heather says. "Would you like us to do the same or would you rather wait until the morning?"

"You have news?"

"Frank called while you were asleep. Emilio escaped from the hospital. They don't know where he is."

"Great," I say with tired sarcasm. "More hassle."

"They want us to stay here until they catch him."

"That's fine with me. I've had enough excitement." I run my hand under the sheets until I find Heather's leg. I hold on to her as I fall asleep again.

I awake feeling refreshed. My wounds do not hurt, despite Heather lying across my chest. She wakes up at the same time as me and pulls herself up so our faces meet. We kiss as I roll her onto her back.

"Good morning," she says in between kissing.

"It really is," I reply. I want to make love to her but I don't know whether she is ready. I roll onto my back and yawn. Heather's chin immediately lands on my chest and her big eyes stare at mine.

"I love you," she says, grinning.

"I love you too," I reply. She is sexy and clever and has a fun-loving personality. Did I mention clever? I find intelligence an attractive quality and I look forward to having Heather teach me advanced physics, quantum mechanics, the Peripheran language and all the other subjects in which I am inferior. I am not sure whether there is anything I can teach her.

"What would you like to do today?" she asks.

"I'd like to take you home."

"Your Earth home?"

"Yes."

"Cook me a meal on your camping cooker?" Heather smiles.

"You're a scientist. Don't you have something we could take with us to get the power on?" I ask.

"I know where we could get a thermal generator," Heather replies.

"How does that work?"

"It takes organic matter and turns it into heat. The heat is then used to generate electricity."

"Sounds perfect."

"I'm not going unless you ask me," Heather says, jumping off the bed. She does a spin and stops by the window, leaning back against the wall. "It must be a date," she adds.

"Right," I say as the penny drops.

"Heather," I say.

"Yes Nathan."

"Will you go out on a date with me?" I ask. This is the first time I have ever asked someone out on a date without worrying what their answer will be.

"Depends. Where would you like to go?" Heather plays.

"I'd like to take you to my house and cook you dinner."

"I would love to go on a date with you," Heather replies. She dives forward onto the bed and crawls up to my face. We kiss briefly.

"I'll need to borrow a thermal generator though," I say.

"Diai," Heather replies. She jumps off the bed and heads into the bathroom. She has so much energy. I hope the Peripheran air gives me some of that energy.

After some breakfast, delivered by an Asten chef, Heather and I meet with Bardel, who suggests we take a couple of armed bodyguards with us. We agree to let two guards follow us but instruct him to keep them distant, because we are going on a date.

We meet the bodyguards on the roof of Asten and they fly us to my home, landing on the road in front of my house - except on Periphera, it is actually a field. Heather transports me to Earth and the bodyguards follow. I am pleased to see my Delorean still parked on my driveway.

"We could go for a drive later," I say to Heather, who is dressed in a long, dark blue dress, with a 19th century military style jacket - seems to be her favourite design. Her hair is tied up in a bun and she is wearing a small amount of makeup. I am wearing a Peripheran man's suit, complete with anana, covering my bum. It seems strange to have trousers with half a skirt attached to the back. The suit includes a dark grey waistcoat and tie. I look smart. Heather looks beautiful.

We head into my home with the bodyguards and wait whilst they search the house. Once they are certain we are alone, they leave and wait outside.

"When is the thermal generator being delivered?" I ask Heather.

"Any time now."

"I'll make us some tea on my camping cooker and then we

can relax in the living room until the generator arrives," I suggest.

"Diai."

I make some tea and meet Heather on the sofa. We sit lengthways, with Heather between my legs, leaning against me.

"What happened in the hospital?" Heather asks.

"They tried to convince me I had been in a coma and that humanity had not been eradicated."

"How did you know it wasn't true?"

"I didn't at first. Lucy visited me. She wrote a code on her arm, which told me your name. I knew then that you were real."

"If they hadn't taken Lucy, Frank would never have found you."

"How's that?" I question.

"Lucy had a tracking device implanted in her toe. Frank organised it after you went missing. He had a hunch they might take her, so he let them."

"They said she had been visiting me whilst I was asleep," I inform her. I sniff her hair. Smells have a big effect on my emotions and Heather's hair makes me feel happy.

"No, the day you saw her was her first day there," Heather explains.

"What about Reeteh. What's he up to?" I ask. I drink some tea.

"I don't know. I think he disappeared. He is still wanted for crimes, despite helping us."

The doorbell sounds, making us jump.

"That'll be the generator, Heather says as she gets up. I head to the front door, with Heather following, and open it to find a man standing with a large box by his feet.

"Thermal generator," he says, smiling.

"Thank you," I reply.

"That is the hardest thing to fend with," he adds before leaving. His armaranos fend takes him back to Periphera.

301

I drag the generator into my home and close the front door.

"Where is your main power input?" Heather asks.

"In the garage. I drag the generator to the kitchen and through the door into the garage. Heather opens a compartment on the generator and pulls two leads out. She attaches them to the meter leads on the consumer unit powering my home. Then she switches the generator on. It makes a low humming sound. I flick the light switch on and the garage lights up.

"It works," I say, grinning. Heather looks at me with a slight frown.

"Of course it works. It's a generator."

"Do we have to throw rotten fruit and veg into it?"

"No, it runs on organic matter but its efficiency is such that one apple will light your home for a day." She lifts a lid on the generator and looks inside. "The hopper is full. That's the equivalent of fifty apples, crushed."

"So fifty days of light?" I query.

"Yes. However, your cooker is going to drain it quicker. Certainly enough power for what we need."

We head back into the house and I switch on the living room lights. Heather visits the bathroom, whilst I turn the stereo on and play some music.

"It's good to be home," I say to myself. I sit on the sofa and finish my tea while I wait for Heather.

The moment I met Heather in North Silestia woods I felt an affinity with her. Even in her medicated state she was attractive. I am sure there may have been human women with the energy and fun-loving personality Heather has, but I only ever met one of them - my late wife. My agreement with Father Time was struck with the wrong entity. Time hasn't healed the wounds; love has. Aphrodite has triumphed over time. My depression has eased a little but it has not gone away. I no longer want to die but, instead, my negative emotions have transferred into a fear - a fear of losing Heather. Even though she is just upstairs, in my bathroom, I miss her and I feel anxious. Twice I have believed I would never see her again and the memory of how that felt lies heavy in my heart. I want to chain myself to her and never let us be apart. Are Peripheran women objective enough not to see that as the will of a psychopath? Should I tell Heather I feel that way? She seems to want us to be open with each other. In previous relationships, I found being open closed certain doors. There are some things you have to keep to yourself.

"Nate, you are such an idiot sometimes," I say to myself.

"Do you have evidence to back that up?" Heather says from behind me. I didn't hear her come down the stairs. I jump up and wonder what explanation I need to give for saying that.

"I was thinking about my depression," I admit. Heather wraps her arms around me and stares into my eyes. Her eyes are the most amazing shade of green.

"Where is your mind right now?" she asks.

"I no longer want to die," I explain. "You know how you said I wasn't scared of anything?"

"Yes."

"I am now. I am scared of losing you. My depression is turning that fear into anxiety. Some women don't want to hear that a man is obsessed with them so early into the relationship. Does that bother you?"

"As a scientist, I always analyse all the evidence before I draw a conclusion. You are not doing that. You have not taken into account the trauma of seeing the human race die. You developed strong feelings for me and on two occasions lost me. You believed it would be forever. You have me back and your brain is telling you that you will lose me again. I understand that. As our relationship develops, we may grow apart. We may fall out of love. Or we may live happily together for the rest of our lives. You need to convince your brain that all of those scenarios are acceptable."

303

"I really can tell you everything about me, can't I," I say.

"I hope so. Relationships don't work if you have to hide something."

"Are you typical of Peripheran women or are you so pragmatic because you are a scientist?" I ask.

"I hope no other Peripheran woman is like me," Heather says, smiling. Her eyes widen and she looks like she is about to do something unexpected. "Otherwise I'm going to have to keep you away from them all."

"That reminds me. I think Frank has a crush on my sister," I tell Heather.

"Ooh, that could be painful," Heather replies. "Does Lucy like him?"

"I don't know. I told her about Jeremy and his affair."

"Good for you. How did she take it?"

"Not great but I think the trip to the hospital has distracted her."

"Frank is no fool. He will treat her well."

"I really hope she is able to start a new, happy life on Periphera."

"She may want to come back to Earth," Heather points out.

"Knowing Luce, she will get involved in rebuilding Earth and clearing up. Fancy a trip to the supermarket?"

"You think their food will be any less rotten?" I feel Heather's hand on my back. Then her chin on my shoulder. I turn and kiss her.

"Some date this is. We have the whole planet and no edible food."

"We could order Peripheran," Heather suggests.

"I wanted to cook for you."

"Order some chicken, onions and peppers and you can make us a curry with one of those jars in your cupboard. Do you have dried rice?"

"Yes."

"Let's go and ask the bodyguards to get what we need."

"Diai," I agree. We head out of the kitchen and search for the bodyguards. They are nowhere to be seen.

"Do you think they got bored and went back to Periphera?" I ask. Heather looks concerned.

"They wouldn't leave us," she replies. As we head into my neighbour's garden I see two bodies lying on the floor by the side gate.

"There they are," I tell Heather. I realise we are in trouble. I quickly spin around to check whether there is anyone near us but see nothing. I take hold of Heather's hand and pull her back to my driveway. I left the keys to my Delorean in the ignition, since there is no one on Earth to steal it. As we approach the car I see Emilio standing by my front door.

"Shouldn't you be in hiding?" I shout at him. I stand in front of Heather to shield her from him.

"I was, but I decided that you were worth the risk," Emilio replies.

"Give up," I tell him. "You lost. Asten knows you are corrupt. The government knows. There is nowhere you can hide. I believe the Peripheran intelligence network is pretty slick. Do the right thing and turn yourself in."

"I may just do that, after I have killed you both."

"Really? Is that what you want? Be a man and accept you lost."

"If you were pushed off a cliff and the man who pushed you was within arm's reach, wouldn't you take him with you?" Emilio asks.

"Don't try to justify your actions with analogies," I say to him. I feel angry. Why can't this man just go away? I notice that Emilio doesn't seem to have a gun with him. How did he kill the guards?

"You once wanted to die," Emilio states. "I now know how that feels. I am ready to die. You pushed me off the cliff and I

305

am willing to fall. But I am going to take you with me." Emilio takes a large knife out of his coat and holds it up.

"No gun?" I ask.

"Gunfire is detectable," he answers.

"What?" I question. Heather whispers to me.

"Asten has devices which can detect gunshots," she informs me.

"So, he just has a knife?"

"Certainly looks that way."

I step forward and approach Emilio. Heather stays close behind me, ready to armaranos fend.

"Come on then, let's end this," I say. Emilio turns his back on me and puts his hands in the air. As I step forward, Heather puts her hand on my shoulder and pulls me back.

"Remember what I told you. If he fends..."

"Diai," I acknowledge. Emilio quickly turns around and thrusts the knife at me. I jump forward and push him against my front door, trying to knock the knife out of his hand. Heather wraps her arms around my waist as Emilio's back lights up and he fends back to Periphera. A second flash transports me and Heather to her home world.

As my eyes recover from the trip I find Emilio and Heather fighting. Heather is pushing him away from me, whilst trying to avoid his thrusts with the knife. I quickly jump into the middle of the fight, pulling Emilio to the ground. I punch him in the face twice. Then there is the familiar flash of pink light and Emilio transports us both to Earth.

"Give up, dickhead," I say, perhaps a little childishly. Heather appears behind me, the pink lightning lighting up the nearby wall. Emilio pushes me off and immediately disappears back to Periphera.

"This is getting tiresome," I say to Heather.

"You want to sit this out?" she asks.

"No, not at all. Take me to him," I reply. I stand up and let

Heather transport me back to Periphera. We find Emilio rubbing his face.

"Give up, Emilio," I shout at the bastard. He jumps forwards and thrusts the knife at me. I manage to avoid the business-end of the blade and I feel Heather jump backwards. I find myself hugging my enemy. I push him back and see blood on his knife. His back lights up again, as he fends back to Earth. I turn to Heather and see her angel wings arc over her head, transporting her back to Earth without me.

"No!" I shout at her but she is gone. I am alone. I check myself but cannot find a wound. The blood wasn't mine.

The aircraft we arrived in is sitting empty on the grass. Next to it is another craft, Emilio's. I run over to my transport and pull the pilots' door open. Inside, I locate a pistol, which I arm and set to maximum distance. I have no sooner set the dial when I see a flash of light as Emilio appears on Periphera. He has his back to me and is looking for me. As he turns around I lift the gun and aim it at his head. He sees me and starts running towards me. I pull the trigger a dozen times and fill his head and body with holes, finally killing him.

Heather is nowhere to be seen. She hasn't returned. I don't know what to do, so I sit on the grass and wait. If she could use her armaranos fend, she would. The fact that she hasn't probably means Emilio overpowered her. She may be dead. I find myself face down on the grass. My eyes well with tears and I feel helpless.

Overhead, I hear the sound of an aircraft. I look up and watch as it lands next to me. The door opens and Reeteh jumps out, along with four armed men. Without saying a word Reeteh looks at Emilio's body.

"Fend me to Earth!" I shout. I stand and approach him.

"You did well," Reeteh says calmly.

"Heather is on Earth and she hasn't returned. I need to see her."

Reeteh steps up to me and wraps his arms around my waist. We are nose-to-nose. His angel wings arc over us and we are transported to Earth. I quickly push him out of the way and look for Heather. I see her lying on the floor by my Delorean. Her face is covered in blood and she is unconscious. I drop to my knees and feel her neck for a pulse. She has one, she is alive. I look at her body and see a stab wound in her abdomen. Other than that she seems to be fine. The blood on her face is from a blow to her head. I slap her cheeks gently to try and wake her.

"Is she alive?" Reeteh asks.

"Yes," I reply. "Can you transport us back?" I look up at him.

"I can do better than that," Reeteh says. He turns to one of his men, who is holding a box. The man steps forward and crouches down next to Heather. He opens the box and takes out a small device, placing it on Heather's forehead. He presses a button and Heather wakes up. She looks confused.

"What happened?" she asks.

"He knocked you out," I say. "Can you remember who you are?"

"Am I Queen Victoria," she says, smiling.

"Don't smile, you were unconscious. You might have brain damage."

"She'll be fine," the man says. "But we need to get her to a hospital to have that stab wound sewn up."

"How do you know?" I question.

"The device has scanned her brain and organs," Reeteh answers. He looks smug.

"How did you know?" I ask.

"Emilio was a loose end I needed to deal with," Reeteh explains. "I have been following him. When I realised he was coming after you I thought you might need help. Besides, it earns me credit to help you. My standing is not exactly exemplary."

"Can you stand up?" I ask Heather. She shakes her head.

"I'm going to need help. Get out of the way, so I can fend back to Periphera."

I stand up and watch as she initiates her armaranos fend. Reeteh steps behind me and transports me back to Periphera.

As his men follow us I notice three more aircraft approaching. I crouch down next to Heather and hold her hand.

"I have to leave," Reeteh says. "Goodbye." He pats my shoulder.

"Thank you," I say to him. As he climbs into his aircraft, he turns and shouts.

"The device my medic used on Heather's head was part of a project I was working on before I became involved in the baltron phase. Heather designed it."

Chapter Thirty-Two
Another Hospital

I find myself lying on another hospital bed, except this time it is a Peripheran hospital and I am lying next to Heather, who is the patient this time. She is in good spirits, despite having just had a hole in her abdomen sewn up.

"The doctor said you can still have children," I tell her.

"Really?" Heather says. "Why would I want to do that? I've already had two."

"Er, well, I was hoping..."

"I'm playing with you," she says. She kisses me and runs her hand through my hair. "If we have children, will you want to raise them?" she asks.

"Very much so," I reply.

"You will need to teach me how to be a mother," she says. And there it is: something I can teach her.

Frank and Lucy enter the room.

"Should you be lying on the bed, Nate?" Lucy asks.

"It's where I belong," I reply. I sit up and drop my legs onto the floor.

"How are you feeling?" Frank asks Heather.

"I'm fine," she replies.

"I have something for you, Nate," he says, pulling an envelope out of his pocket.

"Is it a bill for all the damage?" I laugh.

"No, it's a job. Well an offer."

"A job offer? Doing what?" I ask.

"Well, it's a training position. I thought you might like to join my team and train to be an investigator. You have a few bad habits we'll need to correct but I think you'll do well." He hands me the envelope.

"Thank you," I say, placing the envelope in my pocket. "What's the pay like?"

"Well, as one of the last humans, you are not going to have to worry about money. Verorlanden is passing a bill which will provide for all humans and ensure you all live without need."

"That's nice. Do they feel guilty?"

"Probably." Frank steps towards the door. "I have to go. I'll come back and see you when I get a chance," he says before leaving. He looks at Lucy and smiles. Then he is gone.

"So how are you coping, Luce?" I ask my sister.

"I'm doing surprisingly well," she replies. "Frank has been teaching me about Periphera."

"He's a good man," I tell her.

"I know," she replies. "It is so nice to see you happy," she adds. "You worried me with your need for self-destruction."

"I feel very positive now."

"It shows. You look a hundred times better. I have my brother back."

"Thanks."

"See you later," Lucy says as she heads for the door.

I lie back with Heather. Three times I thought I had lost her. Now that the trauma is over we can really get to know each other. I want to visit Mallam, where she grew up, and meet the people who shaped and nurtured her. I want to start a home with her and eventually have kids. She will undoubtedly be a terrible mother but she will have something other Peripherans don't - a family.

There is an old saying: That, which doesn't kill us, only makes us stronger. I didn't kill myself. I am stronger.

~ **End** ~

~ Contact The Author ~

www.jasenquick.co.uk
http://jasenquick.com/

Lightning Source UK Ltd.
Milton Keynes UK
UKOW04f0137061215

264162UK00001B/3/P